NOTHING TO TELL

SCARLETT FINN

ONE

RUNNING AWAY. Smart. Great, Harper. Real mature.

Alone in the bowels of LA's Grand Hotel, somewhere in a dark corridor, she shook her hands, her arms, fighting to cast off the indignity.

"No. No. No. No! No!"

Good. 'Cause berating herself was productive. She did enough of it in her head, did she have to do it out loud too? Was it her fault madness seeped out when it got too much to contain?

"Is there a problem, Miss?"

Oh, shit.

She stopped pacing.

Alone? Maybe not so much.

The whole idea when slipping out of her sister's engagement party—okay, fleeing like the room was on fire—was to gather herself. Her thoughts. Her courage. Did she have any of that? She couldn't even get seclusion right.

This spot had people.

Person. Alone? Hopefully. Judging from the

pitch, male.

If she stayed quiet and wished herself invisible, would he go away? Probably not. So much for venting in peace.

Broadening a totally fake smile, she spun around. From one indignity to another. Just don't ramble. No rambling aloud. Allowed? Either worked.

"No, uh, I'm sorry." Pressing both hands to her abdomen, she held in the proverbial scream. "I thought I was alone."

Where had he come from? Not behind, the entryway was too narrow. So in front… with him now moving in her direction, she couldn't see what was there. Or him, as more than an outline.

His form stopped a few feet away. And, yep, expectation, his anticipation hung in the black stagnant air between them. Amazing what a person could decipher with so few visual cues. For her, it was damn near a miracle.

"Evidently." Oh, a smirk. Great. No, she didn't see it. His voice didn't hide it. He dropped his gym bag, startling her. Under the circumstances, edginess was justified. It was justified. "What's wrong?"

Oh, just absolutely everything with the world, society, her family… her ex-boyfriend.

"Nothing," she said because what else could she say to a stranger? "Nothing's wrong."

Airing dirty laundry wasn't her style. She wouldn't share her thoughts with this stranger when she didn't even share them with her friends. Or she wouldn't share them with friends, if she had any friends.

Adara was her decompression conduit. Most of the time. This night was an exception. She wouldn't put her sister in the middle of the mess. The woman's engagement party was in full swing. A sibling tête-à-tête wasn't exactly appropriate.

"Are you a guest here at the hotel?"

"No," Harper said. "My sister's engagement party is in full swing upstairs."

"There's a problem?"

"No."

Question after question. All the questions. Was this an interrogation? Move along, Quizzy. Her life was so not his business.

She stepped aside, opening up his view.

Hint, hint, that door right there was the exit. Don't let it hit ya…

"You're not having fun?"

More questions. Why was her story the scoop of the day? Nosey guests should entertain themselves in the pool or with pay-per-view.

Time to change the subject before the flames of shame engulfed her. Yes, that was a real thing.

"Isn't this a strange place to be at this time of night?" That was it, good, stem the tidal wave of his curiosity. "It's almost eleven p.m."

"Guests can access the fitness suite at any time, day or night. They only have to call the concierge," he said. "During the day there is a range of personal training facilities—"

Her cough of laughter stalled him. "Sorry," she said, overjoyed for the distraction from her own shit. "Do you loiter in dark, abandoned areas of the hotel ready to spout the marketing script to anyone you happen upon? Is that your job?"

"No." The rumble of his deep voice anchored her in the mortifying moment. "Habit."

"You're in sales?"

That's right, Deep Voice, answer the question. Forget her embarrassing outburst. Move along. Move along.

"You could say that," he replied. "Are you

married?"

Or don't move along… Damnit, apparently his idea of progress was to get super personal, super fast.

Uh… rude. "Excuse me?"

Was she reading this right? They couldn't see each other's faces, yet he was hitting on her?

Maybe not. Matter of fact, he'd stated what was apparently obvious within seconds of meeting her. Yes, she was unmarriable. Just what needed to be reinforced. Thanks for that. Don't worry, she was under no illusions.

"If you're running from your sister's engagement party the typical assumption would be that you're not married and perhaps envious…"

Okay, she'd missed the mark, he wasn't hitting on her. "I'm not envious of anything."

Was his casual curiosity a reprieve or should she be offended he was prying without tact again?

"Why did you run from the party?"

Ordinarily, putting words to her shame was difficult. Hence why it was her default to avoid the issue. This entitled stranger wasn't being subtle, she got the feeling he'd wait all night for an answer.

This could be an opportunity. Yeah, that's how she should look at it. If she didn't talk about what brought her there, she'd stay down in the dark forever wallowing in shame.

The gloom, the anonymity, gave her a platform. One use only. Speak now, then forever hold her peace.

"I ran into my ex," she admitted.

"Ah."

"I didn't expect to see him tonight." Maybe she should have. "Damon had an affair with my sister's best friend, Charissa. They left the country together a year ago, he works for my dad, and they had this opportunity in Australia…" The stranger didn't care. "Anyway, they're back and I think I'd just…"

Articulating it was tough.

After Damon and Charissa emigrated—for a year as it turned out—the pitying looks did eventually dry up. *Eventually*. For months, she'd been living free and easy and hadn't thought about Damon at all. She sure didn't miss him. Then, bam! Him and Charissa show up, right there, celebrating without shame. One helluva gut punch.

"You're just getting over the betrayal and you didn't expect them to return?"

The stranger got it. He understood.

Thank God someone did.

Maybe she wasn't totally insane. "No, I didn't. My sister, Adara, said nothing about them coming tonight. She and Charissa were best friends. Are best friends. Maybe it's just a shock response. Adara can't have known they'd be here or she would've told me." She would've. "He looks great."

"You're not as over him as you thought?"

"No, it's not that." Her muddled thoughts didn't want to form a line. "Maybe I… I thought I was going to spend my life with him… When I found out about the affair… it ripped my world apart. For him, it's like nothing ever happened. And there he is, just there, back in my social life. If they're here to stay, Damon's going to be at the office." And there was the nausea again. "He'll be everywhere. How can I pretend nothing happened? He's up there dancing with her… he used to dance with me, you know? It's so normal. Like I imagined our whole past." The stranger took a step in her direction, keeping his distance without a word. "Why do I feel like this?" she whispered, pressing her splayed fingers into her stomach again.

"You're not over him," the stranger said.

That explanation was too simple. She didn't want Damon. Didn't feel love or lust. No jealousy or envy. She just felt sick.

"When they came off the dance floor, heading in my direction, I ran." While doing her best to disguise the haste. "Man, I couldn't get out of there fast enough. I can't pretend to be happy for them. I can't. I'm in the same place, doing the same things I did when Damon and I were together. I can't keep a man happy and he knows that. Charissa will look down her nose with pity. I don't want to be pitied. They'll take one look and know I'm a failure. I'm at my sister's engagement party and I couldn't even find myself a plus one… I'm pathetic. No wonder he left me."

"Sounds like you're throwing your own pity party."

Thanks for the sympathy. Don't sugarcoat it, will you?

"I don't pity myself. I disgust myself. If I'd known they were coming I'd have made more of an effort to get a date. I do not want to be the pitied singleton." The only singleton. "Again. If I had someone to dance with… someone to take my hand… let them watch me dance and laugh and be happy." What a fantasy. Pathetic didn't cover it. "If I had that distraction, I could be oblivious instead of drowning in humiliation."

"You did nothing wrong."

Ha, that was a joke. "Yeah? Damon's been my father's favorite for years. There's only me and my sister; dad has no son to take the reins of his business. Damon was that man. I caught them cheating at my birthday party last year. My mother was with me and… she said it's what men do."

"She expected you to stay with him?"

"Is fidelity too much to ask?" Harper sighed. "My father expected us to patch it up… Davis Scott is never wrong. My father is used to giving orders and having them obeyed. When I refused to turn a blind eye and put up with the affair… Damon was already in line to set up the Australian partnership, but I was supposed to be the one to go with him. I found out about the affair and Charissa took my place… in every sense."

"You did the right thing. If he didn't make you happy—"

"I didn't make him happy." That was the embarrassment. "I didn't go looking for a better offer. I didn't have affairs to quench my un-slaked lust." Her throat hurt. "I didn't keep him happy in life. I didn't keep him happy in bed, and both of them know that. Now I have to stand in front of them while none of us state that obvious fact. Will they be thinking it? I will. Does that sound like a fun way to spend an evening?"

The impromptu therapy session was helping. The stranger's intrusion started as unwelcome, but talking it out provided some perspective. Kinda. She could do this. She'd have to psyche herself up to return to the party. She'd be missed eventually and if the partygoers made a big deal about her running away to hide, she'd be even more humiliated.

"Did he make you happy? This Damon guy?"

What did that have to do with anything?

Lifting her head, she wanted to decipher the stranger's expression because his tone was so… knowing. Darkness liked to be infuriating.

"I hadn't thought about it. I wasn't happy. I wasn't sad. I was… indifferent."

"And you were going to spend your life with the man?"

He didn't have to sound so incredulous about it. Grown-ups settled all the time. Love, like real love, the movie kind, yeah, she'd never seen evidence that actually existed. This stranger was a romantic… or an idiot.

"We had respect… or at least I thought we did." The cheating thing sort of flew in the face of that. "Love is… an anomaly, it's not as common as people make it out to be. The majority of us settle with respect, cohabitation. A partner. That's what I thought Damon and I had before I found out about him and Charissa."

"You were wrong about that, maybe you're wrong about love too."

Talk about missing the point. Her turmoil wasn't related to a delusion about a prince sweeping her off her feet. Ha! Ridiculous! Hilarious!

All she wanted? To be left alone to live her life. Unfortunately, the people in her circle prioritized relationships above everything else.

Well, other than her father, he prioritized business. That was the one thing they had in common. Because, truly, what else was worth the time?

"I don't care about love," she said.

"You care about appearances."

"It's what I've been raised to consider."

"How things look?"

"Instead of how things actually are? Yeah."

"So you want it to look good?"

"My relationships?"

"Yeah," he said. "You said you wanted someone to hold your hand tonight. You want to throw it back at him, have Damon think twice about his behavior."

"I don't want everyone to be reminded that I'm the pathetic dumped one. I wish I could just… pretend I didn't care. Have Damon think he's not crossed my mind in the year since they left."

"Cowering isn't going to achieve that."

Again, stating the obvious. This guy had a talent for it.

"No," Harper agreed. "But it's better than the alternative."

"Your sister has made a life-changing decision. Hiding down here, you're missing the chance to celebrate with her. You won't get that back."

Her sister had found a secure relationship. A stand-up guy. The couple would look after each other.

"Carnell worships Adara, he'd never hurt her."

"Sounds like love to me… Get back upstairs, get a drink… you never know what might happen."

His message? That not everyone settled. Was that his point? Adara and Carnell were in love. Yes, that was true. Harper's sister adored her fiancé, but not as much as Carnell adored his fiancée.

"I suppose there's a chance I'll fall flat on my face in the middle of the room. That would begin a new humiliating chapter." A little sarcasm was warranted. Okay, maybe a big sarcasm was too. "I wouldn't want to miss that."

She hated feeling sorry for herself. Work had been busy and she'd already had a drink or two, could that explain the unexpected wobble? Usually she was happy to tell the world to go to hell. Why was tonight so different?

"Don't you want to celebrate your sister's engagement?"

Yes! She did! Missing out on sharing this night with her sibling was heartbreaking. For her, at least. Adara wouldn't miss a beat, she'd be up there having a ball. At the end of the day, wasn't that the most important thing?

"Adara is beautiful and poised. Being social, fitting in, it comes naturally to her. Screwing up is what I do best."

Story of her life.

"No more pity," he said.

The outside edge of his index finger grazed her temple.

When did he get close enough to touch her? To soothe with such a gentle—

"Go upstairs and hold your head high… We

never know which cards our opponents hold. Act like you've got it and they'll believe you do. There's nothing more powerful than the bluff. When you pull it off, it's a high."

The electricity of his departed caress was still warm. It wasn't intrusive; it was intimate. The zing still fizzled on the path his finger traced.

Sheesh, don't make it a big thing. It probably only felt that way because they were alone in the dark.

Giving her no chance to speak again, he opened the door that led back to the stairwell. Struck dumb, she followed his unspoken invitation to use it.

Like an apparition, he didn't follow, he just drifted away.

Okay. Back upstairs.

She could do this.

TWO

Bastian

FURTHER WORDS HAD weighted her lips. Even without seeing them, he'd sensed she wasn't done sharing. Urging her into the stairwell was the quickest way to regain his sanity.

In theory.

The unique aroma of her intoxicating perfume tempted him to whisk her away from her family, her ex, and all her troubles. What was he thinking?

The gym was supposed to tire him, not set him on a personal mission.

Let it go. It was a bad idea. Forget her. And her troubles. And the breathy little gasps that peppered her desperate words.

He stifled an internal groan.

In less than five hours, he was expected to host a fleet of executives seeking partnership. He didn't want to partner—no, open mind. Keep an open mind. His friend Breck's advice. Caspian concurred. Both knew what they were talking about.

There, in the hotel, *his* hotel, he'd be the consummate host for his professional guests. This was his world. His home ground. On balance, he probably spent more time in hotels than he did in his own home. Pushing through was where he excelled. Business, his life, it gave him an outlet for the mental energy he couldn't expend elsewhere.

Though even that had been dragging of late.

Insomnia plagued him. Irritation was never good for business. Everything was on the up, he had no excuse for worry or preoccupation. Recently, for some reason, an unfamiliar weight burdened his shoulders. Something was there, something he wanted. Something he could feel but couldn't see. Until he could figure out what the hell it was, he couldn't pursue it.

Damnit, he was a man of action. See the goal, head straight for it, no distractions.

Success often meant being surrounded by people. Yet the number of bodies in his periphery was irrelevant if there was nothing to embrace, no challenge, no peace. God, what was wrong with him?

He needed to get laid.

Nope. Even that failed to inspire a smile. Sex was easy. What about laughter? Conversation? Connection?

He and Robyn had called it quits a while ago. Some might attribute his insomnia to that, but it wasn't. If anything, getting out of that entanglement was a relief.

No, the hunger clawed long before they ended things. Something wanted to race him, he wanted to race…

Shit. No one could have it all. With the business taking up most of his time, his personal relationships often suffered. This was it. Life. Fucking handle it.

What was her scent? What did she…? Sweet, clean, fresh… playful. Like new season berries and mango, peach… the most incredible mouth-watering fruit salad. What the fuck did that mean?

The sweet woman sought something too.

Pride. Confidence. Security.

She wanted to be in a room with a companion, someone there for her.

Someone without ulterior motives. Someone to take her around the dance floor.

He got that. Singles often experienced social occasions from the margins. Judged. Silenced. Pitied.

Miss Sweet wanted someone to be there for her. A plus one. A person catering to her needs. A crutch to lean on instead of propping herself against a wall in the corner hoping to remain unseen.

Working social events under the guise of business networking, he understood the perspective. As he talked industry with staid associates, couples talked, laughed, reveled in each other. Discussing debentures and dividends didn't fall into the category of fun.

After Sweet disappeared into the stairway, he used the employee elevator to get to his floor. Workout forgotten, now he was fastening his Rolex and running his hands through his dark, damp hair. It wasn't perfect but it would do.

Heading out, he was soon back in the employee elevator. Singles needed to stick together. That pressure she spoke of, applied by others to "fix" those not in relationships, had been aimed at him a time or two.

This Damon guy did a helluva number on Miss Sweet. On her own, she had no way to combat or deflect that. Joining her was impulse. Good idea or bad? One thing was for sure, Damon would never pity Miss Sweet again.

All he had to do was seek out her scent in the ballroom… which would reek of perfumes and cologne. That'd be a breeze. He was nothing if not determined. Why not give it a shot? Right now, the mysterious woman needed a helping hand.

It would be a game, a fun distraction. He'd wriggled out of tough spots in his life and now had the chance to pay it forward. Maybe he'd catch that smile that evaded her.

THREE

ANOTHER COMFORTING PAT on the arm, another faux smile. Shit, she could give damn lessons on gritting teeth and accepting familial sympathy. A "grr" seemed appropriate.

"You keep your chin up," Aunt Mabel said. "He'll find you soon."

He being the white knight, saber drawn, ready to save her from spinsterhood. Did knights have sabers? Probably not. Besides, if anyone asked, spinsterhood didn't seem too shabby. Though being subjected to a lifetime of pity… Hmm, that went in the con column.

Stretching her smile until the octogenarian was gone, she breathed out and spun to lean over the bar.

"Jack Daniels on the rocks." Her order tumbled out fast. "Wait—" What was she thinking? "Forget the rocks and make it a double."

The bartender's smile told its own story as he went to fill the order. His wasn't of pity but for sure it reinforced her pathetic aura. Before her instinct to throw something at the bartender's head took hold, a voice rose behind her.

"Harper."

Her eyes closed in resignation.

Shit.

Shit.

Did she say shit?

Damon was a meteor on course to strike. No avoiding or escaping it. Fate had a sick sense of humor… she would have appreciated the alcohol first. Was that too much to ask?

A deep breath and another fake smile, she twirled one eighty degrees to face the speaker.

"Damon," she said, quashing an impulse to hiss like a triggered feline.

Just shy of six foot, Damon resented the dusty blond hair and fine features that gave him a boyish look. The suit was perfect, though not professionally tailored. Hmm, how much of his money had Charissa spent?

"You look great," Damon said.

Did he mean that? She should appreciate that he took the time to check her out, even if it was by rote. Whoa, wait, why? Why should she appreciate it? Because that was how women were conditioned from birth.

Check her out, don't check her out, who the hell cared? She just wanted the agony of awkward embarrassment to end.

"Where's Charissa?"

And still he was checking her out. Or… he was taking a last look at what he could've won and congratulating himself on the reprieve of pulling that lever one more time. Charissa was a better prize. Harper wasn't naive enough to think otherwise. On her best day, she could never be described as graceful. Someone may think her height of five six and petite stature would lend itself to elegance. Yeah, no, her and sophistication never met. Ships in the night and all that.

On the other hand, Charissa was sleek and absolutely flawless. A perfect prize. A woman women envied because it was just so… effortless.

Shut up. Comparison is the thief of joy. Huh, if that was true, she'd been robbed hourly since birth. Joy? What was that.

Focus. "She's talking to Adara," he said with a time-passing head-bob many folks would recognize.

Geez, this was awkward. Small talk. Okay, uh, how did a person shoot the shit with their smarmy ex?

Be polite. Make your momma proud and all that.

She mustered a, "That's nice."

Bring back Aunt Mabel, please, pretty please. At least she was practiced at handling that class of torture.

"Your father offered to put us up at the house, until we get settled again."

Her father had… Holy shit, he didn't—that was why this slimy warthog was making the effort to talk to her. She should've known. Absorb the outrage. Shrug it off. Meant nothing.

Jerk.

"Settled, yes," she said, bile rising in the back of her throat. "Right, sure."

What a rookie move. Where was her forethought? This should've been anticipated.

Damon despised confrontation, he much preferred to stab someone in the back and walk away. He'd never come over to chat just to be nice, of course he wanted something.

For at least a year before the affair was uncovered, Charissa lived at the Scott house with Adara. A six-bedroom house wouldn't be nearly big enough to avoid the happy couple if they moved in.

"I told him we can't accept without discussing it with you first."

Oh, yeah, 'cause he was known for being so

gracious. This wasn't his idea. Damon didn't care about her comfort or convenience, or anyone's comfort or convenience. This was Adara, she'd put money on it.

"So you came over here…" she said, fighting an impulse to grind her teeth within her frozen smile. "We haven't spoken for a year, and you came over here to ask if you could move into my house?"

"Your father's house," Damon said. Like that distinction mattered when it came to sharing a kitchen. Why did they have to live in such an expensive city? "It's not out of line. It was my house too."

He lived there with her. *With* her. Damon lived there with her, as her partner. Not that she'd say that. Davis Scott, her father, liked to keep his daughters close and rewarded them for complying. Adara would move out after she was married. At this rate, Harper would be in that house until her dying day.

"Are you coming back to the firm?" she asked, mentally crossing her fingers.

"I never left the firm," Damon said.

Just her.

Right.

Seeking her whiskey, she fumbled for the glass on the bar behind her. Snatching it up, she took that medicine with the ferocity of an asthmatic sucking on an inhaler. Instant death averted.

"No, you didn't."

"I think everyone's past this now." Damon's hand came toward her in a move too reminiscent of the aunt's conciliatory pat. Nope. No way. She veered aside, going around him, putting her back to the room, forcing Damon's back to the bar. Ha! Escape would be easier from that angle. "Harper…"

The pity was coming. It was coming. Brace for impact. Brace. Brace. Brace. She didn't want to flinch, but holding her head high was becoming more and more difficult. Her stupid ex was about to feed her a "there, there" speech.

In the corner of her eye, Charissa approached on an intercept course.

What the fuck? Glancing down, she half expected to be naked. This was the worst nightmare of her life.

Damon's pity and Charissa's gloating at the same time? Who was capable of enduring that without losing their sanity?

"Sorry I'm late."

A masculine voice materialized behind her.

Damon's demeanor changed. Pity gone, offense tensed him. Oh, he wasn't happy. Check out the snarl.

Something touched her elbow, a warm hand. Huh. A quick glance over her shoulder and, yep, confirmed, there was a man standing behind her. Not just behind her like that's where he happened to be, but actually behind *her*.

"Bastian Hunt," the voice spoke again.

The hand left her elbow and reached around, offering itself to Damon. The voice, the hand, both belonged to this stranger at her back.

"Damon Twaddle," her ex said, accepting the shake.

Oh, well, the guys had been introduced. Great! Good for them, maybe now someone could clue her in.

Wary, Damon seemed confused, for which he could be forgiven, hers might be contagious.

"What…"

Another glance back, their eyes met, and her words disappeared.

This guy was maybe six three, hair thick, dark, damp. And he knew something. Something she should know too. Except she didn't.

His square jaw ticked like maybe her

bewilderment was amusing. Laugh it up. Was he a jerk? One asshole was enough. Damon filled that quota all by himself. No supplements or understudies required, thank you.

The edge of his index finger glided down her temple and… it hit her. She gasped. This was the guy, the stranger from downstairs!

Oh. Oh. Oh!

"What's going on?"

Charissa's voice flared by Damon, snapping her attention to the couple. The curious Charissa tucked her hand into Damon's elbow, laying intrigue on the man at her back.

This Bastian Hunt was still there. The wall of his form solid against her spine, he was definitely with her. But… why? What was she missing?

"Harper?" Charissa asked. Kudos, Charissa's smile was almost genuine. Almost, but not quite. "Who is your friend?"

"Bastian Hunt," Damon said, a little spaced out.

What was going on? He hadn't been that drunk a minute ago and she'd never known him to take drugs. Living with Charissa may have driven him to it, especially if she was eviscerating his savings.

"Nice to meet you both," Bastian said. "My apologies but I have to steal Harper. I have some groveling to do. I promised I wouldn't be late and I let her down. I'm lucky she puts up with me."

When his fingers linked between hers, she didn't resist him relieving her of the liquor or leading her through the room onto the dance floor. She even let him hook both hands around the back of his neck and slide his own onto her waist.

"We have about a minute and a half to get our stories straight."

FOUR

"WHAT ARE YOU doing here?" she whispered, glancing at the couples around them as though proximity alone would reveal this Bastian's scam.

"You wanted someone to dance with."

What she should do was push out of his arms. She should slap his face and tell the creep to get lost. Should. Instead, her hands skimmed higher until her fingers twined in the ends of his hair.

He wasn't a creep. Though unexpected, it was sweet that he would do something selfless like this for her, to save her.

"You came to dance with me? To be my white knight?"

A fairytale moment brought to life.

"I had to get changed first," he said. When she managed a yap of laughter, his straight white teeth flashed in a smile. Ah, and a dimple, cute. "Harper is your name?"

She nodded. "Harper Scott."

"Bastian Hunt," he said. Yeah, she'd got that

much. "What do you do?"

"I'm a corporate event coordinator," she said. "I have my own business, though I work from my father's office complex."

Absorbing this, his expression became more serious. "What does your father's company do?"

"Scott Solutions. They sell bespoke IT and multimedia installations to small and mid-sized companies."

"Installation," Bastian said. "Computers?"

"Pretty much," she said, amused by his simplification of what Damon liked to pretend was complex. "I thought you were in sales."

"A spade's still a spade."

She laughed again. That was true. Salesmen had the gift of the gab. She guessed he was off the clock and could afford to be honest.

He drew her closer to nuzzle his nose in her hair. "Your perfume is intoxicating, what is it?"

"I'm not wearing perfume."

His disposition shifted a little and she loosened, prompting him to hold her closer.

Now this guy's suit was definitely tailored, no doubt about that. Expensive too, just like the watch on his wrist. An air of success shimmered around him… Was it just confidence or could he back it up? What had he said about bluffing? Given he was an advocate for faking it, maybe it wouldn't be smart to trust him too soon. Though even fake, it was impressive. He really sold the confidence and affluence, honest or not.

"Where do you live?"

"With my mother, father, and sister," she said. "And apparently now my ex and his girlfriend."

"They're moving into your parents' house?" Bastian asked, making eye contact without separating their bodies. "How big is the house?"

"Six bedrooms." Harper couldn't afford not to answer his questions now he'd shown up as her plus one. People would assume they were seeing each other, or at least that they knew some things about each other. She had to fill in the gaps… and fast. "It's big but…"

"You weren't wrong about your father's opinion of Damon. Why would—"

"They're just back from Australia," Harper said. "Charissa lived with Adara at my parents' for a long time before they went away. Damon was staying there too… with me…" Ultimately, "It gave him easier access to Charissa."

In response to her shiver, Bastian splayed his hands on her lower back, comforting her with strength.

"Don't think about them," he said. "Think about us. Let them watch."

"I don't imagine they'll be watching," she said, resting her face by his lapel.

The soft fabric and unmistakable scent of man wrought a different kind of shiver. Damon's arms were never this safe, she'd never felt this special with him. Then again, Damon never once went out of his way to care about her needs. Ha, out of his way? Her needs could be jumping up and down right there on the path in front of him and he'd still manage to avoid them.

"Oh, they are," Bastian said. "Trust me, Sweet, they're watching."

She'd take his word for it. It wasn't like she could check out the people around them. God knew what would happen if any of them made eye contact. She'd probably combust… or find herself naked in that nightmare. From bad to suspicious, it really could be she was having a psychotic break. How common was it that hot, sweet guys swooped in to play white knight? Maybe she was in a coma or high on drugs.

"Thank you for doing this," she said, clinging to

hopes of reality. "If I can ever repay—"

"The night's not over yet," he said with obvious cheer. If he was aiming for inspiring optimism, he'd misjudged his audience of one. "We're just getting started. What's your drink?"

"Vodka and cranberry," she said. The whiskey was for emergencies and Dutch courage only. "What's yours?"

"I drink Scotch," Bastian said, squeezing her closer, scanning the room. Getting a measure of those he'd have to perform for? "You don't need to know that. I take care of you."

"I couldn't ask you to actually—"

"What?" he asked. "We'll dance, and drink, and talk to anyone who wants to gawk. You're home, Harper, enjoy the night while it lasts."

He'd been delivered by her secret fairy godmother. That had to be it. Or drugs were still a possible explanation. Would it be rude to ask Bastian if she'd been spiked?

"Okay," she said, having no reason or inclination to argue.

It didn't matter that this man was gorgeous or way out of her league. That night, he was there for her. What the hell? Why not enjoy it? Chances were this was the last opportunity she'd have to delay facing Damon and their past. It sure wasn't going anywhere... unfortunately.

Bastian wasn't done with his questions. "When would you introduce a man to your family?"

"Sorry?"

Getting their stories straight meant no time for pleasantries.

"How far into a relationship would you usually invite him to meet your family?"

"They already knew Damon before we started

dating, but a guy they didn't know… maybe three or four months, why?"

"Then that's how long we've been seeing each other."

Oh, this wasn't a first date? Interesting slant. With one glaring flaw.

"Seeing each other…" she said. "I don't know anything about you."

Shit, huh, she should formulate some questions of her own. This guy was used to driving. Something about him screamed "in charge." So far, he'd led, and he, apparently, didn't expect that to change.

"Tonight's about you, Harper. Our stories need to match enough to fool your family," Bastian said. When the song ended, he retreated to take her hand. "Let's get you a drink."

Drunk. Yes. Stupefied. Blurring hard edges sounded good right about then.

This guy was attentive… or dangerous. In a room full of friends and family, she wasn't afraid.

"Are you trying to get me drunk so you can take advantage of me?"

Bastian's sure stride faltered and he turned fast, blazing scrutiny beneath his stern brow. He had to be trying to gauge if she was joking or accusing. When she smiled, his tempting dimple relaxed.

"Maybe that's the payment required," he said in the spirit of the tease.

"Man, then you really would be hard up," she said, deliberately walking in to nudge him, meaning to hasten their arrival at the bar.

Except he didn't budge an inch. The feather-light caress of his fingertip on her temple dazed her until the intensity of his smolder was all she could see.

"Yeah, I imagine I would be."

Corny, but she laughed. "I need to be drunker for

talk like that to work."

"Good tip," he said, curving an arm around her shoulders, pinning their bodies together for the final leg of their journey.

On arrival, Bastian slid her between him and the bar, trapping her in a protective circle, ordering their drinks over the top of her head. This was a bold move. Shielded by his body, Bastian staked a claim, keeping her safe and away from the possibly wicked intentions of others. Did he know that or was it incidental? Was she reading too much into it? Probably.

She'd taken one sip of her drink when Damon came barreling over.

"Can I talk to you, Harpy?" Damon asked, completely ignoring Bastian.

"You are talking to me," Harper said, licking her lips before sucking more alcohol up her straw.

Bastian's hand flattened on her abdomen to urge her back against his torso. Physical contact. Support. Solidarity. Leaning on him... she liked it.

"It's important," Damon grumbled.

Whatever was going on, Damon didn't want Bastian involved. That only encouraged her to keep her new friend close.

"You can stay at the house, Damon," Harper said. "I can't exactly say no. My father would probably kick me out before he would evict you anyway. But you can tell him you were noble and considerate, though you know I would never have said no."

Sass was run of the mill for her smart mouth when it was feeling confident. And with the monolith that was Bastian supporting her, the assuredness came flooding back. Would it last? Maybe. Maybe not. But it felt good then. Which was an achievement given she'd almost vomited when Damon first raised the proposition.

"Can I say no?" Bastian chipped in. "I don't like the idea of you living with an ex."

Tipping up her chin, she couldn't see Bastian's face but addressed him anyway.

"Damon doesn't want me, he's in love with Charissa," Harper said. "He dumped me, remember?"

"Thanks for screwing up," Bastian said, propping his chin on her head. "She's mine and staying that way."

Damon gaped. "You're Bastian Hunt," he said as though he couldn't quite believe it.

"Yes, I am." Bastian lowered his mouth to her hair. "Where would you like to sit, Sweet?"

"Your choice," she said, sipping her drink again.

"If I had my choice, we'd be upstairs in bed and you'd be sitting on me."

FIVE

SHOCK BURST IN her stomach, opening her mouth, dropping the straw from her lips. No man had ever said something so daring. Not about her, and definitely not in company.

And her reaction was new too. Her inner thighs tingled, a rousing heat jolted up through her core. This was good, it was… Who was this guy?

Okay, yes, it was a ruse for Damon's benefit. Intellectually, she knew that. Uh huh. Yeah. Yet her body squeezed backward, following its instinctive need to get closer. Something primal in her liked Bastian's direct words and the conjured possibilities. At that point, she was a passenger to her body's awakening.

A man as charming and attentive as Bastian could never be enamored with her for real. Tonight was simply a chance to dream. She'd take it.

Fizz of desire aside, it was no hardship to see Damon at such a loss either. Ha! Take that!

Damon scoffed. "I can't believe—"

"I've heard a whisper," Adara sang, appearing behind Damon, beaming at the group. "It's great to see everyone getting along." Adara pinched Damon's cheek much to Damon's chagrin. Ah, what a cutie-cutiepie. "And it looks like that whisper is true."

Adara didn't disguise her open appraisal of Bastian.

"Bastian Hunt," he said.

Again, he reached around her body to offer a hand.

Though Adara gave it a loose shake, her narrowed eyes weren't so sure. "Yes, I heard that," her sister said. "But what are you to our Harper?"

"The whole world," he proclaimed. With a nudge, she cast a smile in his direction. "No point lying to them, Sweet."

"Your significance is shrinking by the second," Harper teased, enjoying the theme of their banter.

"No, it's not," he murmured on her scalp, though the others must've heard it.

Was that for show or could he sense her bubbling hormones? Please embarrassment, take a vacation.

She laughed and nudged him again, which tightened his embrace just as Carnell came to join them.

"This is Carnell," Harper said to Bastian who shook the man's hand. "He's the hopeless puppy marrying Adara."

"After you plan the big day," Adara said to her, cozying into her fiancé.

"I am not a wedding planner," Harper said. "How many times do I have to tell you that?"

"You organize parties and stuff," Adara said. "You wouldn't help out your own sister?"

"I'll help you as much as a sister can, but not to the detriment of my business."

Her sister filled in some blanks for the three men. "She's freaking out about this big launch event thing next month."

She sighed. "I am not freaking out," she enunciated every word.

Not that her sister was listening. "She was up at four thirty this morning working. Four thirty! What on earth would possess anyone—"

"It's always office hours somewhere on the planet," Bastian said.

"Thank you," Harper said to him while glaring at her sister. Though she didn't do much, or any, international business. "Someone finally gets it."

"Like peas in a pod," Adara said.

Much as she loved her sister, they couldn't be more different. "We can't all be happy in Mani-Pedi World."

She and her sister teased each other about their life choices. Only teased. Adara played up to the pampered princess persona, but the truth was, she cared, she listened, Adara had a good heart. Though she didn't always know what to do with it.

"Yes, I am entirely shallow," Adara said without shame. "But, please note, this is my engagement party, proving that I, at least, get something out of my superficial life. I got my guy. You work, sweat, and break your back. Why? To get more work. It's senseless."

Her ex couldn't resist the urge to get in on the action. "Harpy's always been a workaholic."

"I am not a workaholic. What is this? Attack Harper hour? Is this one of your planned party games?"

"You know we're only teasing," Adara said, wearing a smile that faded when she side-eyed Damon. "You'll stop when you find the right man."

"Will I?" Harper asked appreciating the veiled insult Adara sent Damon's way.

Charissa pushed through Carnell and Adara to once again put her hand in Damon's elbow, asserting her ownership. Yeah, she could have him. Good luck.

Charissa had a right to be insecure about the relationship given the way it had started. What was it? Once a cheater, always a cheater.

"Your father wants to speak to you, Harper," Charissa declared.

Damon bristled. Where was his attitude coming from? That answer would have to wait. Her father would too. She so wasn't in the mood for family judgment... more family judgment.

"I bet he does," Carnell murmured.

Meaning...?

"Where's Mom?" she asked her sister.

Adara sighed. "With Carnell's parents."

"Trouble?"

"Only in so far as they're already arguing about our marriage." Adara swallowed down some of her pink drink.

"The wedding?"

"No, the marriage," Adara corrected her. "They're picking out locations for where we should live. Dad wants to build something for us."

"That's generous," Damon said.

"It's only to keep us close. We'll end up in a backyard pool house."

"Still generous."

"Yeah." Adara didn't have much patience for Damon. Served him right. "Like you'd have been happy living on their doorstep if you married Ha—oh..."

Without Bastian at her side, that would've reignited the mortification. With him there, meh, who cared? Man, she really owed this guy. Maybe she could pay him to be her full-time ego float.

"It's okay," Harper said. "The cat's out the bag."

"You told Bastian?" her sister asked.

That she'd been cheated on and cast aside? Yes, she had. Though if she hadn't that question would've dropped her right in it.

Bastian soothed her sister. "It came up in early conversation."

Early was right.

Adara's blush faded as she addressed Bastian. "He's a bastard but she's my best friend. Talk about a rock and a hard place. I'm surprised you haven't hit him in the face… Harper did."

"Too many witnesses," Bastian said, jovial.

At least, she thought so until Damon straightened up.

Wow, whatever expression Bastian wore, it could turn a guy to stone.

"Your father wants to speak to you, Harper," Charissa said again, a parrot stuck on repeat.

"Dad wants to speak to me about you two moving in."

Her relationship with her father was tenuous at best. It had never exactly been robust, but since she'd refused his offer of a job at his firm in favor of going out on her own, yeah, most of the time she was dead to him. As highlighted by his affront that she'd rejected Damon and his cheating, choosing self-respect over her father's legacy. Oh, she was such a disappointment.

"Or about your new boyfriend," Adara said. "Is he your boyfriend?"

Everyone's curiosity about the stranger was justified; she hadn't mentioned being involved. In her defense, she wasn't involved until less than an hour ago.

Instead of perpetuating the lie, she joked. "He's a gigolo." Harper stroked the hand he had around her. "I just hired him for the night."

She still held a drink, Bastian apparently didn't have one because both of his hands were on her.

Adara's lips curled in a tease. "Leave me his card."

"Excuse me?" Carnell asked, quickly placated by the kiss Adara pressed to his cheek before wiping away the gloss she'd left.

"You've kept quiet about this, sister," Adara said, giving Bastian another look over. "He's expensive."

"Only the best quality."

"She was kidding about the gigolo thing," Damon said.

Trust Damon to explain something everyone understood.

"Doesn't make him any less expensive," Adara said. "Men like him want to take a woman to the opera and the ballet." Damon and Carnell snickered. "Not exactly Harper's style."

"We're only using each other for sex," Harper said, quietening the snickers in an instant.

Adara grinned. "Then have at it," she said. "You deserve a break. You haven't had the best of luck with men."

"Passive-aggressive doesn't suit you, Adara," Damon said.

Pinning him under an icy glare, Adara snarled, "Would you like me to hit you? I have no problem being direct."

"Everyone knows that," Damon said, kindling his confidence. "That's how you worked through every man in ScoSo management before settling on this sap."

Adara was bold but delicate and didn't deserve that.

"Take that back, you asshole!" Harper jerked out of Bastian's grasp. "Apologize!"

"Everyone calm down," Carnell said.

Typically, Damon was unapologetic. "Just stating facts."

Shit, she wanted to hit him again so bad. "What is your problem?"

"I have no problem." Damon shrugged. "It's true. Who's going to deny it?"

"Your father wants to speak with you, Harper," Charissa said, apparently having nothing else to contribute.

Carnell's arm went around Adara as she tucked her face in at his chest. Oh, God, she'd be crying in a minute.

"You're a snake," Harper hissed at Damon. "There was absolutely no need for you to talk like that. What exactly did you think—"

"Come on, Harpy, you're the Contrast Sisters," Damon said with the nerve to actually smile. "The slut and the prude."

He always had the worst sense of humor.

"Damon," Charissa chastised, which was at least some proof she had a mind of her own.

Not that Damon heard her.

His arrogance might not be surprising, but it did disgust her.

"Never more of a man than when you're stepping on those around you to get up top. Do you feel good?" Harper asked. "Do you feel better about being less than slime? We'll all feel better when we remember what a jerk you are, but for you... repulsive is for life."

Carnell took Adara away. Good. Everyone should be far away from him. Her included. She strode off, unable to be near her bastard of an ex for another second. The jerk had ruined Adara's night, her very important night.

Storming away was needlessly dramatic, especially when, uh, she didn't have anywhere to go. Still with her, Bastian must've sensed her lack of direction. He captured her hand and used her momentum to sweep her around into his arms on the dance floor again.

Burying her face in his jacket, her composure

needed a minute.

"That guy's a piece of work," Bastian said. "You're still not over that? You've got some taste in men, Sweet."

"Don't goad me," she mumbled, pressing her face against him. "I feel awful... dirty and violated that he ever touched me. My dad brought him into our lives, but... I'm disgusted with myself."

"Did you really hit him?" Somehow the way she moved against him relayed confirmation. "Good. How did you restrain yourself? He deserves so much more than one hit." She managed to sob out a laugh. "Are you crying?"

Resting her palms on him, she couldn't bring herself to lift her head yet. Being there was nice, in his embrace, nestled in close, hands on his chest, either side of her face. Was it too much to ask to exist in this safe place for a while longer?

Crying wasn't the right descriptor, maybe on the inside. Everything was such a mess. Her life was such a mess.

"I won't ruin your suit," she said, easing back to curl her fingers around his tie. "I promise."

"Screw the suit, Sweet," he said, squeezing her.

Oh, it felt good. No man ever held her this way. Should they be so familiar so soon? It didn't feel wrong. Maybe it should.

"It's a nice suit."

"I have plenty of them. Do you want me to hit him? We can pay off the witnesses."

Another laugh bled from her lips. This guy had some talent.

"Bastian..." she whispered as he stroked her hair.

"Yeah?"

"Thank you for tonight," she said, hazarding a

glance up to his concern.

Far from sight, his dimple was hidden somewhere behind his frown. Already she missed it. Weird.

"You're upset. You shouldn't thank me when—"

"I'd forgotten…"

Damon crashing unwelcome into her life again had distracted her from the truth that should've saved her from embarrassment.

"Forgotten what?"

"Who he really was. I'm grateful to Charissa for saving me from that. If it hadn't been for tonight… for you, for this… thank you."

"Then my work is done," he said, skimming the tip of his index finger down to her cheekbone.

"I suppose it is," she whispered.

Singledom was just fine with her if a man like Damon was the alternative.

Bastian flashed his dimple. There it was. Her smile quickly followed. She wasn't ready to leave his arms and settled close. The dance gave her cover to enjoy the man sharing their secret.

They'd never cross paths again. Eventually the music would fade, just as Bastian would from her life. For a short time, they'd belonged to each other. Bastian might not realize it, but he'd given her a gift she wouldn't forget for the rest of her life.

SIX

Bastian

ANYONE COULD BE forgiven for believing he'd stopped thinking about her. He hadn't.

In his office, at his vast oak desk that separated him from his rambling mother, Bastian shouldn't be distracted by memories of Harper's scent. Yet there he was.

"Bastian," Carolyn Hunt said to her son. "Are you listening to me?"

No was the quick answer. His mother wouldn't like that truth and she'd raised him better than to be so harsh.

"Yes," he said instead, drawing his focus from the grand floor-to-ceiling windows beyond the conference table to his right. "I'm listening. It's the same story you've been spouting for months. I don't need to hear it again."

Months? Since high school.

"We're worried about you," she said.

His mother's heart was in the right place. Still, he could do without the interference. Stress didn't feature in his life, it didn't fray his nerves. Except right then, the hounding sensation plagued him. Insomnia. Irritability. Why was he so on edge?

That something he was missing… Something? Someone?

"Great." He pushed away from the desk to stand up, hoping she'd do the same. "Thank you for your concern. I appreciate that you care."

"We do care," Carolyn said, remaining seated. He should've known. His mom wasn't easily handled. "Though I wonder why when you're being glib."

He didn't mean to offend, he just had other things on his mind. His love life, existent or not, was one of Carolyn's favorite hobbies. More of a priority for her than him.

"I'm sorry," Bastian said. Relenting to his mom's sincerity, he sat again. "You have nothing to worry about."

"We do," she said. "You've been distracted. You're not happy, son, a mom knows."

His mom doted on him and his sister, Keely. They'd grown up without a nanny, unusual given their affluence. Carolyn inherited a fortune after the death of her parents. That money didn't stop his father working hard while Carolyn fulfilled her dream, dedicating her days to motherhood. They were her world then, still were, if he was honest. Most of her time now was dedicated to non-profit organizations. Often she pursued causes in league with her best friend, another rich woman who dedicated herself to her ever-growing family.

He shrugged, like a teenager unable to figure out what answer would appease his parent.

"Things are great. I'm great. There's no reason for me to be unhappy."

"That doesn't mean you're not, sweetheart."

It was difficult to argue with her at the best of times. When she was right, it was nigh on impossible. The truth, from an objective point of view, was he had no right to be unhappy. His life was privileged, always had been, he'd never wanted for anything. Money. Success. Family. His life was a stream of home runs. He'd been raised right with solid values, and never experienced hardship. Yet his insomnia continued. If anything, it was worse now he had a specific thought keeping him awake.

The scent of Harper filled his senses again. Shit. Why couldn't he stop thinking about her? Get it together, man.

At the engagement party, they'd danced one, then another; three, maybe four, went by. Neither of them would leave the sanctuary of their embrace. The sensation of holding her calmed him. So much so it quelled his overwhelming urge to deck that Damon bastard.

When Harper lifted her head that final time, he'd known it was over. With a single nod, he had taken her hand and kissed the petal-soft skin of her knuckles. God, she had the most beautiful smile—

"Bastian!"

He snapped from the daze. "Hmm?"

"I said you should invite Nicole to the Valentine Ball."

Rich and powerful men all over the world paused to listen when he spoke. His mom? Wasn't intimidated. He had never unlocked the key to that or shaking her from a cause. Tenacity ran in the family.

"Mom," he said, intending to temper her expectations. "I know you liked her—"

"I didn't like her, I don't know her," Carolyn said. "I hardly got a moment to speak to her. But if you like her, you should pursue her. It's been so long since we've seen you happy with a woman. Not all women are out for what you can give them like that Robyn. You know that, sweetheart, don't you? You've been successful in every business endeavor you've pursued. But your wealth isn't the sum of you. We want to see you happy and settled down with someone special."

Nice sentiment, slightly overshadowed by the fact that...

"You want grandchildren."

The smile they shared proved how well he knew his mom.

Keely, his sister, was thirteen years his junior. His parents struggled with fertility issues. It wasn't until they'd given up on the idea of a second child that his younger sister chose to make an appearance.

The lucky surprise that never stopped giving, Keely was bright, optimistic, and spoiled rotten, but she had a good heart.

"One or two before I'm too old to chase after them," Carolyn said, having made no secret of her wish to be a grandmother. "That aside..." She got serious again. "I want you to be happy. You've never been the typical rich playboy type."

"I was too busy," he said, holding his hands up to the expansive office they sat in.

Grand Holdings was his life and had been since he bought a small chain of mediocre hotels in his late teens. Before he'd even left school, he started working to expand and build a reputation for himself and his hotels as a top-of-the-line luxury chain.

A good foundation of money and support helped. His mom invested in him, showing nothing but confidence in his ability. Making it under the steam of hard work was important to him, as was not disappointing his family. He'd paid his mother back every cent and shown his father he'd be able to take care of his sister no matter what.

After his parents were gone, he and Keely would inherit their father's business interests and their mom's old money. But Bastian wanted to be a success in his own right. His parents never interfered with his business interests or discouraged him.

Being his own man was key, and he sure had learned, many times over, from his mistakes. He started small, studied every detail, tweaking his own models until profit was optimized.

His interests went beyond the hotels these days, his stock portfolio was rewarding and he owned an airline that catered to the wealthier end of the market. Life was good. But a booming business didn't leave much time for soulmate searching.

"The playboy lifestyle never suited or appealed to you."

Another fact. Though he knew a few, he'd never understood men who partied all the time, frittering away their money, changing girlfriends every week. Talk about counterproductive and exhausting. A man could put his time and energy to better use.

Despite that, disappointing his mom stung deep. By not prioritizing his prospective family, he'd done exactly that.

Linking his fingers, he chose to appease instead of tease. "When I meet the mother of your future grandchildren, Mom, I promise you'll be the first to know."

Did that make her feel better? His mom went through these phases all the time. She'd leave him alone for months and then, from nowhere, start to panic about his lack of a wife. That would cue a stream of harassment, well intentioned harassment, intended to prompt him into getting serious about a girlfriend. Eventually, he'd calm her down, or his father would, and peace would return for a while. As he got older, the frequency of the episodes increased.

His mother may feel urgency, but he'd never been inspired.

The buzzer on his phone's intercom alerted him to Tina's imminent contribution. Please be a reprieve…

Tina's voice chirped down the line. "Mr. Hunt, I apologize for the interruption, but…"

"Yes?" he asked after Tina's words trailed off.

Given the discomfort in her voice, he'd guess she was squirming. Tina was quick and efficient, two vital qualities in her role as his executive assistant. If she didn't want to deliver whatever news she was sitting on, it couldn't be good.

"Your girlfriend is in the hospital," Tina said.

Turned out squirming was catching; making eye contact with his mom was a mistake. Great, now she'd think he was hiding a romantic relationship. The matriarch's lecture wanted assurance he wasn't neglecting that area of his life. If the girlfriend thing was true, it would be cruel to keep it to himself. For both his mother's sanity, and his own.

"My girlfriend?"

No way his mom would believe it, but, as far as he knew, he didn't have one.

The voice in the speaker hesitated again. "Yes, her sister called to say she's in the ER," Tina said. "She was mugged."

And, still, he drew a blank. "My girlfriend?"

"Bastian…" his mom warned.

His hand wasn't in the cookie jar, he'd swear it in front of a judge.

"Mom, I promise you—"

"Harper," Tina interrupted. "Her name is Harper. Is that right?"

Bastian was already out of his chair. "I'm on my way."

SEVEN

"THIS IS THE MOST embarrassing moment of my life," Harper muttered when Bastian walked into the ER exam room.

Perfect, just as she remembered him. He didn't disappoint. So few men had that quality. That was something, right? She should have at least one nice memory before she combusted in humiliation.

A woman entered behind him. Older. Shorter. Reeking of sophistication.

Not that Bastian noticed the others in the room. She, seated on the end of the hospital bed, got his complete focus.

Purpose sped his gait until he stopped in front of her. "Look at me."

They only had a private room because Adara insisted on it. What a fuss for nothing. Talk about unnecessary. She'd expected her sister and Carnell to come back into the room alone. Bastian? Really? Bastian? How had that happened? She'd murder her beloved sibling for this.

Since they arrived, Carnell sported a permanent frown, much like the one Bastian was wearing too. Adara had been teary and apologetic. Drama? No. There was no need for all the emotion. This was one big misunderstanding. A purposeless palaver.

The sooner she could get out of there, the better.

"No," she said. Bastian didn't hear her or he didn't care. He cupped her face and brought it up against her will, forcing her to meet his eye. "I'm fine. Don't fuss."

"We'll give you guys a minute," Carnell said and left with an arm around Adara.

"Where are the police?" Bastian asked. "What happened?"

Her gaze darted around. Something else, something else, anything else, the ceiling, the cabinet, oh, a sharps container. How interesting.

"Nothing happened," Harper said because, unfortunately, she couldn't avoid his question forever. "Don't fuss."

The entitlement of his touch suggested he wasn't afflicted with the same awareness that zipped through her whenever they touched.

"Where's your doctor?"

"Bastian," she whined. "This is mortifying."

Nope, nothing got through.

The woman who'd arrived with him slunk over to crowd in beside them. "Are you going to introduce us?"

"I told you to stay in the car," Bastian said to the woman, without losing his focus.

He pushed the hair from her temple, uncovering the bruised graze that hid there. His jaw twitched and strengthened, clamping tight.

"You didn't have to come," Harper said, curling her fingers around his wrists as his hands continued their caress.

"You were mugged," he said. "Did you expect me to hear that and ignore it?"

The presence of the strange woman made it impossible to have an honest conversation.

"I didn't know Adara called you. I don't know how—I wouldn't have let them. They must have called when I was with the doctor."

"Good, I'm glad they called," he said. "Someone needs to drum some sense into you. What happened?"

She tried, unsuccessfully, to duck away from his touch. "It's not a big deal."

He leaned forward, forcing her to slope backward. Dropping his weight to his fists on the mattress at either side of her, Bastian was intent, completely at ease with their proximity.

Her heart, on the other hand, couldn't handle it. It hammered so hard she could almost hear it screaming to jump from her chest and hide. Shit, the last thing she wanted to do was start panting in his face. If she was going to have a heart attack, guess a hospital was the place to do it.

This man, this deliciously, unconstrained, consuming man, wasn't shy about using his size and effect on her to demand what he wanted.

Somehow, he loomed closer. "Then you won't mind telling me what happened."

Wow, well, when he was set on something, he didn't let up. Was this battle winnable? Not if she wanted it over as fast as possible. He was so damn assured and unapologetic. Being the sole point of his commanding concentration was both humbling and arousing. The power of his fixation alleviated the pain in her skull, diverting it to the tingling between her thighs.

Swallowing, she licked her lips, accepting Bastian wouldn't retreat until he had the truth.

"I went out for dinner with Adara and Carnell," Harper said, tracing a fingernail around the face of his watch.

Her nail kept exploring, moving to the links of the metal strap, sliding in and out. Fidgeting refocused her bouncing endorphins. It was the adrenaline of the night. That was the agitation. She shouldn't read anything into it, he shouldn't—was she a billboard of humiliation?

"And?"

"I went outside to make a phone call and… a guy ran up and snatched my purse." His eyes rose to note the purse on the bed behind her. Yes, that purse. Okay, she knew what he was thinking. "I didn't let him have it."

After a long, unimpressed blink, his eyes opened on hers again. "Of course not, that would've been too smart. Do you have secret nuclear launch codes in there? The Football wears Prada?"

If he wanted to get sarcastic, she'd get defensive. "No," she said. "But it's mine."

"You have a sentimental attachment to it?"

It was a purse, like any other, one she liked, but it wasn't an heirloom or a gift. "That's not the point."

"What if he'd had a gun?"

Her attacker didn't have any kind of weapon, except his fists, which were the reason all parties found themselves in this moment.

"He hit me in the face."

"I can see that. What if he'd had a knife, or another weapon, something that caused more than cuts and bruises?"

"He didn't."

Bastian was overreacting, everybody was overreacting. It was done and she was safe. End of story. A mugger had no right to put his hands on her or her things. To be honest, she was surprised everyone else seemed so eager to capitulate.

"You didn't know that," he said. "Why would you take the risk?"

"It's mine!"

Though his exhale was audible, she gave him points for mentally counting to ten before responding. No, there was no need to fuss, but it was sweet of him to come despite their lack of an actual connection—a genuine connection at any rate.

"You're more important than a purse, Sweet."

Instead of fighting with the man displaying such concern, she appreciated his proximity and sought something she'd missed.

"Show me your dimple," she murmured, her palm finding his cheek.

Even if it was against his better judgment, he relented and smiled. They weren't going to fight; they were calling a truce.

"You're trouble," he muttered. "Aren't you?"

"You didn't have to come," she whispered.

He traced his forefinger down her jaw while she cradled his face. "I did."

Their bubble burst when the door opened and Adara came in with Carnell in tow. Bastian retreated to see the new entrants.

"Thank you for coming," Adara said to Bastian. "I can't believe she… I can't believe this happened. It's my fault."

"Adara…" Her sister's apologies had been coming all night. "This is not your fault."

"I should've been outside with you," Adara said. "I chose the restaurant."

Carnell put a hand on his worried fiancée's shoulder. "This is not your fault."

"Are your parents on their way?" Bastian asked the group.

"I didn't phone Dad." Adara blushed. "I can't

phone him."

"No, that would've been embarrassing," Harper said, directing her words at Bastian. "I'm fine. You're worrying about nothing."

Fumbling behind her for the broken strap of her bag, she wound it around her hand.

Except Bastian preempted her and blocked her before she could get off the bed. "Where are you going?"

"I'm going home," she stated in clear, plain English to the whole room.

"I'll come with you," Adara said, scurrying over to Bastian's side.

"No," Harper said. "You were staying over at Carnell's tonight. I don't need a babysitter."

"I'm not going to Carnell's," Adara said. "I'm not leaving you alone after this. Oh my God."

Everyone was looking at her. All expectation narrowed. Harper. Harper. Harper. The internal mental chant squeezed from every angle. Life was a shitstorm. Did they have to gawk? She already felt like a zoo exhibit. Okay, they wanted to look out for her, she got that, but the notion of her independence being curtailed… That aversion released a little sass.

"Statistically, the chances of me being mugged twice in one night are low," she said. "I'm safer than all of you."

"You shouldn't be alone," Adara said, being a worrywart. "The doctor said you might have a concussion. We can't tell Mom and Dad what happened; they won't know to look after you."

Despite living with them, she saw little of her parents and was used to staying out or secreting herself in her bedroom. More so these days given the chance of running into Damon or Charissa.

"My head is harder than the sidewalk," Harper said. "I'll be fine on my own."

"You could go home with Bastian."

That from the now-smiling woman he'd brought with him. Wham! Knocked it right out of the park! What an opener.

"Mom!" he barked.

Oh, God! Oh, God! Oh, God! No, no, no!

Mortification loosened her jaw. "She's your mother? Of course she's your mother."

Because what else would be more mortifying?

"Carolyn Hunt," the woman said, holding out her hand.

Harper shook it, as was the polite thing to do. The rest of her body quaked.

This lie just got bigger.

So far parents had not been directly involved. At the engagement party, she'd avoided presenting Bastian to her parents as… anything. They'd danced and then he'd left, that was it. Job done.

The stupid mugger had a lot to answer for. Her purse? Who cared? But that one moment dominoed into the next until Bastian's poor mother was dragged to her side, forcing them deeper into the lie.

"Lovely to meet you," Harper said because what the hell else could she say?

"You too," Carolyn said. "I'm sorry to hear about your trouble tonight."

"Really, it's no trouble, just one of those things."

Carolyn nodded with a head tilt of sympathy.

Bastian interjected. "Would you two stop chatting like you're at a society luncheon? We're in a hospital."

"I'll go home with Carnell," Adara said, "if you go home with Bastian."

What an ultimatum.

Carolyn smiled again and this time, the countenance put her on edge. Placated expressions had replaced the angry, worried, guilty ones, that was a plus. See the good. Ignore the bad. Be positive.

This mood was, at least, an improvement.

"Okay," Harper relented.

"Really?" Bastian, Adara, and Carnell all said at the same time.

Bastian didn't hinder her slipping off the bed. "If it will make you all feel better."

"Will you promise to take care of her, Bastian?" Adara asked. "I'll tell my father she's with you. I know he'll understand."

"I bet he will," Carnell said under his breath.

So her father was going to believe she was sleeping over at the house of a man they'd never met. No, she didn't need her father's approval to have a relationship, but this was going to raise questions she'd rather not field.

How would she pass it off? Booty call? Better that than reveal the truth of the mugging.

"Good, now we have an agreement," Carolyn said. "Do you need a doctor to sign you out?"

EIGHT

PAPERWORK OUT OF the way, they left the hospital as a group. After fussing greatly, Adara and Carnell got in a cab destined for his apartment.

Two down.

Who was left? Her, Bastian… and his mother.

Well, this was awkward. Great. Just great.

Bastian kept their fingers twined on the walk through the parking garage. A black BMW nestled discreetly in the corner flashed when they approached.

"Good thing he didn't bring the Porsche. I'll sit in the back," Carolyn said. "Your place is with Bastian."

As his mom got in, Harper drew her eyes from Bastian's. Her place? By not correcting Carolyn's assumption, their dishonesty sucked them farther into the fraud. This was wrong, it was just wrong.

She got in and said nothing as they drove out of the garage.

The trip itself was benign, or it would've been if she wasn't hyperaware of Bastian's hand so near to her knee when it rested on the manual gearstick. The space in the front was too small for both of them, too small for two people, she was sure of it.

Grown men were supposed to fit in this car. It didn't matter that she was dwarfed in the seat. No, something about the sight of his hand curled around the gear knob, so firm and strong… Space wasn't it, oxygen, that was what it lacked. Why was the air so thin? Was it getting hot?

Eventually, he pulled up to a grand black gate that was already opening. When they drove on, the crunch of gravel beneath the tires surprised her. Something wrong with asphalt?

This wasn't her neighborhood. No, that was far, far away. And felt so much further when they passed some trees and a broad red brick building came into view. The entrance portico, flanked by bold Roman columns, also sported Victorian-esque lamps. Chic.

Nice.

In its day, it would've been just as majestic and stylish. These days, buildings like this were converted into apartments or retirement homes.

Bastian stopped parallel to the front door and got out to round the car.

"It was good to meet you, Harper," Carolyn said as Bastian opened the back door. "I hope we'll see you again soon."

Smiling was the polite thing to do. Still, the lie clawed at her throat. "I apologize for the inconvenience tonight."

"Nonsense. I'm glad Bastian was able to come to your aid."

Bastian took his mom's hand to help her out and up the stairs. The pair exchanged words for around a minute before Bastian opened the front door and ushered his mom inside.

What was in his head? He was in no hurry to

return, he paced back and forth a few times before running back down to the car. They got to the end of the driveway and back onto the street without exchanging a single word.

"I'm sorry," she said when she couldn't take the silence anymore.

His scowl stayed pasted to the windshield. "Forget it."

If he was pissed off, he should've spoken up to correct his mother's assumption, or told Adara he didn't care about the mugging when she called.

"You didn't have to come to the hospital," Harper said. A big believer in taking responsibility for one's own actions, she wouldn't have expected Bastian to be the sort to whine or play the victim. "I'm sorry that Adara—"

"It's not you. My mom's on my case about… I'm sorry. You have nothing to apologize for. This wasn't your fault. I wanted to be there for you tonight. I was there for you once. Why wouldn't I be there again?"

So he wasn't pissed off about what happened? Yeah, Harper, stupid. Kind of presumptuous to assume it was all about her when his own life was on his mind.

"I didn't expect it to become a habit," she said. "I didn't have your phone number. Why would I think that my sister—"

"Are you implying I gave my phone number to your engaged sister?"

"No!" she said, having not accused him of anything. "I didn't say that."

But he was smiling, not angry. "It doesn't matter," he said. "You're safe, that's what's important."

Everyone had their health? Was that the sentiment? Low bar, but they scraped by. Sighing, she put the night's events out of her mind.

"Do you know the Hounslow Building? It's on

the east—"

"I know Hounslow."

"Can you drop me there beside—"

"Drop you?" he asked, focus leaving the road for the first time. "Am I your car service?"

"No," she said, admiring the interior of the vehicle. "I would never be able to afford you. You must have a hell of a boss if this is your company car."

"We're going to my place—"

"Please," she said, deliberately not letting him finish. "This night has already been one of the worst of my life. I don't need your pity—"

"You're obsessed with pity," he said. "I don't pity you. I said I would look after you and that's what I'm going to do."

Obligation wasn't justification for forcing herself into his life.

"We don't know each other, Bastian," she said. "That night was… a glitch." A dream or fantasy never meant to be repeated. "It was sort of perfect on its own, wasn't it?"

"We didn't know each other then, we do now. It's my place or back to the hospital… Only other choice is your parents."

They didn't know each other now. Not know, know. Except they did. Kinda. A little. She was terrible at this stuff. They'd sort of been on a date, a fake date, sure, but the sight of it was enough for her family to call him in an emergency. He'd offered to care for her without hesitation. Which, now that she thought about it… At the very least, they should be able to use the friends label for their association.

Only… getting this guy in deeper wasn't fair. She'd be in debt to him forever for what he'd done at Adara's engagement party. Going back to his place, asking him to play nursemaid, would be too much of a liberty.

"You can let me out here." The point everyone missed was there was nothing wrong with her. This buddy thing was unnecessary, pretending otherwise was dishonest. She had perpetuated too many lies already that night. "I'll walk."

"Yeah right," he said, gunning the car.

Pushed back in her seat, she searched the streets for a cop. A ticket on top of the inconvenience... Bastian would want rid of her fast.

"You don't have a very tight grip on your emotions, do you?"

"I am the epitome of control, Sweet, trust me."

"You can't kidnap me," she said. Control or not, she clung to her independence at all times. Freedom. Choice. Independence was what separated her from her sister and many of her father's employees. "I'm telling you that I want to leave this car."

"No, you don't," he said, unmoved by her vehemence. "You're saying that because that's what you should say. We're alone and you feel there's no need to carry on the charade."

Their audience was gone, there was no one left around to perform for.

"Exactly."

"That doesn't mean you want to get out of the car."

"The car's not the part that worries me," she admitted.

He glanced in her direction, probably trying to figure her out. "Worries you? You have nothing to fear. Do you think this is about sex? Is that what you're scared of?"

Whoa, well, that was a leap. Where did sex come from all of a sudden?

"I don't think you want to have sex with me," she

said and folded her hands on her damaged purse in her lap.

The movement attracted his eye. "What's in there that's so important?" he asked, nodding toward her purse. "Why wouldn't you let him have it?"

"It's mine."

"You tried that line in the hospital."

"It is," she said, sitting up straighter.

"It has to be more than that."

"It belongs to me; he had no right to touch it. I don't care how desperate he was, that doesn't give him the right to bully me. Bullies do what they do because no one stands up to them. I won't let them get away with it, not with me."

"Principle," Bastian said, bobbing his head. "You stood up to someone who could've killed you on principle?"

Maybe he was being sarcastic, but she didn't retreat.

"Yes," she said. "What better reason is there to stand up to someone?"

No? Nothing. No response.

They just kept driving. Whatever his opinion, he didn't share it. Good. They didn't need to bond or get to know each other. She'd find some way to tell Adara that Bastian was no longer a part of their lives and that would be that... If he ever let her out of the car.

Which he wasn't going to do. With each new corner and stretch of road, he made it clear he wasn't stopping.

As she was on the cusp of succumbing to sleep, he pressed a button and slowed the car.

God, her eyes stung. They'd been open too long or her makeup blurred them. She hadn't even looked in a mirror since before the attack. She was probably a complete mess. Closing them tight, she let her hands hold her head for just a few seconds of peace.

When the motion of the car stopped, she raised her head again. A garage.

Okay.

Bastian shut off the car and they sat in complete silence for more than five seconds.

Harper yawned and sat up straight. So… what now?

Bastian opened his door and got out of the vehicle to unlock an internal side door on the far wall. A low light came from beyond, just a halo around the doorway, no details.

Should she stay there or get out? She sat static when he rounded the hood to reach her side and open the door for her.

Instead of offering a hand to help her out, he crouched, blocking her exit. "Give me your driver's license."

So she'd been wrong about the statistics. "Are you mugging me?"

She didn't follow what was happening.

Was government ID the price of admission?

"If you're concussed, I'll need to ask you questions," Bastian explained. "And I'll need to know the right answers."

Logical, but unnecessary. "I'm not concussed."

"I'll be the judge of that."

"Are you a doctor?"

"No," he said. "Are you?"

Touché.

Harper exhaled. "Bastian…"

Opening his palm, he wasn't expecting a hand, he wanted her ID. Grumbling, she shoved her whole purse into his arms.

"I don't need your bag."

"My day-planner is in there," she said. "You can

ask questions about friends and family birthdays, events, you can ask about my business meetings, my menstrual cycle. After I get them right, you'll know I'm not concussed, then you can call me a cab. Can I get out of the car now?"

Acquiescing, he rose. "You're not leaving," he said, slamming the car door behind her.

NINE

WAS THAT A THREAT? A reassurance? A promise? Damn her inability to interpret tone. His fingers laced between hers to lead her through the door halo and into, ah, a kitchen. A huge kitchen with granite counters and a plumbed central island. It kept on going. A twelve-place dining table, then a seating area with couches and end tables in front of the glass wall at the end.

Wow.

The windows were inky black, filled by the mystery of night. What lay beyond? Wasn't that the question of the moment? Hardly fair he could ask her personal questions and she couldn't ask about the yard. Did he have a pool? Was there a patio? Did he own or rent?

Her questions stayed unanswered. Bastian took her into an enclosed, ascending stairway.

At the top, he gestured at the door straight ahead. "That's the bathroom."

"Bathroom, got it."

"I'll sleep in here," he said, touching the door to

the left. "Room on the right is yours."

Room on the right was so big, she'd guess it was the size of the garage beneath. A bed in the center of the room took up most of the area.

"This is a big room," she said admiring the solid oak furniture while he closed the curtains.

Shedding her shoes, she curled her toes into the thick carpet, opening and closing, squishing the pile that could almost be liquid, gobbling her up.

Bastian put her purse on the bottom corner of the bed. "I'll get you something to sleep in, and a toothbrush."

A toothbrush? Like a spare toothbrush? He must entertain a lot. Thinking about it, and his irrefutable hotness, it wasn't a leap to assume he entertained women a lot. Like a lot. There wouldn't be many immune to the dimple.

She stayed put, toe squishing the carpet. It kept her entertained. Though it was taking a lot of effort not to drop down there and bury her hands in it too.

That would be wrong.

What would be right?

Etiquette for these situations was not in any dating guide.

Not that they were dating.

As promised, he came back with a tee-shirt, a pair of shorts, and a toothbrush still in its pack.

"Bastian," she said, taking the items. "Why are you being nice to me?"

In one backward stride, he put more than physical space between them.

"Trying to seduce you," he muttered without an ounce of sincerity.

They both relaxed when she laughed.

Hugging the clothes to her chest, she exhaled. "You didn't sign up for this."

"Get changed," he said. "I'll get you a glass of water."

When he left the room, she stripped off and pulled his tee-shirt on over her head. The shorts wouldn't stay up. Letting them fall to her ankles would be more embarrassing than going without. The tee-shirt fell to her thighs, keeping her decent, so the shorts got folded away with the rest of her clothes.

Bastian knocked. At least, she assumed it was him. He wouldn't want to walk in and see her naked.

"You're good," she called out.

Crawling onto the bed, she kneeled in the middle as he entered with a glass of water that he set on the nightstand.

The only thing left was to say goodnight. For some reason, that wasn't appealing.

"You never told me why you were in the Grand the night we met," she said. "We can't be more than an hour from there now. Why would you be in a hotel if you live so close?"

"Back-to-back meetings," he said. "I had a dinner appointment and a pre-breakfast meeting in one of their conference suites. It made sense to spend the night."

Made sense, but the Grand wasn't cheap. Her immediate family considered spending the night of the engagement party too. Until they calculated how much that would cost. With that, Adara also crossed it off her possible wedding venue list. Their father made good money, but not good enough money that they could afford to blow the entire wedding budget on one ballroom and some champagne.

"Do you like hotels?" he asked. "Did facing Damon in one put you off?"

"No," she said, sinking into the luxurious linen spread on the bed. "I don't stay in hotels often. Work takes precedence over play."

"So Adara said." Bastian came over to rest his legs on the side of the mattress. "I can respect that. I've been accused of the same."

Conversation in the privacy of the bedroom wasn't usually held like this, with one party lying down and another standing up. Falling into the obscure seemed to be their thing.

One undeniable point rose above the others…

By loitering, Bastian betrayed he wasn't ready for goodnight either.

"You don't have to be afraid," she said, lifting a hand toward him. "Lie down with me."

What did they have to fear? He'd never pressured or harassed her. If they were what people thought they were, they'd have done the same, or more, several times. No one was watching, they didn't have to perform. Would that put him off?

No. He toed off his shoes and took her hand without hesitation to lie at her side. It shouldn't feel right, their intimacy was a lie conjured for others. Yet her body, her mind, her hormones responded as though it were all true.

With one liberty came another and she rested her head on his chest. They'd been this close when dancing. Nothing wrong with it. Nothing strange. Did horizontal matter more than vertical?

Listening to his heartbeat soothed in the silence. One, two, three. Sharing heat, the sure arm he closed around her shoulders kept her safe.

He inhaled the scent of her hair. It should be strange and creepy, yet she couldn't remember ever being so at peace. Bonding didn't have to be sexual or conversational. Being in this private space, in the intimate position, she closed her eyes and brushed her palm up and down the shirt buttons that concealed the flesh of his torso. Learning his shape, his scent, his rhythm only made her hungry for more.

"Your mom is nice. I see where you get your kindness from."

"I'm sorry for her tonight," he said. "I don't know what she was thinking, suggesting that you come back here."

At the time, the suggestion surprised her, but lying there with him, she couldn't be sorry.

"You've met my family," she said, "but I know nothing about yours."

"What do you want to know?"

Was that an invitation? One he may come to regret.

"You sure you want to do that? Ask such an open question?"

"I don't know," he said. "Ask and I'll see."

Was there a tinge of humorous dubiousness? Is that what she heard? Emotion, why was it so damn difficult to decipher? Amusement? Reluctance? She needed to know this man better.

"Are your parents still together?"

"They are."

"Siblings?"

"Younger sister."

"Is she married?"

"Not last time I checked."

"Do your family live in town?"

"Yes."

"You see them regularly?"

"Yes." He laughed. "Wow, you really are good at this."

Interrogation?

She sat up because looking at him might give her a better clue of his tolerance. Might.

"Sorry, I just…"

"No, it's okay," he said, his fingertips drifting up

the arm she planted to keep her upright. "Ask whatever you want, I have nothing to hide."

"Families always confuse the hell out of me. We're born into this bloodline that—most people don't even like their families."

"Well, I'd say I like mine, most of the time, despite what my mother did tonight. She can be determined."

"With a smile though," she said. "That makes a difference."

"I guess it does."

"Acting with love is well intended."

"Where my mom's concerned, it's more to do with her than me."

"Meaning?"

"She looked after me and Keely, raised us full-time while my dad worked. Our futures are something she's been dreaming about a long time."

"And she's ready to see them?"

"To know how they're going to play out? Yeah."

"Because she wants to know you'll be okay." He shrugged, still caressing her arm. "That's very caring. I can see why you like them."

From the affection in his tone, it was obvious his family was important.

This was too far away. She relaxed her arm to return her head to his body.

Since the moment they met at the engagement party, his altruism was palpable. In the various moments she'd thought of him since then—which numbered higher than should be admitted out loud—she never thought she'd have the chance to quiz him on his motivation.

Now they were lying there together, being honest, she got her chance.

"Why did you do it?" she murmured, loose,

salved, and sated. "Why did you come to Adara's party to rescue me?"

Beneath her cheek, he took a deep breath. "I don't know. It was a… drive. An impulse I couldn't ignore. I've been single most of my adult life. Like you, I prioritize business. Fielding questions about why you're not coupled up, deflecting attempts at matchmaking, I've been there. You deserved a night off from that crap."

How many times had he wished someone would swoop in and save him?

"That's very sweet." Her caress slid lower, just grazing his belt. His explanation made sense for their first encounter, didn't for the second. "Why did you come to the hospital tonight?"

He stroked her back. "I've been thinking about you. I'd be lying if I said otherwise."

So she wasn't the only one. "I didn't think I'd ever see you again." Believing his selfless act was a one off. "I'm happy I did."

He'd asked nothing in return for supporting her. Amazing in this day and age. Bastian wasn't like other men.

The bed was warm and the embrace comforting. Shirking the last shred of tension, her body sank into his. Long time since she'd fallen asleep with a man. Bastian may not have signed up for this, but when her hand stalled on his abdomen, she went with it.

Bastian exhaled. "So am I."

"Will we see each other again?" she murmured on the cusp of slumber.

"I don't know," he answered, his finger grazing her jaw before his hand settled over hers. "I don't know, Sweet."

Her eyes closed when she tucked her head deeper under his chin. "You're a good, kind man, Bastian," she murmured nuzzling closer. "A good, kind man."

TEN

Bastian

IF THE BEAUTY in his arms read his thoughts, she wouldn't have said those last words. Holding her, stroking her hair, he breathed her scent in and out. Damn, it went deep, and so would his cock given half a chance.

Fuck. What the hell was wrong with him?

Lying in the dark with this woman felt inexplicably right; a part of her reached out and coiled around his heart. Tight. Harper had zero expectations. The opposite, in truth, she relieved the pressure of life, business, family, all of it. She didn't need to be entertained or humored; he didn't nod along with her as he had done with women in his past.

A friend. Were they friends? They weren't clearly defined, which meant the lines weren't either. Hence finding himself in bed with her, unable to make a move. Shit, he'd teed this up wrong.

Harper was a person he enjoyed spending time with, for no other reason than to share oxygen with her.

When they breathed the same air, an odd closeness enveloped them. Friendship?

In that darkened bedroom, holding her, fully clothed, against him… He'd never even kissed her… not yet.

Couldn't he be honest in his own head if nowhere else? He'd wanted to kiss her since he'd first caught whiff of that intoxicating fragrance. What wrung that scent from her pores? He'd find out if he slipped into her shower and—

Oh, he was going to her place now? Into her shower? In what kind of friendship did one fantasize about the other naked? Come on, he deserved some slack, the woman lay in his arms, that sweet little body tucked in so close he could feel the cushion of her breasts against his ribs, what else should he be thinking?

One of her shins lay over his. Temptation gritted his teeth. One smooth lift of his knee would urge her limb higher, he could keep on going until it made contact with the painful erection behind his fly.

Fuck. Jerk.

She'd been attacked and didn't want to be in his home.

There was where they'd found themselves. No matter how tempting, he'd never take advantage.

In the hospital, his mother's suggestion he should look after Harper startled him, no denying that, and he'd resisted… for maybe half a beat. He should've fought harder.

Their night at Adara's party was perfect on its own. That's what Harper said. If fucking only. Yeah, it was perfect, he agreed, with only an ounce of sincerity. She'd plagued his thoughts all week.

Whatever impression he gave her that night, he should've left it at that. Except the risk of ruining that perfection could reap the ultimate reward. Sex? Was that the sleaze he'd become?

But, damn, he had to know. He wasn't good at letting things go or living with the unknown. Until right then, he'd never entertained the idea of pursuing her. His thoughts were of her as an apparition. In that fantasy, because their contact had been so brief and intense, she'd be anything he wanted her to be. Could be he was making her, them, into something they'd never be capable of sustaining.

Still, fate dropped this opportunity in his lap. When had he ever snubbed one of those?

Harper Scott wasn't meant to be an unrealized dream. Reality, that's where she belonged, in his reality. If he didn't play this through, nothing in his life, no woman in his future, would live up to the prospect of Harper Scott.

The idea of seducing her unsettled him as much as it inspired.

Before he could insinuate himself into her life, and maybe her bed, he'd need to clear up their misunderstanding.

What was that? That this was no more than two platonic citizens helping each other out. No, they were something bigger.

She didn't know who he was.

Damon did. When he'd introduced himself, the spark of recognition hit the prick. Oh, he'd seen it the world over. Not just recognition, but the flare of promise. Given what some of his associates endured, he wasn't sorry his notoriety was limited to the business world.

Adara, or Carnell, must've figured it out too. They'd got in touch with him at work—thankfully. None of them, it seemed, told Harper, which made sense. Her family believed them to be in a relationship. People in relationships usually knew what each other did for a living.

From his limited experience, he'd gleaned Harper was a private person. If her family, or anyone, tried to butt into her life or bring him up, she would shut them down. And given their shared lie, that was smart. Wasn't so easy to answer questions about someone you'd known for a couple of hours.

This woman needed someone on her side, looking out for her. And, fuck, it was clear she'd be capable of looking after what was important to her too.

Independence was her stalwart, along with guarding her vulnerabilities. He wanted to be her safe haven, needed to be.

That night in the dark Grand corridor, she'd opened up to him because she had no one else to open up to. And despite being the younger sister, Harper proved she would defend her sister when Adara couldn't do it for herself. At the engagement party, she stood up to Damon. The man she cut loose, refusing to accept his infidelity.

Hell, that night, she'd taken on a mugger. What did that tell him?

Harper was strong and used to being the only one looking out for her. Her relationship with her parents was so weak that it didn't warrant telling them about her mugging. What else didn't they know?

Adara had other things to worry about. Her relationship with Carnell, their engagement, their upcoming wedding. The woman's life was full.

How could he wheedle his way in? Whatever it entailed, he'd be there for Harper Scott as much as she would let him.

Carnal impulses could wait. What she needed was uncomplicated. A friend. Someone to trust.

That was it. The first priority was friendship. A solid foundation they could build on.

Desire would be sated later. If that was what she wanted. Now he just had to make sure his dick controlled itself until it was time to take possession of this woman.

ELEVEN

MIND WANDERING, Harper relied on autopilot to complete her invoices.

It was Monday for crissakes, she'd left Bastian's place on Saturday. Get over it already.

Bastian's embrace took up too much space in her brain. Stupid. Stupid.

On the Saturday morning, she'd woken in his embrace. Cool, right? No big deal. Yeah, maybe if that was all she did. That wouldn't have been totally audacious. But this was her and she didn't do things by half. No, she ratcheted entitlement up to a whole new level.

How?

She'd been on top of him, her whole body on his, sleeping on him like he was her own personal mattress.

Shit. And there was the incredulity again. Who did she think she was? They'd fallen asleep, that didn't give her license to climb on top of him like some kind of animal.

In that mortification, she extricated herself from his arms, slowly, carefully, so as not to wake him. She'd gathered her things and crept out of the bedroom to dress in the silent kitchen.

Shame. Shame. Shame.

From there, she slipped out through the garage and ran down the concrete driveway without daring to look back.

Period. Over. Forget it.

Why couldn't she stop thinking about it?

Embarrassment flamed in her cheeks all over again.

It was funny how something acceptable in the intimacy of a dark bedroom became mortifying in the stark light of day.

Saturday hadn't been a total bust. After a quick stop at home for a shower and change of clothes, she'd gone into the office and buried herself in paperwork. Sunday too. Work grounded her, everything made sense inside her four little walls. Keeping busy was better than obsessing about her audacity.

With the weekend gone and Monday lunchtime approaching, her father's building was in full operation mode. Her small office on the ground floor was functional, little more, nothing fancy. Still, she was grateful her father let her work there given her business wasn't any part of Scott Solutions.

Bastian.

Damn.

Where did that thought come from?

She had to forget about him.

For those first few seconds, after waking in the security of his arms, in his bed, bathed in his generosity, she'd been at peace. The guy had done nothing but help her out, and she'd gone and made a fool of herself. Typical. She couldn't kid herself it was the first time.

It started with her meltdown over Damon and now she'd mounted him in his sleep.

No, they'd never see each other again. That decision was easy. She'd asked him the question before sleep. After? She'd rather poke her eyes with pins than risk humiliating herself in front of him again. God knew what she'd do next if given half a chance.

Done. Finished. No more. Bastian? Bastian who? That was it. A stranger. They were strangers.

A tap on her office door raised her head. Great! A distraction that—when Damon peeked in, optimism fled.

God, she couldn't catch a break.

"Do you have a minute?" her ex asked.

For him, the answer would always be the same. "No."

"I want to apologize," he said, coming in despite the lack of invitation. "I think we should talk."

If he was going to carry on talking anyway, why bother asking permission?

No surprise. This was Damon, he heard what he wanted to hear.

Another knock on the door spared her his homily. Optimism again piqued her spine straight. Come on, be a reprieve, be a reprieve. She had nothing on her schedule, but she'd take a meeting with any surprise visitor on the planet who wasn't Damon Twaddle.

Would she ever learn not to jump to conclusions?

The refined woman who stepped into her modest office drenched her with a horror that forced her to her feet.

"Mrs. Hunt," Harper said, running a hand down her hip.

Carolyn Hunt surveyed the desk, the file cabinets behind her, and the poster on the wall above... Oh, God. There wasn't judgment there, that she could read, but half her problem was being unable to do just that, with anyone.

The blinds on the window were closed because Harper didn't like passersby on the sidewalk to see her working or in meetings with clients. The covered window precluded natural light lessening any illusion of space. Not that there really was such an illusion.

The tiny, gloomy room didn't frighten away Mrs. Hunt's smile. No, like a pro, it remained in place, even when she glanced at the bristling Damon.

"Can I tempt you out for some lunch, Harper?" Carolyn asked.

"You're lunching with his mother?" Damon spat, striding to her desk.

Mrs. Hunt saved her from responding. "Ah, you know Bastian too?" Carolyn asked, something false flavoring that particular smile.

"We've met," Damon ground out the words while maintaining his glare.

"Good," Carolyn said. "It's important her coworkers know she's off the market."

Smiling was an art form for this impressive woman. Somehow, Carolyn managed to appear tame and courteous while exuding a severity that betrayed no one should mess with her.

No doubt she was a formidable mother. Though Harper struggled to imagine anyone disciplining Bastian with any kind of success. He was too kind to be naughty anyway.

Bastian. Yes. She only had to consider his opinion on this situation for a dozen seconds. There was no way he'd approved his mother showing up there in advance. No way would he let his mother cultivate a relationship with his fake girlfriend.

She couldn't encourage this. Carolyn had the wrong impression. It would be dishonest to lead the innocent matriarch on. And, honestly? She wasn't cut out for subterfuge.

The words. The words. How to let Carolyn down gently…

Deliberating, she moistened her lips. "Mrs. Hunt—"

"Call me Carolyn."

"Sure, but—"

"It's just lunch, a little luncheon. Nothing inconsiderate in that, is there?" Innocence seemed far from that glow in Carolyn's eye. "There's someone I'm dying for you to meet."

TWELVE

SOMEONE TO MEET?

The first person she'd considered was Keely. Which was why sitting still in Carolyn's fancy chauffeur driven car was so difficult. His sister? Bastian adored his sister. That wasn't a bond she wanted to jeopardize with their lie.

Getting away from Damon was a plus. No denying it. Leaving him gaping had been kind of fun. Carolyn deserved thanks for swinging that. Maybe if her ex hadn't been around, she'd have put up more of a fight to avoid the lunch. She should've called Bastian to let him know what was going on, except… she didn't have his phone number. Another thing she couldn't admit to that particular audience.

Not that it necessarily would've made a difference. Harper wasn't cut out for winning battles against members of the Hunt family. They were a determined bunch.

Instead of running out on him Saturday, maybe she should've first discussed with Bastian how to address telling the truth. Until they had that conversation, her hands were tied. So much for never seeing him again. The last thing she wanted to do was damage the son's relationship with his mother, but she had no idea how to play this.

They stopped outside a restaurant she'd never been to before. Had they meant to stop? The road was suddenly busy as vehicles slowed. Why? Another car was parked at the curb too, surrounded by a mob that washed the full width of the sidewalk, rippling this way and that like a sudden riptide.

What caused the commotion?

Or who.

In LA, it was usually a who.

The back door was opened and both she and Carolyn were helped out of the car. Noise gathered from the bustling group, roaring and screeching, all baying for the attention of… A couple of big guys barged people out the way, creating a corridor to free another few burly guys and out emerged a beauty wearing a boatneck dress and oversized sunglasses.

"Right on time," the tiny brunette said, adjusting to head for the door as another guy opened it. "Let's get inside."

That woman had been in the current and got out alive? Security sure were pros.

At the restaurant door, the beauty lingered to wave at the crowd. She and Carolyn were ushered to a table in the far corner, next to the glass walls showcasing a private rear courtyard.

"This is beautiful," she said.

Someone helped her with her seat, another helped Carolyn. The pair raced to get the third seat as the brunette joined them. Slipping off her shades, a sigh left the woman's lips when she sat.

The woman. Brunette. Familiar. Why would—

"This is the intrigue?" the stranger asked Carolyn with a smile that never strayed.

"Yes. Harper Scott, I'd like you to meet Roxanna Kyst. Oh, or should that be Lomond?"

"Officially, we're hyphenating, a nod to the caveman thing, but it doesn't matter. Whatever is fine. I know who I am. Course my guy may not say the same. We all know what he's like," Roxanna said, rising just a little to reach over the table. "Roxie."

"Harper," she said, accepting the handshake.

On letting go, Roxie dropped back into her seat. "We could've done this at the club or back at the hotel. We're paying the competition here."

They were separated from the rest of the room. Tables around them were empty. On purpose? Maybe. Maybe not. The restaurant wasn't full, only a dozen or so tables were occupied, yet, hmm, they did appear to be drawing some whispering interest. Security guards formed a perimeter, standing ready, for what? Anyone who may invade their sanctuary, or Roxie's sanctuary anyway.

Carolyn lowered her volume. "We're flying under the radar."

Drawn in, Roxie got closer. "Oh, we are?" Glee wrapped the beauty. "I love a good caper."

"Bastian doesn't like it when I meddle in his love life."

"What? Are you kidding?" Roxie exclaimed. "That's half a mother's job." Her head went sideways. "Although, if my mother tried that…"

"She'd be in cahoots with your husband."

"My parents do prefer him over me… Like the rest of the planet's population. It's the eyes, all in the eyes, and his smile… the jaw, the ass… Let's not talk about the rest of the package." She combed her finger down her long bangs. "Though the package… mmm."

Carolyn laughed. "You found true love all by yourself." True love? "And you're never in one place long enough for your mother to meddle. I dread to think how she sleeps at night."

"She sleeps because my dad and Z are bros now. You dread to think? I dread to think what they talk about and have never been brave enough to ask. Hope it's not our sex life. Z talks about sex a lot."

"Says the woman with the stream and enough followers to land her own TV show."

"Sexploitation will get you just about anything in Hollywood," Roxie said. "And you can quote me on that."

On a laugh, Carolyn gestured at Roxie, who immediately ordered when the server came over.

"Roxie just got married," Carolyn explained. "At the Grand. We've dragged her away from her new husband."

"What do you want to eat?" Roxie asked. "I'm starved. Z and I have dinner reservations later, so he says, I don't know. I'll need to carb up to get through the night's marathon either way. That's a whole other kind of ravenous."

She quickly grabbed a menu and ordered fast. Roxie probably didn't want to be away from her guy for too long, hence the haste.

"Congratulations," she said when the server left.

"Congratulations for…" Roxie's eyes rolled in their sockets. "The show? Oh, no, the wedding? Right! Yes!" She laughed. "Sorry, I'm a little out of practice with the real world… And anyone who isn't Z really, and he's taken me on for life. He gets no apologies."

"Is it a relief?"

"To be married or over *The Wedding?*" Roxie asked. "Jane took the heat for the Big Day, the stress was all hers."

"Jane got married too," Carolyn filled her in. "They're close friends."

Nice, but… relevant?

"Enough about my nonsense. Should I assume Harper is Bastian's squeeze?" Roxie said, taking the time to scrutinize her. "She's pretty. Is she smart? Funny? How's the sex?"

The… his mom was sitting right there! Shock had to be written all over her face.

"Roxie has few filters."

"Who needs filters? It's honesty in full stereo. Bastian may believe you're chaste, Mrs. Hunt, but you're a woman, same as me. And I've met your kids."

"Keely?" her sudden question jazzed the other two.

"She's a fabulous woman. Incredibly smart. Incredibly kind," Roxie said. "I'm putting her on my list."

"Your list?" Harper asked.

Again, it was Carolyn who illustrated. "Roxie likes to help."

Okay, that didn't give her the full picture. "Help?"

"Women, in relationships, navigating into them, out of them, around in them—"

"Hey, I never coerce anyone. I'm a listening ear… and sometimes I nudge. Love just happens around me."

"And you have a list…?"

"Of single friends who may, or may not, be lined up for love."

Okay, that was… She didn't know what that was. Was it a hobby or a full-time occupation? She still hadn't figured out why Roxie was so familiar.

"How do you know each other?"

Carolyn didn't seem like the fangirl type.

"Our charitable work overlaps."

Charity? She got that. People from all walks of

life contributed to charitable causes. From volunteers making minimum wage through to the upper echelons of society donating billions. Charity was a great equalizer. And it was a big part of her work too. At a certain level, anyway.

"Good cover for meeting too," Roxie said. "If Bastian asks, this is about Lola's Liberty."

THIRTEEN

ROXIE'S ATTENTION WENT to Carolyn. "Did you talk to Tripp about repping Lighting Darkness?"

"I don't think he's in the country at the moment."

"As long as he's on the planet, his mom is happy. That's what he says."

Tripp… Wait, Lola's Liberty—ah-ha!

"You married Zairn Lomond," Harper said, interrupting when clarity smacked her.

"Against my better judgment. I was drunk at the time," Roxie joked. Was it a joke? "He has naked pictures and threatened to leak them to the press. What choice did I have?"

She did know this woman. Not know her, but how…?

"Crimson is the hottest ticket in town."

"If you ever want in, give me a call."

Ha, yeah, right. Organizing events may be her thing, but not on the level of Crimson and Zairn Lomond. Carolyn had interesting connections. Yet another reason she should tell the truth.

Bastian wouldn't like her lying to his mother. Not in such a direct and—could be interpreted as—self-serving way. This could be exploited by some as a back door into a world she had no chance of getting a foothold in without this networking opportunity.

Carolyn was ready for her son to settle down. He'd told her as much himself and the woman made no secret of it in person. Leading her on was cruel. The only way to approach this without being abrupt was to play down their relationship. Let the mother know, they weren't serious, that they had no future. Be vague, non-committal, subtle in her creeping retreat.

That would open a path for Bastian to reveal the truth.

"Mrs. Hunt—"

"I told you to call me Carolyn. Please," she said, sitting back a little as servers came to pour tea. Tea? Actual tea in a pot with teacups and everything. "You look well, Harper. Are you over the worst of your injuries?"

Injuries? Oh, the mugging, the last time they'd seen each other. "Yes—"

"My Bastian looked after Harper," Carolyn said. "After she was mugged."

"Oh my God," Roxie exclaimed. "You were—do you want security? You should have security. Have some of mine, I have plenty spares lying around. Did the mugger take anything important?"

"Nothing," Carolyn said. "Harper fought back."

"Go, you, girl." Roxie's nod was impressed. "You're not from Chicago, are you?"

"No." Was that important? "I just… what gave him the right?"

Picking up her teacup, Roxie gestured. "I like her."

"As does my Bastian—sorry, I suppose he's not

my Bastian anymore is he," Carolyn said, wearing a private smile. "He's yours."

Ouch, Harper winced. This was going to be harder than she'd hoped. "Carolyn—"

"He cares for you a great deal," Carolyn said. "I wouldn't want to make you uncomfortable, Harper, but…" The older woman turned her address to Roxie. "I've never seen him that frantic over a woman before."

Oh, Carolyn was a wily one. These twists and turns kept her guessing. Did Carolyn know her son wasn't really in a relationship? Was she being called out? Perhaps this was a matchmaking exercise. Either that or Carolyn really thought she was getting to know her potential future daughter-in-law.

Revealing the whole truth was out of her reach, that didn't mean all honesty was off the table.

"He's a good man," Harper said.

There, that was fair. True. And shouldn't bolster expectations. Bastian couldn't get mad at her for that statement. Diplomacy: a balancing act.

"Yes." This time Carolyn's smile was all pride, nothing puzzling about that. "He is."

"You raised him well," Harper said, on a roll. "He's grateful and proud of how he grew up."

"As I am of him," Carolyn said, raising her teacup to her lips.

"He's proud of Keely too," Harper said, tasting her own tea. This was easy. Just say true stuff. She had this. "He pretends she's an inconvenience but it's teasing, he loves her very much."

"I actually am an inconvenience to my brother," Roxie said, licking her spoon before placing it in the saucer under the cup. "Have been since the day I was born."

Servers came over with their food and a fresh pot of tea. Tea was a big deal there, apparently, or it was a special request. Maybe Roxie was really into tea.

Would they move on from talking about Bastian now? Even if they did, that didn't save her thoughts straying back to him.

When in bed, with Bastian, his veiled pride in his little sister wasn't well disguised. So far, everyone she'd met kind of exuded a rambunctious pride in the youngest Hunt. Keely must be a joy in all their lives.

"Bastian has always looked after his sister," Carolyn said. "You'll see how close they are when you meet her this weekend."

Wait…? Ease evaporated, went the same way as her smile. What…?

"I… I will?"

"Yes, you'll be coming to the charity ball with Bastian."

What…? A…

Had she talked herself into an invitation? Was his mom setting them up on a date? Wily didn't cover it, she'd have to watch herself around this matriarch.

"Oh no," Harper said. "I won't be—we're friends, good friends, but—"

"Things are so different now," Carolyn said, putting her delicate cup in its saucer. "My parents were strict. That taught me I didn't want to be an autocratic parent. I showed, or tried to show, Bastian and Keely the overt love I didn't understand from my own parents."

"It shows. Bastian loves you."

Carolyn sighed. "Children these days. They have all these words for relationships that aren't relationships."

"Friends with benefits," Roxie said after swallowing. "Situationships. Hook-ups. Fuck buddies."

Oh God.

"I can't keep track of it all. Flings and affairs were complicated enough."

"You found your guy young though, Carolyn.

And guys were much more stand up then."

Carolyn laughed. "Yes, a long, long time ago."

Harper stated another truth. "Bastian's a stand-up guy."

"Roxie didn't think so when they first met."

"I did… I warmed up to him."

"You didn't like Bastian?" Harper asked.

How could that be possible?

"You hear lots of stories about a guy and sometimes… it feels too good to be true. No guy is truly a picnic."

"Except Zairn?" Carolyn said, still amused.

"God, no, not him. He snores and hogs the blankets, he's no picnic." The warmth in Roxie's eyes said different. "Love blinds us to their faults. And, so far, everyone I've met loves Bastian Hunt."

"People love Zairn too and Tripp."

"Not in the same way, they have reputations to uphold. Bastian's just known to be… perfect."

No one was perfect. If that was how he'd been sold, she understood Roxie's initial suspicions. Especially given her bunch of single friends looking for love. When friend circles merged those situationships and hookups tended to be inevitable.

"He's responsible," Carolyn said. "Always has been. And, Harper, please don't be deterred. I don't know the specifics of your relationship with my son. Bastian would rather I didn't get involved. He doesn't like meddling, but some meddling is a mother's right. He cares for you. Perhaps you have a friendship, or more, maybe it's casual. As I said things are different now than they were in my day."

Which implied…

Harper frowned. "I don't understand what—"

"All of his life he's had women fawning around him. He isn't interested in the plucked and preened with their shallow intentions. They pass the time sometimes, I suppose. That's not his future. I know what I saw when you two were together and no one will convince me otherwise. You are special to him. When he heard you were in the hospital, he couldn't get there fast enough. The way you relate to each other, how you talk, there's a familiarity much deeper than any friendship or shallow acquaintance."

And there was the proof this innocent little lunch was anything but innocent. Was the intention to push them together or scare her off?

"If you're asking about my intentions—"

"No," Carolyn said, holding up a hand to halt Harper's words. "If Bastian thought I was interfering he would be livid. He's very particular, and protective of those he cares about… You do care about him too, don't you?"

An invisible warning light flashed behind Carolyn, conjured by her dilemma. There was no easy, honest way to back up out of this cul-de-sac.

"He's a good man," Harper repeated herself, searching for kind, circumspect things to say about Bastian. "He helped me when he could've walked away. Yes, I care about him. But I… I wouldn't want you to make assumptions about—"

"No, of course not. I won't assume, I promise."

The words should provide relief. Except the whisper of a smile on Carolyn's lips didn't inspire confidence. The assumptions were already there.

The lunch conversation moved on to Harper's business and Roxie's new reality show. They got around to their charity work, something they all had in common. Though her connections were more of the professional kind than the personal.

That conversation led to the exchange of business cards. Though when she tried to give Carolyn hers, she learned Adara had already done that at the hospital.

Nice. Thanks, sis. At least that enlightened her on how Carolyn found her.

The check was paid, and, huh, lunch was over. She shouldn't be disappointed. She'd tried to avoid coming, now she didn't want to go back to work. Shame they'd be unlikely to ever do this again.

Roxie was waylaid by a server to sign things. One led to two and so on…

Pushing her chair away, her butt barely left the seat before Carolyn slid a rectangle of heavy, embossed paper across the table.

"What's this?" Harper asked, flipping over what turned out to be an invitation to the charity ball.

"He won't enjoy himself alone. He suffers through these things to support me. But if it's not women throwing themselves at him, it's the men trying to probe him for business advice. It would be nice if you could join him, give him a night off… He needs someone to dance with."

Did Carolyn know those were the magic words?

Sidelining her embarrassment about sleeping on top of the man for a minute, what would be the right thing to do? He'd put his own dignity aside to join her at Adara's engagement party for that very reason. Someone to dance with.

Saving her from being the pitied singleton, he'd granted her fairy tale wish. Not doing the same in return would be wrong. Damnit.

Only… what would Bastian think of her showing up unannounced?

She couldn't decide. "I don't know if—"

"What would Roxie do?" Roxie exclaimed, returning to them. "That's what you have to ask yourself. And as Roxie…" She leaned in. "I say sex is almost guaranteed. ”

"Think about it," Carolyn said, urging the invitation closer. "I won't mention it to him, and if he invites you himself, we can forget this conversation ever took place. He's proud and never wants anyone to assume he needs saving."

The notion was familiar. "I'll think about it."

FOURTEEN

AVOIDING DAMON BECAME the challenge of the week. Wasn't always easy but was worth the effort. During business hours, she worked away from the office. Choosing to conduct meetings at clients' offices and scouting possible locations for events, she swerved the Scott Solutions complex at every opportunity.

Her father had been called away on business midweek. Having nothing better to do, her mother went with him. Normally fewer people in the house meant less noise, more space was a good thing.

Problem was, without her parents around, Harper was the single gooseberry watching two couples have a pleasant double-date night after night. Though she'd pick being a gooseberry with two couples over Adara and Carnell eating out or at Carnell's apartment. By sticking around, the engaged couple did her a favor. Imagine being alone with Damon and Charissa. Yeah, gave her the shivers too.

Damon spent most of the week scowling and snapping at a meeker-than-usual Charissa. So much so, she felt sorry for the woman. That was saying something.

With the house being nothing but tension, the decision to go to the ball had been a breeze.

She needed to get out.

Away from this house.

The event would be as much of a reprieve for her as she hoped it would be for Bastian. Grabbing her clutch, she stuck her feet into the delicate grape-colored sling-backs that went with her strapless silk dress. With its slit from ankle to high on her thigh, this dress was one of her favorites.

Spritzing perfume on her neck and wrists before leaving the bedroom, she hurried down the stairs. The cab was likely outside already.

Her path to the front door was blocked. Damn, she'd hoped to make a clean getaway.

"That dress… for dinner?" Charissa asked from the bottom of the stairs where she stood with Damon.

"I'm going out," Harper said, checking her purse for her keys, card, and invitation.

Damon side-stepped, getting between the women. "With him?"

His dislike of Bastian made zero sense.

"Not that it's any of your business," Harper said. "But, yes, Bastian will be there."

According to Carolyn anyway.

"He's not picking you up?" Damon scoffed, glancing at Charissa as if seeking support for his judgment.

"Are you that desperate to see him again?" Harper asked, pleased to have the unexpected opportunity to mock her ex. "I can give you his number, but I don't think you're his type."

A knock at the door interrupted. Damn, and she was enjoying that. Had the cab driver come to hurry her? Had she been that long? The guy must have the meter on, what did he care if she took all night?

Charissa was the one to go open the door. Her hand dropped from the handle as the door swung to a stop. She couldn't see around it, just watched as Charissa's jaw loosened.

"Good evening," a male voice, who…?

It wasn't Bastian, maybe the caller wasn't for her at all.

"Char?" Damon said, going to grab the door and open it wider.

"Is Harper ready?"

Harper? It was for her and… her own chin swung south. This was not—he was not.

"Zairn Lomond," Damon said, disbelief bleeding the words from his breath. "You're…"

The guy, yes, Zairn Lomond, who ignored those in front of him to raise a smile for her.

"Are you ready?"

How did he…? How did they…?

She did nod, she knew because her hair brushed her cheek, not because she could consciously control her actions… Zairn Lomond.

Purse still in hand, she drifted down the last stair and across to be swept out the door by Lomond, his arm curving behind her in a swoop that never actually made contact.

The waiting car was no regular cab. But the guy was wearing a tux—and a billionaire—what did she expect? The man standing by the limo opened the door as they approached. Zairn gestured for her to get in first.

It didn't occur to her not to slip inside. It didn't even occur to her that this guy was a complete stranger. Funny how celebrity could grant such familiarity between people who'd never otherwise met.

Helped that Roxie was inside. "Honey!" the hostess exclaimed, patting the seat next to her. "Come sit. Champagne?"

Zairn sat alone on the backseat while Roxie put a flute of champagne in her hand.

"Thank you."

"See, I knew she'd be ready," Roxie said to the man opposite them. "A woman knows."

"You never know when Toria's going to be ready," Zairn muttered, retrieving a phone from his inner pocket.

"No one knows when Toria will be ready, Toria included."

She swallowed. The delicate glass between her fingertips gave her something to look at. The little bubbles, slight foam—

"Would you prefer something else?"

It took her a second, Roxie to Zairn, Roxie—Zairn was talking to her.

"Something else?"

"To drink," he said.

"Yeah, we can stop at the club," Roxie said. "Zairn'll mix anything."

"Oh no, I…" Crimson, they were talking about their nightclub. "Thank you, I—"

"We don't have to stop at the club," Zairn said. "Don't overwhelm the woman."

"She's not overwhelmed. We're not overwhelming."

"You're overwhelming."

"Me?" Roxie asked with a cluck of exhaled outrage. "What have I told you about looking the way you do around women? And men? Everyone in fact. Weren't you going to do something about that, husband?"

Though it sounded like Roxie was chastising him, his eyes slunk up over the top of his phone. One corner of his mouth curled in feral amusement.

"Been busy the last few days, wife."

"Sex is no excuse. That's your marital duty," Roxie said, opening the fridge to whip out a bottle. "I can mix Gin and It."

Zairn tucked his phone away to then outstretch the empty hand. "Give it to me."

Maybe that had been Roxie's plan all along. Decidedly the cat that got the cream, Roxie arched across her to put the bottle in her husband's hand, pushing her shoulders back to accentuate the cleavage revealed by her dress.

"It's fine," Harper said, though Zairn took the bottle and Roxie righted herself. "I don't need a drink."

"Yes, you do," Roxie said, putting the champagne aside and linking their hands. "These parties are always filled with sycophants and brownnosers."

"Aren't they the same thing?"

"Mix, man," Roxie said to her guy. "Protect and provide."

"Yes, dear."

"You look great." Roxie's focus came back. "The dress is just right. Beautiful. I love it."

That was at least something. "Thank you. I like yours too."

"Thank you. Good, now that's out the way, let's get down to it."

"It?"

"Carolyn is a wonderful woman," Roxie said. "Just not always the most perceptive."

"You have a nose for it," Zairn muttered, doing his thing.

"I have a nose for it," Roxie repeated.

"I don't understand what—"

"Have you talked to Bastian since our lunch?" Uh… "That look on your face right now. That's it right there."

"It?"

"You've never had sex with him, have you?" Roxie tossed in that grenade like it was no big deal. "Are you even dating him? If you were dating him, he'd have beat us to the punch. Why isn't he picking you up?"

Screwing on a bottle cap, Zairn exhaled. "I should've known…"

"You should've known, husband, yes."

"This is one of your capers."

"It's not a caper. You picked up a beautiful woman from her house, what's so wrong with that? Are you hard-done-by?"

"You said I'd never pick up another woman."

"Different context and you're welcome," Roxie said. "There you are, marriage hasn't taken it from you after all, stud."

Okay, she was a little adrift. "I don't understand what—"

"Don't worry about it, we're here to see you through," Roxie said. "Just think of us as your guardian angels." It wouldn't be so bad to have those. "You have to excuse Carolyn, she can be pushy—"

"*She* can be pushy?" Zairn scoffed. "You've got a goddamn Olympic medal in that sport, Lola. Top of the podium."

Roxie ignored him. "Her children mean the whole world to her. And if Carolyn's pushing you for Bastian, you've made a good impression. Are you into him?"

"I don't know what—this is all happening fast."

"Okay," Roxie said, squeezing her hand. "Take it slow. Tell me what happened. Step by step."

"I shouldn't—Bastian—I shouldn't… I haven't talked to him about discussing this. Did you tell Carolyn?"

"No! Your secrets are safe with me," Roxie

insisted. Harper glanced back at Zairn capping the cocktail shaker. "Don't worry about him. He knows better than to repeat anything he hears in our bed." And that was… they weren't in bed. "You can trust us."

Maybe she could, maybe she shouldn't. Though letting out some of the insanity rather than caging it all might help guard against screwing this up.

"It was my sister's engagement party…"

For the next hour or so, she told the story of just how she and Bastian ended up in the mess. She talked about Damon and Charissa, the mugging, her wish to extricate herself without hurting good people.

"Bastian was doing me a favor and now… I don't want his mom to be upset when she finds out it's not what she thinks it is."

"Yeah, 'cause she thinks you're fuck buddies."

"Strong foundation for any marriage," Zairn said, still on his phone as he had been for most of the trip, in between mixing them cocktails.

"They're not getting married," Roxie said. "You have marriage on the brain."

Zairn explained. "If Carolyn's trying to maneuver them together, she sees a future."

Could Carolyn see a future for her and Bastian's relationship? That made things all the more dicey.

"He was doing me a favor…"

"Which is why you're doing the same for him tonight." Roxie had her hand again. "Don't worry about it. We're with you, we'll look after you."

That wouldn't do anything for letting Carolyn down gently.

"I'll talk to him tonight." If she could. "He knows his mother, he probably already has an exit strategy."

Though it wasn't completely clear if Bastian knew she'd been invited to this event. They slowed to turn onto a driveway. As the house was revealed, she regretted her decision to be there.

The black night around the large white building was lit with exquisite twinkling lights. In a line of other vehicles, they waited their turn behind limos and sports cars being attended to by valets.

Dread crept in, cooling and marring her skin with goosebumps.

Parties were a part of her work life. Other parties, not parties like this. And as much as her father liked to make out he was rich, which he was compared to many people, this wasn't their league. Not even close.

This was the league of the super-rich. The one percent. Women dripped with precious jewels and every suit was hand-tailored to perfection.

Thank God she'd settled on her long, silk dress; her alternate option had been a short, red, halter-neck. Far from appropriate.

If she got out of this car she'd be stranded, without an avenue of escape. Except there was no going back. This wasn't her car. She couldn't order it to turn around and take her home.

At the head of the queue, Zairn got out first. Roxie stayed right behind her as she inhaled and stepped out.

It was her imagination. It was. It was her imagination that everyone turned to look at the stranger getting out of a car, and with Zairn Lomond too. She'd gone there to make Bastian feel better and so far only managed to make herself feel worse.

This wasn't about her.

Her chin rose. She wasn't there for herself, or to make herself feel good, she was there for Bastian. These people could think anything they wanted about her; she would never see any of them again.

Bastian had risked humiliation coming to her aid

once, twice actually. Now it was her turn.

Roxie took Zairn's arm and he offered her the other. Friendship. Comrades. Telling them the whole truth could be something she came to regret. But right then, walking into that intimidating space, she was grateful not to be alone.

No one even asked for her invitation. Maybe it was gauche to worry about paper and bureaucracy, though there was a man at a podium by the door. More likely it was her companions who paid the price of her entry. Would anyone get in the way of Zairn and Roxie?

Grand double doors framed the gleaming marble floor and balustrade beyond. The domed ceiling had to be fifty feet above the floor they gazed down upon from a circular mezzanine around the upper perimeter. A double staircase led down to the shimmering main floor, as bright as the breeding that coasted around on castors. With her skirt in one hand and her clutch around her wrist, she descended to join them. An interloper. A phony. An intruder.

Bastian better be pleased to see her… if she ever came across him.

The whole place was abuzz. People dancing, drinking, smiling, laughing. Waiters circulated with champagne flutes and waitresses carried canapés.

How many drinks had she already had? Alcohol was her friend. Weighing the merits of drinking on an empty stomach, she didn't give much weight to the con side. If nothing else, it would help her to blend in. She snatched a flute of champagne from the next tray that passed.

Sipping the alcohol, she scanned the surrounding faces. None of them were looking at her. Nope. Roxie and Zairn attracted a lot of attention, maybe they weren't the best escorts after all.

Locate Bastian. Right. Yes. Where was he? There

were so many people, and the space was so large, she could spend hours looking at the ever-moving crowd and never lay eyes on him. She'd be lost in the snow. Alone surrounded by white noise. Ensconced in the mist of bodies.

People came closer. Roxie hurried in front of Zairn, stopping him while addressing Harper.

"Do you want to dance with Zairn?" Because she should take first shift? That wasn't right. "He's good."

"No, thank you," she said, sort of afraid to look up at the husband the wife was offering. "You go ahead."

"It gives people a chance to adjust to his presence," Roxie said. "Sure you'll be okay? Just for a couple of minutes."

With the way the newlyweds looked at each other, touched each other, absorbed each other, she could almost divine their need to be close. Apparently, the post-wedding sex didn't quench their thirst. And, damn, that kind of lust was enviable.

As the couple headed for the dance floor, she slunk through various bodies and groups to stop on the edge of the room. Maybe she should go back upstairs. It would be easier to observe from the mezzanine above. Though spotting him and reaching him couldn't coincide if she was way up there No way would she jump up and down or call out to him. No, the point was to save him from embarrassment not cause it.

"You look lost," an unfamiliar masculine voice materialized at her side.

Turning to the source, a broad gentleman reeking with confidence smiled at her.

"No," she said. "I was just looking for my friend."

"We can't have a beautiful woman without a companion, can we?"

FIFTEEN

Bastian

BASTIAN LOOKED AT his watch for the tenth time in as many minutes.

"Relax, son," his mom said. "Stop scowling."

Much as he didn't want to sound like a teenager, he groaned. "I've written a check, Mom. I don't understand why I can't leave. Dad's around here somewhere, he'll entertain you."

This ball supported one of his mom's many, many charities. He didn't have the same quota of time to spend with her bunch of non-profits.

"Your father is dancing with your sister," Carolyn said. "We're all here together, Bastian. This is family time."

That was the card she played when she wanted to guilt him into quieting down. Her parents, his grandparents, believed business was more important than anything. Any time he displayed similar tendencies, his mom slapped him into line. Fast. Figuratively speaking.

"There are two or three hundred other people here," he said. "It's not the best time for us to bond."

Cynicism didn't infect his mom. Never did. He'd never been able to manipulate Carolyn like she could manipulate him, his father, and his sister without breaking a sweat. His mom might not have been a career woman, but she was the smartest Hunt by far.

"You promised your sister you would be here."

Citing Keely was another choice maneuver. Another point to Mom. So far, he had no points. Unless the check counted.

"I didn't say I would stay." Semantics were his final line of defense. "I'm here, aren't I? Can I leave now?"

His mom sighed. "How do you expect to settle down when you don't take the time to look around? You never know what beauties you might stumble across."

Stifling the urge to groan again, he should've known this was about more than "family" time.

"Is that what this is about?" Bastian asked. "You want me to find Princess Charming?"

"It wouldn't hurt to have a look around at who's on offer, would it?" she said, twisting to scan the women around them. "There are a lot of beautiful women here tonight."

Shit. Lloyd Newton was heading their way. Instinct spun him around to face the opposite direction. Walk on by, Lloyd, keep on walking.

Leaving things to chance wasn't his style, and he didn't like being a sitting duck.

"Damn," Bastian muttered. Reaching behind him, he caught his mom's shoulder to guide her over in front of him again. "Do you want to dance?"

"I promised the next one to your father," Carolyn said, still glancing left and right as she sipped her drink.

She was probably trying to figure out the cause

of his shifty behavior. He wouldn't enlighten her. Just for sport, she'd wave Lloyd over if he told her the truth. His mom's sense of humor often got him into trouble.

"It's still this one," Bastian said. "It's not the next one yet."

"There are maybe three lines of music left."

"Bastian!" Fuck. Lloyd came to his side and patted his elbow. "I was hoping to pin you down tonight."

Damn it, on his list of people to avoid, Lloyd Newton sat right on top.

"The Poole investment, I know."

"Have you had a chance to look over the materials?"

No, he hadn't because Lloyd Newton was a buffoon in business. If he'd been anyone else, Bastian would have told him straight. Unfortunately, Lloyd was a friend of his aunt's. His sensitive aunt who tended to take things personally.

"It's in the inbox, Lloyd."

"I know. I know. A man like you is very busy, I understand. I appreciate that you're taking the time to look at my proposal at all."

Lloyd Newton was at least twenty years his senior and still begging for table scraps. Was there a point at which a man decided to give up on the idea of achieving pinnacle success? Everyone's definition of success was different, but Bastian couldn't imagine conducting himself with the desperation he sensed in Lloyd and other men like him.

Surely there came a point where Lloyd should accept where he was and stop striving for more. Wasn't that what Harper said about love?

Shit, Harper… she was never far from his mind.

Gaining a new respect for Lloyd, in another context, fighting even when the battle seemed impossible could be necessary.

The music stopped and a familiar sound drifted to his ears over the susurration of the party.

That enthralling laugh.

Harper.

The music began again, but his ears were pricked to identify a different sound. Had he imagined her? Was he hallucinating?

Lloyd was still talking, but it was down to Carolyn to listen. From the way his mom responded to deliberately draw Newton's attention, it was clear she'd seen his concentration waver.

Scrutinizing the crowd one way and the other, he passed right by the sight of her figure only to pause and return fast.

Yes, it was her.

Harper Scott was at the edge of the room laughing with Ricardo Whey.

Lloyd became instantly irrelevant. Had to be fucking Ricardo Whey? His feet moved before his mind formed a plan. Rudeness be damned, he strode away, intent on his goal.

Nothing in the room, in the world, was more important than the smiling woman in his crosshairs.

The party, the guests, all of it blurred when he got to her side. "Sweet?"

She turned, smile lighting her whole face. The vision of her was a sucker punch to the abs. Breathe, man, don't forget to breathe.

"Bastian!"

Harper stepped in to press herself against his side. Her automatic impulse to make full body contact— yep, he'd forgotten his own name. Her arm slid around him under his jacket until she hooked her thumb into one of his belt loops.

"Looks like he found me," Harper said to

Ricardo. "I should've known if I stayed in one place long enough he would."

"Your friend is Bastian Hunt?"

Bastian registered Whey's incredulity. Let him wonder. Harper kept on smiling, being polite, but he could sense her desire to get away from Whey.

"Someone has to take pity on him," Harper said, resting her head on his chest.

She wanted everyone in the room to believe she belonged to him. Good. Worked for him.

"Good to see you, Bastian," Whey said.

"And you," Bastian said, shaking Whey's hand.

"No Colliers in the room tonight."

"Not that I've seen."

"A lot of low profiles these days."

"Which profiles are you thinking about?" Bastian asked, knowing exactly who the man didn't want to see.

"I heard Zairn's still in town. Not seen him around."

"Since the wedding?" Oh, that's right, Whey wasn't invited. They both knew it. And, boy, it gave him some pleasure to see the man bristle. "You'll be disappointed if you came tonight to see him. Last I heard, Roxie's keeping him busy across town."

"No," Harper said, interrupting the men's flow. "They're dancing. Roxie and Zairn are dancing."

"They're…" How the hell did Harper know Zairn? Time to get her alone. "If you'll excuse us, I promised this beautiful woman a dance."

Whey lifted his glass in concession and took Harper's when she held it out.

Check that out, not many people would ask Ricardo Whey to pick up after them.

Arm still around her, he held her tight all the way to the dance floor. Like it was choreographed, when he swept her into his arms, Harper slipped her thumb from his belt and relaxed her hands on his chest.

Absorbing her scent, he loosened. Thoughts of leaving evaporated. This had suddenly become the hottest ticket in town and the only place he wanted to be. Thank God his mother was his mother.

"What did you think you were doing?" Bastian asked, inspecting those circulating close, being less than subtle in their scrutiny.

Not that Harper noticed anyone else.

"If you're upset I'm here, it's easily remedied," she said, bringing her hands closer to the center of his chest. "I can leave."

Good, chastise her. Great. Where did that fit in with the plan to win her over? He'd never been so happy to see a person in his life and, somehow, he'd put the opposite in her head. If Harper left right then, they'd probably never see each other again. Severing ties wouldn't make him happy. New plan, erase any doubt.

"I'm not upset you're here."

"You sound upset," she said, tipping her head back.

He did, but it wasn't because she was at the party. "I'm upset that you came here without me."

"I hoped you would be here."

If that was true, she'd made a misstep crossing paths with Whey.

"You were talking to Ricardo Whey. He would say anything to take you home to his bed."

Another smile, and, shit… Time to check out the others again. Anything to distract himself from the stunning sight. Resisting an urge to growl and squeeze her closer wasn't easy.

"Bed didn't come up in the conversation, and he didn't make a move."

Talking was move enough. Too close. Whey had been on the approach, of that he had no doubt.

Harper didn't understand she belonged to him. That wasn't her fault, he hadn't told her yet.

"You're a beautiful woman deserving of attention. Too many other men know that."

If he'd known her intention to be there, he'd have picked her up and kept her on his arm all night. How was it she'd never been at one of these parties before and then she was there with him?

It couldn't be that he'd never noticed her in this crowd before. He wasn't blind; he'd have noticed. Many would. The same faces passed every time. They all attended these events, spent their money, then saw each other again the next time. The butter was always churned. Everyone knew the steps to this dance. Polite. Smiling. Dancing. Mind-numbing… until Harper. Yet if she moved in circles with Roxie and Zairn…

The party started two hours ago. Had she been wandering through the crowd all that time? Any man could've picked her up and he wouldn't have been around to interrupt the seduction.

"You don't have to look after me," she said. The heat of her delicate hands seeped through his shirt. "You helped me out at my family party; I thought I would return the favor."

Wait… what?

He stopped. Her presence wasn't serendipitous, it was orchestrated?

"You're here for me?"

The glitter in her eyes dazzled him. "I said that, didn't I?"

SIXTEEN

Bastian

THIS WAS GETTING COMPLICATED.

He'd never refuse any opportunity to dance with Harper, to hold her. Any excuse to put his arms around her worked for him. The only downside? The more he held her, the harder it became to comply with his hands-off policy. Especially when she looked at him with that intimate adoration and pressed her body into his.

"Our families think we're dating," he said because they'd have to address it.

One conversation in a hotel basement had flung their lives onto a totally new tangent. Permanently or temporarily? It was no longer a one-off illusion; their connection was turning into something.

Brave and fearless, Harper didn't shrink. "I know, you don't have to remind me," she said, brushing her fingers across his jacket. "Though my parents are out of town, so we've caught a break there."

Standing still on the dance floor was conspicuous. Shit. He picked up the dance again. What was she thinking? Bringing up their families was supposed to start a conversation that would give him an idea of her position.

Being uncomplicated meant not pushing her. It didn't mean he shouldn't encourage her to share. Her home life had to be fraught, and it was his job to listen to her worries.

"You're left at home with Adara?"

"And Carnell, Charissa, and Damon, yes."

Every time he heard that dickhead's name, he regretted not taking his chance to punch the jerk. Forget that, Harper was opening up, trusting him, without hesitating. This was good. Time to return the favor.

"I don't like you staying with him."

"Damon?" Harper asked. "He wasn't happy that I was coming here tonight."

No surprise there. "Damon?"

"Yeah," she said. "I think he has a little crush on you."

Didn't take a genius to figure out the guy's problem. "Or on you."

Men like that jerkoff wanted to be important. They strutted, wanting what they couldn't have. It wasn't about love or lust, it was about control. He'd wanted Charissa because having two women on the go made him feel important. It was sickening. Damon probably enjoyed the idea of Harper being heartbroken and humiliated. The recent hint that maybe Harper was over him and moving on with her life would be piquing Damon's interest in her again.

Harper wasn't so quick to accept the possibility Damon wanted her.

"He cheated on me."

Like that made any difference. Screwing around wasn't a reflection on Harper, it was another indicator of Damon's weak personality.

"Doesn't matter." He slid his hands lower on her

back. "He knows you've moved on and that makes you attractive again."

"So I should have sex with him to prove your point?"

Where the fuck did that come from? Definitely not. What? No! The thought churned his stomach. The idea of any other man touching her was nauseating.

"You should never have sex with him again."

Or any other man. He left that part out... for now.

"I don't think there's any chance of that," Harper said.

Giving Damon airtime in their conversation would stoke the guy's ego. Time to move it along.

"Your bruises have faded since the hospital."

"Yes," she agreed. "With the wonder of concealer I'm back to normal."

Deciding to be part of her life when lying in bed in the dark was easy. Coaxing his way into her affections wasn't as straightforward.

She wouldn't want a scene and with success came notoriety. Protecting her from the eager attention of others was another priority. That ruled out grand romantic gestures.

Her presence might be a surprise, but it was also an opportunity to ingratiate himself, and betrayed he was still in her thoughts. Good.

It wasn't on her to make this happen, a man should chase his sweetheart.

"I wanted to call you," he said. "I planned to leave a respectable interval before hunting down your number. Wouldn't want you to think I was...?"

"Creepy?" she asked. "That's nice of you to say, but there was no need to call. I'm fine."

That had become her catchphrase. And it couldn't be true given how their last encounter ended.

"You ran out on me," Bastian said. "We spent the night together, then you ran out on me. There's something wrong if you felt the need to do that. You didn't trust me?"

"Trust you?" she said, touching her nose to his lapel, avoiding his gaze. "I woke up on top of you, Bastian. You're the one who shouldn't trust me."

During their shared night, he'd woken with her body covering his. He'd wrapped his arms around her, relishing the intimacy of the possibilities it conjured for their future. For a guy who spent most nights struggling to sleep, it was a relief to find a comfort that relaxed him.

Before Harper, he tossed and turned. Having her in his arms changed all that. Already addicted, the woman was better than any drug. She brought him peace.

"I didn't mind," he said in a major understatement. "You kept me warm."

Her laugh wasn't more than an exhale but restoring her smile was a helluva reward.

"I've never had a mattress with a heartbeat."

"Any time I can help…"

"You made it!" Carolyn called, dancing closer with his father.

Great time to interrupt their conversation and shatter their intimacy. Thanks came out more like a curse under his breath. His mom had a knack for involving herself in his life at exactly the wrong moment.

As much as he loved his mother, tact wasn't on her list of admirable qualities. Carolyn was likely to say something that would scare Harper off or give her the wrong idea. That was the last thing they needed.

"Do you need something, Mom?" Bastian asked, minding his manners while landing a glare on the smiling woman who'd birthed him.

"Don't be rude to your mother," Harper said, sliding one hand down from his chest to his diaphragm.

That was damn polite, acknowledging Carolyn was more than he wanted to do. Harper's soothing hand eased some of the irritation. If she wanted him to try harder, he would.

"He was talking about leaving before he spotted you," Carolyn said. "I don't think he'll worry about that now."

"It's a wonderful event," Harper said.

Where did the power of that smile come from? No mistaking it had control of him. That was something he'd consolidate within himself, he wouldn't fight it.

"This is the girl?" his father asked Carolyn.

So his mom had clued in his dad? No surprise there. Since childhood he'd witnessed his parents on the dance floor whispering, holding each other close. Shouldn't that affinity give them more consideration for what they'd busted up between him and Harper? Apparently not.

"Oh yes," Carolyn said, patting her husband's arm. "This is Harper Scott. Harper this is my husband Thomas, Bastian's father."

"Very nice to meet you," Harper said.

Thomas Hunt took her hand and kissed her knuckles. Man, not a nice sight. Until he had the pleasure of laying his lips on that body, no other man should have the privilege. Taking Harper's hand from his father, Bastian laid it back on his chest where it belonged.

Thomas' eyebrow slid up. "Jealous of your dad, son?"

"Just don't kiss her."

His family would have a field day with this. He shouldn't have done something so obvious. Too late to take it back now.

Thomas Hunt's grin spread. "Carolyn, you were right."

"Right about what?" Bastian asked, but his

parents only smiled. "Do you know what they're talking about?"

"No idea," Harper said, but wasn't paying much attention to the conversation because she was frowning at something beyond them. "Why is there an art exhibit in the corner?"

Harper came to this function for him. That should've been obvious from the get-go.

"It's not an exhibit, it's an auction for the charity," Carolyn said. "Bastian can take you over and show you the lots. It's not just art, there are various donations made by companies and individuals. His sister has already requested the canary diamond. It's seven carats I believe."

His sister did have an eye for the shiny, extravagant lots.

"Keely can request all she wants," Bastian said. Carolyn shook her head and shared a smile with Harper. "What?"

"Nothing," Harper said, patting his chest.

"He's already put in a bid for it," his mom said. True, but how did she know? "Doubt anyone else will top it."

"Why not?" Harper asked, but no one answered.

"Unless perhaps Roxanna wants it," Thomas said. "Her and Zairn are on the dance floor."

"First public appearance since the wedding," Carolyn added. "Rubies are more her thing, and Zairn gave her jewels for their nuptials."

Thomas took his wife back into his arms. "You two enjoy yourselves."

When his parents were mingled in with the crowd again, Harper asked, "Is your sister here?"

Keely was a society princess; functions like this were the highlight of her week.

"Somewhere," Bastian said. "She'll introduce

herself when she finds you. She has no shame."

His sister brimmed with optimism and had all the patience he lacked.

"She gets that from your mother, I suppose," Harper said. "Which reminds me, your mother was talking about The Faith Wish Foundation. I told her I could hook it into the Charity Launch Circulator, a newsletter shared by coordinators. If the charity gets the nod in there it will automatically be—"

"Talking about it when?" It hadn't come up in the car on the way back from the hospital. Her mouth snapped shut and her nose touched his lapel again. Suspicion deepened his voice. "Harper, talking about it when?"

"At lunch."

Fuck. He almost didn't believe it. Almost. Except his mom was more than capable of sneaking around behind his back, especially when it came to his personal life.

Harper wouldn't have sought Carolyn out, no way, of that he was sure. But his mom, yep, no doubt about it, she loved to meddle.

"You had lunch with my mom?"

Paling, she became rigid in his arms. "I thought she would've mentioned it."

"Damn, what did she say to you? She told you about tonight?"

"Yes."

The pieces fell into place. Harper was here because his mom had encouraged her to come. Under normal circumstances, he would give his mom shit for interfering. This time the impulse was less certain. Having Harper there worked for him. He couldn't be too mad about it. Not that he'd show his mom any overt gratitude, she didn't need the encouragement.

One thing he didn't like? A meeting occurring

without his knowledge. God only knew what his mom said.

"My mom can be intense… she's worried about me, or she claims to be. She wants grandkids."

Harper relaxed, hitting him with a zing of pride. "Don't worry, I told her we weren't long-term."

Damn, why would she have to tell Carolyn that? The conversation must've been more than charities and functions.

"You did?"

Some of her confidence became confusion. "Well, I tried to but…"

That didn't bode well. Once his mom decided to hear one thing, convincing her of another was difficult.

"But what?"

Her head tilted. "I think she thinks we're fuck buddies."

"That's much better," Bastian said insincerely.

Never had those two words together entered his mind along with Harper's name. But he had to give her credit, saying them at the first luncheon the women shared proved Harper had cojones.

Unless…

"Were you alone at lunch?" he asked. "Or was there a newly-minted Mrs. Lomond at the table?"

She winced. "They're hyphenating."

Bingo. So she hadn't known Roxie before, but she did now.

"Roxie's not my biggest fan."

While his mom talked him up, it was just as likely Roxie talked him down.

"She thinks you're too good to be true," Harper explained, much to his surprise. "She doesn't dislike you, just worried one of her girls might fall for you and be disappointed." Another smile glittered. "I don't think it would be possible for you to disappoint anyone."

And she was the one person he didn't want to disappoint. Chances were high that Harper didn't realize she was now one of Roxie's girls too. Mrs. Lomond—sorry, Mrs. Kyst-Lomond, didn't take long to adopt women into her circle.

"Roxie's as full on as my mother."

"I like Roxie, but I am worried about your mom?"

"Worried about her?"

"I told her we were friends and that she shouldn't make assumptions. But she kind of cut me off and said you weren't interested in shallow acquaintances. I didn't want to disappoint her by telling her straight, Bastian. She loves you so much and I… I didn't want to get her hopes up. I couldn't lie to her either. She said you cared about me, and asked if I cared about you and—"

"I'm going to kill her," Bastian grumbled.

How dare his mom be so blatant in her questioning. Carolyn wasn't a deceptive person, but she was usually more discreet than to interrogate his girlfriends. This wouldn't wait.

Snatching Harper's hand to hurry them off the dance floor, his long strides couldn't get them there quick enough. Trotting behind him, Harper kept up without much of a choice to do otherwise.

"Stop it!" Harper said, trying to break free.

Emotions were running too high for him to just stop. His mom's interfering was too much, he'd told her plenty of times to keep her nose out. This time she'd gone too far.

"She had no right—"

"You're hurting me," Harper said.

That changed the game. His fury hooked a hairpin. The whimper in her voice stopped him immediately. In apology and reassurance, he looped an arm around her, keeping her against his side.

Turned out the journey was over anyway. His mom and father approached and may not get the reception they expected. His mom had to stay away from Harper and quit interfering. He'd make that clear. Harper had enough trouble with her own family. She shouldn't be getting it from his side too.

Without his express permission, his mom shouldn't be anywhere near his woman. Sharing lunch with Harper wasn't a pleasure he'd had. It was wrong his mom got to date his girlfriend before he did.

"I'm going to kill her," he muttered with renewed annoyance when his parents weren't four feet from his side. "Mom—"

Harper snatched his face and pulled him downward until the cushion of her lips caught his. Awareness was instantly visceral. That sweet little body of hers bowed beneath his. Her hands slid to the back of his neck, pulling him down to urge herself up higher as he tasted her mouth for the first time.

SEVENTEEN

Bastian

HER ENCHANTING SCENT was nothing in comparison to the saccharine of her mouth. Intoxicated, he'd never get enough to quench the hunger she stirred in him. Without permission, his tongue slid between her lips. In the tangle, he sampled the flavor he'd sought all his life. He'd never known he needed it until that moment, now he couldn't remember surviving without it.

She initiated the kiss and ended it too. Thank God. If she hadn't kept a rein on sense, he'd have taken her there, damn their surroundings.

"Well…" he managed to say.

That single word was a struggle. The disorientation of her unexpected, but so very welcome, kiss, sent his brain cells scrambling.

She curled her lips into her mouth in a vulnerable show of apology. Oh no, baby. No reason for contrition. The flush in her cheeks was there for him. Their kiss did that to her. His guts burned in blinding envy of her teeth, her tongue, and all those places he wished to explore behind her plump lips.

She touched her nose to him, pressing her body closer too. A habit that was becoming his favorite.

"Sorry," she whispered.

His parents must have kept on walking because they weren't around anymore. He didn't care, he couldn't even remember why he'd sought them.

Every face in their periphery gawked with open interest. Not that he cared. No. Pride was what filled him. Harper wouldn't be so used to the rubbernecking.

Legend had its drawbacks.

The spectators were aghast. He'd never kissed a woman in such a public place, certainly not a kiss like that. Other than superficial air kisses, no one kissed like that at these events, it just wasn't done.

Her impulse was to move away, he could feel it before it happened. After sharing such an intense moment, he wasn't ready for distance. He hooked his arm over her head, across her shoulders, to hold her body against his.

He didn't want her to flee. If she did, he couldn't follow, not with the reaction she'd caused behind his fly.

Putting that aside, he examined the different hues of each strand in her exquisite locks, appreciating how well she fitted against him. He could get used to this, *would* get used to this, when she was ready.

Getting physical with her was on his agenda, secondary to ensuring her wellbeing.

"Are you okay?" he asked the top of her head, his lips tickled by her mocha tresses.

"I didn't mean to do that... to kiss you. You can't blame your mother for thinking there's something between us. This is our mess. We got ourselves into it. If you start pointing fingers, we'll only get invested."

"Are you telling me we're not invested already?"

When she looked up, the answer was written all over her face. Distress matched the certainty, but he was invigorated. It wasn't just him; she felt this thing bubbling between them.

"Bastian! Bastian!"

Keely ran up behind Harper who he kept close despite his sister's bouncing and grinning. Elation buzzed around her all the same.

"What are you so happy about?" Bastian asked.

Her million-dollar smile glowed. "Are you kidding? You're making out at parties? No one else would get away with that. Honestly, it's so… naughty."

Trust his sister to know exactly the wrong thing to say in her excitement.

"Keely," he warned, aware of quashing anything that might discourage Harper.

His embrace grew cold when Harper turned away. She didn't run and hide; her posture didn't suggest being self-conscious. His guess? She was curious about his intrusive sibling.

"I'm Keely," she exclaimed. "Your new sister."

Keely grabbed Harper into a hug.

He tried to pry the two apart with little success. "Leave her alone, Keel," Bastian said. "She's not your new sister."

Only when they were good and ready did the women let go of each other. Automatically, Harper leaned on him again. Excellent.

"When Robyn hears about this she's going to be ma-had," Keely prodded Bastian.

Great. Fuck. Sometimes Keely was… Keely.

"Robyn?" Harper asked, withdrawing to put a foot of space between them. "Who's Robyn?"

"Oops," Keely said. "Got to go."

His sister was fast swallowed by the mass of other partygoers.

"She's an ex…" he said. "Robyn is my ex."

Already aware of the distance between them, he didn't like it when she increased it with another backward step. Most people wanted to be near him. In the past, women had gone to extraordinary lengths to touch and fawn. Not Harper. Her perception wasn't biased by his success.

Any inkling of infidelity would poison Harper's perception of this. Integrity was vital to her.

"You don't sound sure," Harper said, mortified and alert. "Oh my God, why didn't you tell me you were seeing someone? I would never have come here if I knew…"

Robyn was ancient history. Keely never liked his ex and rejoiced that they'd split up. His mom was more diplomatic but probably felt the same.

"I'm not seeing her," he said.

Dampening the surge of testosterone-fueled possession that flooded him when Harper twisted away from his reach, he had to remember she didn't actually belong to him, yet.

The squirm of her gaze spoke to her discomfort.

She lowered her volume to a breath. "I didn't even think to ask. We were only supposed to be together that one night. I told you it was perfect at that." She sighed. "Now everything's complicated."

He had experience with calming women down. With a drama queen sister and a vocal mother, he'd been training for it most of his life.

"It's nothing," he soothed, stroking the silken skin of her upper arm. The pure texture boosted his testosterone again. "I'm not seeing her, Sweet. It's just us, you and me… Fidelity's not too much to ask, remember?"

That wasn't the reassurance she needed. All he needed was her close to him again. He failed them both.

"You can see anyone you want," Harper whispered. "We both know this isn't real. The problem is that others don't. Your mother would never have encouraged me to come here if she knew you were serious about someone else. All she wants is to see you happy, Bastian. You let her know about this woman and she'll feel better. Right now, she's telling me that you're passing the time, screwing around with a bunch of women. She knows that doesn't make you happy."

His brows rose. "So now I'm screwing around with a bunch of women? How many is a bunch?"

The ebb and flow of this fascinating woman's emotions led to captivating conversation. As long as they were talking, she wasn't going anywhere.

"That's not my business," Harper said. "But you should've been honest, with me, with your mother, and with your family. They want you to be happy."

Learning her buttons and how to stimulate them would come in useful later.

With that in mind, he had to ask, "Why are you so upset about this?"

Her blink was shock.

She leaned away, crossing her arms in front of her. "I'm not upset."

Man, she was beautiful when she was defensive. It didn't help ease her embarrassment when he smiled, but he couldn't help himself. Finding this woman had been a blessing.

"Could've fooled me."

Would needling her provoke a jealousy confession? That implication energized his attraction. Most women who got upset about his associations were dramatic about it, giving him the sense it was a cry for attention.

Not Harper.

Their potential future relied on her admitting

their attraction. From what he could tell so far, she was fighting it.

Staying rigid for half a beat, she gave no hint of what was in her head. Then, just like that, she relaxed.

"Fine, yes, I'm upset. I thought you were my friend and naïvely assumed that included honesty."

Oh, hey, that might have backfired.

"I've been nothing but honest with you, Sweet."

For the first time, he wanted to answer to a woman, this one, and he wanted her to step up and claim that right.

She got more confused and shook her head downward, only to then tip it back.

"You shouldn't have come to me that night," she said. "This whole thing was a mistake. We've been sucked in deeper than we—screw around with whoever you want. But don't expect me to be the façade protecting your secrets."

That was almost laughable. Never took Harper long to get him smiling.

"You don't want to be the dutiful wife while I screw anything under twenty-five in a skirt?"

Tensing, she clearly didn't see the funny side.

"If those are your requirements, find yourself a different front."

No sense of humor, huh? No prizes for guessing why.

"You're punishing me for his mistakes," Bastian said. "You do see that, don't you? You're still smarting over Damon and waiting for it to happen again. You're pushing me away so I can't get close enough to hurt you."

"This isn't real," she said.

He couldn't disagree more. What he felt might be sudden and unique, but that only enhanced his certainty.

"Feels real to me," he said, backing her into a corner.

Angling them in the confined space wasn't planned. It just happened. Alone as they could get in this crowded space, it was the only place he wanted to be.

Harper shook her head. "What are we doing?" she whispered. "One kiss and then we're at each other like cat and dog."

Bingo! She felt it too. Though her reaction contrasted his. Their magnetism enticed him while it unsettled her. When her palm went to her forehead, he rested his forearm on the wall above her head to crowd in closer.

"I'm not seeing anyone else."

"I know," she said, dropping her hand to his chest, igniting heat in his body beneath her dainty fingers. "It's none of my business anyway. I have no reason not to take you at your word. You're right. I'm lashing out because… because I don't want to be made a fool of again."

Wasn't on his agenda, but he was prepared to make one of himself.

"Sweet," he murmured, tracing his finger down her temple. "I won't make a fool out of you."

"Do you promise?" she said, curling her fingers until her nails bit into him, just a little.

There was something so intimate about that act, like her subconscious wanted to pull him to her. His body was willing to go. More than willing.

"Harper!"

The feminine exclamation turned them both around.

"Roxie," he said but the woman was already reaching past him.

"Not here for you, Hunt," Roxie said, taking Harper's hand. "Girl talk time."

EIGHTEEN

THEY KEPT ON going until the bar stopped their progress.

Roxie slapped a hand down as the bartender came their way. "Two piña coladas, please." The guy frowned. "Got a problem?"

"No, ma'am," he said and retreated to mix the drinks.

"Sit, sit," Roxie said, hopping onto a stool of her own. "How are you doing?"

"You heard about the kiss?"

"Saw it, baby," Roxie said. "Nothing wrong with lovin' your man."

"I embarrassed him."

"I don't think you did. Did he say that? If he's got a problem—"

"No, he would never say that. I'm just... an idiot."

"Why?" Roxie asked. "Not a bad thing to be so into a guy you can't contain yourself. Resisting that can be painful. Honestly, it's bad for your health."

"Yeah, and what's everyone going to remember about me? What a great first impression on his friends."

"Okay." Roxie laid a hand over hers. "Yes, Bastian probably knows most people in this room, but they're not his friends. Not the ones that matter."

"You know his friends? His real friends."

"Yes, and they're not here."

"Will they hear about this though? I'll forever be the woman who molested a stranger in polite company."

"For starters, he's not a stranger—" Roxie turned toward the bar when the server brought their drinks. And that tension in her brow wasn't promising. "Where's my umbrella?" The guy blinked in surprise but met Roxie's eye when she looked up. "This should have an umbrella."

"I—"

"Mandatory umbrella," Roxie said. "If it doesn't have an umbrella, I can't drink it. Are you a qualified mixologist? I should have a little paper parasol, right here."

"I'm sorry, Miss Kyst. I don't think—we don't have cocktail umbrellas."

Roxie sighed. "It's not your fault. Someone will be hearing about this though. Imagine sending your mixologists into the wild without paper umbrellas. A travesty." She waved the guy away. "Go on. Back to work." The drink wrinkled Roxie's nose. "My boyfriend better never hear about this."

"Your husband."

"My—right, my husband! I'm surprised that doesn't feel icky." Roxie pushed the second drink closer and raised her own. Okay. They were drinking. "To spontaneity." That was one word for it. After drinking, Roxie licked her lips a few times, concentrating on the liquid. "Not bad. Not perfect. But not bad. To my palate, Z's would be a whole different story. He's pernickety."

"He knew who you were."

"He knew—the bartender? Yeah, a lot of people know who I am these days."

"Have you met before?"

"No, it's a Crimson thing."

She'd recognized Roxie too, maybe not too accurately, but the face was familiar.

"I don't know how you do it, go around with everyone… Don't you worry what people think?"

"I do," Roxie said, straightening her spine. "My Casanova. I worry what he thinks. He's really the only one who matters. These days. I trust my girls to think positive and my guy to open the confusing labyrinth of his mind to me without prompting."

"Have you met his family?"

"Yes."

"Did they push you together?"

"No," Roxie said, laughing after another sip. "No, the people in his life were wary of me to begin with. I was an unknown factor. A crisis event waiting to happen and I've fulfilled that role many, many times."

"I had it with Damon," she said, stirring her drink with the straw. "My family wanted us to be together. My dad wants—none of that matters now."

"Exactly. None of that matters. Dickwad Damon doesn't matter. On with the show," Roxie exclaimed, tossing an arm in the air. "What comes next? Who comes next?"

Roxie's confidence was enviable. She liked to think of herself as strong, assured, in some areas of life: love wasn't one of them.

"Do you know Robyn?"

"Never met her." Roxie directed her straw between her lips, the depth of liquid in the glass went down, paused, and down again. This woman could hold her liquor. "But I know they broke up. By all accounts, she and Bastian weren't that great together. If you want to meet her, I can make it happen." Roxie twisted fast and grabbed the arm of someone passing by. "Is Tripp in town?"

The bewildered person took a second before answering. "Madrid, I think."

"Thanks." Roxie let them go and returned to her drink. "I'll call him later."

"Tripp?" she asked. "Who was that person you stopped?"

"No idea, never seen them before in my life." And Roxie must've read her confusion. "Everyone knows Tripp Breckenridge. He's probably not in Madrid, but I buy he's not in town. I haven't spoken to him for a while—since the wedding, I think."

"You think?"

"Ah, parts of the last week or two are a little… hazy. Zairn has not been shy about handing out those orgasms. Not that he ever is." Confident. Proud. Together. The enviable list went on and on. "I'd call Tripp but my phone is dead…" The beauty's head turned this way and that. "Probably. Wherever it is."

"I didn't know Bastian was seeing anyone." And why should she? Their contact was supposed to be fleeting. "I don't want to step on toes or cause issues for him."

"They are not together." Roxie took another drink then linked their hands. "They broke up way before you… Before you, anyway, I don't know exactly when. I can find out."

The openness, the kindness, it was humbling.

"Everyone in Bastian's life is so nice."

"Not everyone. Z's more in his life than I am. I'm closer to Carolyn."

"He's apologized for her being so bold, but I'm amazed just how much she loves her children."

"Who loves their children?" Another female

joined them: Keely. "Who are we talking about?"

"Your mom," Roxie answered without hesitation and gestured to the bartender for another drink. "Not everyone grows up with such a dedicated mother."

"This is cause of Bastian, right?" Keely asked, the warmth in those big, beautiful eyes nodding one way then the other. "Is he mad at Mom?"

"No!" God, she was worried about embarrassing the man, now she had to be aware of stirring up mischief in the family too. "He's not mad."

"It's difficult to tell with him," Roxie added. "He plays his cards close to his chest."

"Yeah, he never talks about relationship stuff," Keely agreed, going to the stool behind her, putting Harper in the middle. "Mom tries to talk to him, I do, even Dad. He just doesn't like talking about that stuff."

"He doesn't want to let anyone down." The sweet liquor coated her throat. "Your mom is eager for him to settle down, he doesn't want to give her false hope."

"You don't want to settle down with my brother?"

Her horror went to Roxie first, the woman raised her brows.

"I didn't say that," Harper said. How was she digging herself deeper…? Again! "Your brother is a wonderful man."

"Wonderful? Is there a less sexy word to describe a guy?" Keely said, grinning when the bartender came with her cocktail. "Thank you…" She picked it up to drink. "I love it when you come out to play, Rox."

"I love it too." Roxie touched the surface of her drink. "When are we going to hook you up with your forever guy, Keely, honey?"

"Bastian will never accept any guy. I'll die a spinster."

Roxie leaned in. "Who says he has to know? Come stay with us in New York. We might even hook you up with a Breckenridge."

Keely laughed. Her drink dropped a little as she shook her head. "Oh my God, that's practically incest!"

Ew, okay, the less said about that…

"Your brother is sexy," she said in hope of leaving a better lasting impression. "Too sexy."

"That why you made out with him? Bastian's not usually… naughty."

"Harper brings it out in him."

"People will be talking about that for months. Years! You'll be legendary."

And that was exactly what she didn't want to hear. Years? Long after she'd returned to her mess of a life, when Bastian was just trying to get along, people would remember…

"Nothing wrong with that."

No? She felt sick. "Years?"

"Geez…" Roxie said, putting down her glass and twisting her stool around to scan the space. "Let's clear this up now…"

"Clear it up?"

"Watch and learn." Roxie kicked out her leg as she pounced off the stool. Her set pace and determination cleared people from her path, opening up a direct route to her husband—Roxie swept away his glass so fast that it fell from his hand. Then she was grabbing him down, kissing him like—oh and there was the leg to his hip, a bounce and… Wow, Roxie was—wow.

Keely's giggle came with a sigh. "I love her so much. Isn't she amazing?"

Zairn would wonder where such passion came from so suddenly. Or maybe he wouldn't. They weren't a couple who apologized for their love and were proud of it everywhere.

Maybe she could take a leaf from their book and learn a few things… If she didn't terrify Bastian in the process.

Wait. No. Not Bastian. She wasn't with Bastian, she was… they really needed to figure this out.

NINETEEN

A NIGHT FOR THE BOOKS. With Roxie, Keely, and the attentive man currently driving her home. Oh, but she wasn't ready. He'd been utterly focused on her all night without crowding her. With his dad and Zairn part of their group, the men did their own talking while she got to know Keely and Carolyn better.

Despite only meeting Roxie once before that night, it already felt they'd been friends for years. Something about Roxie just put her, and everyone else, at ease. The woman was a magnet for people and could talk to anyone. Literally anyone. Except Ricardo Whey. He got the stink eye with a slight side-smirk, the two must have history.

Every once in a while, Bastian would sweep her away to hold her tight on the dance floor. It gave them time to talk alone, without lies. Those moments reinforced their duplicity. What a view they must've made to those who believed their mistruths.

At the end of the night, as the Hunt parents and Keely said goodnight and left the hall, Harper gathered her clutch, ready to tell Bastian she was going too. Before a word left her lips, he wrapped her in his jacket and draped a possessive arm over her shoulder to lead her outside.

A valet brought his car around. He helped her inside and moments later they were on a long, dark road.

"Did you have a good time?" he asked.

The smile on her face probably said it all. Though tired, the night still stirred her blood.

"Yeah," she said. "Better than I thought I would."

"You were worried about coming out with me?"

He'd been the simplest part of the whole night.

"No," she said, slipping her feet from her shoes. "But when we drove up to that house… everyone looked so… refined."

"You look amazing," he said. "That dress plays peek-a-boo with your leg. Drives me crazy."

Without their audience, he didn't have to be sweet with her. The habit would wear off.

"Not while you're driving," she said. "Speaking of which, you can drop me anywhere and I'll get a cab to—"

"Why would you get a cab?"

"You can't drive all the way to my parents', and it would be a heck of a long walk. It's forever away."

For a second, neither of them said anything. The silence was his acquiesce… wasn't it? Except their route didn't change.

"You told Damon and Charissa we had a date tonight."

And if she'd needed a slap to get back to reality, talking about Damon was it. Did Bastian really need to go there?

"Yeah," she grumbled.

"Everyone thinks we've been seeing each other

for four months."

"Or thereabouts."

"Hypothetically..." he said. "If you've been seeing a guy for four months, you've met his family, and he's met yours. You've just been on a date, drinking, dancing. You've teased him with that dress all night, got him thinking about what's underneath... It's the end of the date, he's got you in his car... what would happen next?"

Hmm... The usual goodnight kiss on the doorstep phase would be over by four months.

"You think we'd be having sex," she said, but couldn't subscribe to the assumption. "We would be over the 'screwing like bunnies' phase."

"By four months?" he asked, taking his eyes from the road. "Are you sure about that?"

Yes, she was damn sure about it. That phase never lasted long. She and Bastian were too invested in business to be distracted by anything like sex for too long.

"We only see each other once a week," she said. "And last week I was injured so I doubt that would've included anything adventurous..." Truth was, she was pragmatic about sex. "It's what I said the night we met, people settle for respect, cohabitation. A partner."

Bastian didn't agree. "Indifference," he said. "Like you had with Damon, you think our relationship would be like that?"

She twisted the wrist strap of her clutch around. They were trapped in a confined space again. Just like the night he'd brought her back from the hospital, claustrophobia closed in. Their choice of conversation wasn't helping alleviate the growing humidity. Was it all in her head? Maybe she was sick.

In this car and nowhere else? Other than in Bastian's arms on the dance floor. Any time she was up close it got hotter and a little squirmy.

"Not to be rude but… I don't see how it could be any different."

"I'd be faithful for one thing," he said.

Shit, she hadn't meant to offend him. Being compared to Damon could sour anyone's mood. Though, in fairness, she hadn't been the one to bring up her ex. It wasn't like she was making a direct comparison anyway, that should be obvious given the difference between the two men.

"Of course," she said. "What I meant was the feeling, the emotion involved, the general day-to-day goings on of any relationship will be similar."

"After four months with Damon you'd stopped having sex?"

Embarrassment chilled her. What was it with this guy that she kept walking into these conversational cul-de-sacs?

"This is mortifying," she whispered to herself.

"I want to know," Bastian said. "Are you telling me that after four months of access this guy could keep his hands off you?"

Seemed the conversation was happening no matter what, with or without her. Bastian was perfectly at ease. Good for him. What kind of gentleman asked questions like this of a woman with a few glasses of champagne—and maybe three or four cocktails—in her.

"Yes."

"I don't believe it."

She scoffed. "It's true," she said, happy to be offended if that was where he wanted to drive her. "I have no reason to lie."

"What was wrong with him?"

What was that supposed to mean?

"Nothing," she said. "There was nothing wrong with him."

"There had to be if he was passing up a night in bed with you."

Okay, uh… another surprise. Being kind when there was no one around was one thing, but deconstructing her relationship with Damon wouldn't achieve anything. Then again, Damon hadn't made the best first impression on Bastian. She guessed that fostered negative feelings. Damon upset Adara the same night the two men met. As a brother himself, Bastian could probably identify with how it felt to have someone insult a sibling.

"You don't have to do that, you know. It's sweet of you to say—"

"It's not sweet at all. You wanted honesty? This is it," Bastian said. "That guy could have you any day, any time he wanted, and he didn't take full advantage? There has to be something wrong with him."

His vehemence wasn't meant to be vicious, she sensed it came from a place of certainty, which only compounded her own humiliation.

"There isn't," she said.

"There is, there has to be—"

"It's me!"

Neither said a word for a few seconds.

"Right," he said, seeming to figure it out. "You kicked him out of bed. That I get."

"No." She sighed. "You heard his joke about the Contrast Sisters. It's a known fact that I'm no good… in bed… And now that I've confessed that horrifying truth to you, drive me into the ocean."

"You're no good in bed."

Gawping, she probably squawked, but shock deafened her.

"You didn't have to repeat it!" she said. "What kind of gentleman are you? Now when I fall asleep tonight I'll hear you saying that sentence in my head over and over again."

"You are good in bed."

Her thoughts spun out with the speed of that turnaround. She didn't get it. While she slowly died inside, Bastian just sat there like they were talking about the weather.

Exasperated, she swallowed air for a minute before sputtering, "How could you possibly know that?" Suspicion crept in. "Is this a guy thing where you try to goad me into proving you're wrong thus you get sex of some variety while I get to be correct?"

His dimple was quick to distract her. "I'm not goading you into anything, Sweet. I'm giving you my opinion."

He hadn't sold her. "I appreciate the ignorant compliment, as well intentioned as it may be, but you can't know that."

"Sure I do."

Never short of confidence, Bastian's certainty bordered on cocky.

She didn't get it. Just what was in those cocktails?

"Did we have sex and somehow I missed it?"

"No," he said on a laugh. "But I have shared a bed with you and I have no complaints."

Rather than laugh, she went for dry sarcasm instead. "Yes," she said. "I do my best work while unconscious."

He wasn't deterred. "Sweet, there are three things I know about you for sure. All of them contradict whatever that inadequate, unthinking idiot might have said to you."

This should be interesting.

She folded her arms. "Three?"

"You're beautiful," Bastian said. "You have a killer body that screams sin even when you're trying to cover it up. You're engaging and interesting. Your instinct is sharp. You're entertaining, funny, and curious. You have a wonderful mind brimming with thoughts and questions enough to enrapture any man. You're caring. Have a voice that diverts male blood south and would even if you were reciting the Constitution. And when you laugh I want to taste every morsel of that delectable mouth and beg for more. You're responsive, keen, so aware of what's going on but focused on your priority. A man doesn't have to guess when he's with you. Every squeak and whimper lets a guy know exactly what's right, and what's wrong. You're better than every dessert on the cart; you're prime rib rare enough to make a guy's mouth water. With you, Harper Scott, there's no such thing as no room for more."

And that was…

Her mouth wouldn't close but her—she—they…

"That was more than three things."

Flattered and overwhelmed, she had no idea how to… All she could do was accept her certainty was his. She'd never been so grateful for, or to, another person. Showing him that wouldn't be easy. She slid her hand over his on the gear stick. When he opened his fingers to accept hers between them, she begged him to understand.

"Stay the night," he said.

"Okay."

There was no way she had the power to say no. Whether what he'd said was true or not didn't matter. He gave her what she needed. Every time, somehow, he managed it.

He picked her hand up to kiss her knuckles. "I promise I'll leave you alone this time."

Did she want to be left alone?

Their connected hands muddied the conviction that this wasn't real. They weren't together. She wasn't even sure they were friends. They were acquaintances, associates… partners in crime, offering each other a mutual alibi. That was it. Nothing more. Nothing.

TWENTY

LIKE ON HER FIRST visit, he gave her a tee-shirt, shorts, and a toothbrush. Not just any toothbrush. *Her* toothbrush, the one he'd kept since her last visit. He kept it. Wonders never ceased. That suggested he'd expected her back.

She had a toothbrush. At Bastian's.

Sorry, that required a moment of… huh.

As promised, after setting her up in the same bedroom as before, he left her alone. She didn't stop him from leaving, even when he hesitated. No matter how much she wanted him to stay, she did not want to wake up on top of him… again. Liberties like that shouldn't be repeated. Once was an accident, twice was pathological.

Despite the warmth of the room and the luxurious covers, her second experience sleeping there didn't match the first. They weren't in the same ballpark. Not with him so tantalizingly close, yet completely out of reach.

Kind, generous, understanding. A man like

Bastian shouldn't be alone.

Everything about him suggested a desire to share, to care. He needed a companion. He deserved children, friends, family. He was built to be part of something. Half of a whole. For whatever reason, he'd decided he didn't want a romantic relationship with anyone. It had to be his conscious choice. No other explanation made sense. His determination and perseverance were apparent in everything he did. He didn't leave things like that to chance. If he wanted romance, he'd have gone out there and got it.

Maybe Robyn hurt him and he was still raw.

Guilt crept in. Bastian knew almost everything about her personal life. He'd asked questions and been so attentive. To her shame, she hadn't paid the same attention in return. She would fix that. He'd been her confidant, now she would be his.

That was her last thought before falling asleep and the first when she woke up. On leaving her bedroom, she ran down the stairs.

"May I borrow a pen?" Harper asked, reaching the kitchen.

At the opposite side of the kitchen island, Bastian stopped chopping fruit. His concentration ebbed. The flash of his dimple reinforced her faith. Did she put that there? Could he be pleased to see her? Sheesh, talk about excitable. Calm down.

"Did you sleep well?" he asked, popping a fruit segment into his mouth.

"I did," she said, smoothing her hands from waist to hip.

It hadn't occurred to her to be self-conscious about coming downstairs in his tee-shirt with mussed hair, not until she was faced with him.

"Good."

Oh, it would be so easy to lose herself in his

mesmerizing dimple. Tugging the hem of his tee-shirt down on her thighs, she was grateful to have, at least, donned underwear. In her defense, appearing for breakfast in a cocktail dress wouldn't have been much better.

"Did you?" she asked. "Did you sleep well?"

He half-shrugged and put the chopped fruit into the blender. His tee-shirt was far too big for her. When the neck slid down her arm, she didn't bother pulling it up. It would only fall again anyway.

"What does that mean?" she asked. "That shrug?"

"Are you hungry?"

Damn man was bullheaded. He was really going to ignore the question and expect her to let it go without getting an answer. Getting to know him would be more difficult if he resisted.

She wasn't going to yield that easily. "What's the shrug?"

"I'm an insomniac."

Great, now she felt even worse. "You didn't sleep?"

"I slept a little; it comes and goes."

"You should've woken me," she said, rounding the center island.

"What would you have done?"

"Bored you to sleep," she said and smiled. "I'm a tongue twister expert. I know them all. It's my party piece."

Stealing a hunk of fruit from beside him, she popped it in her mouth just as he turned his smile her way. The unexpected whirr of the blender startled her, though not as much as the splatter of fruit that followed.

"Shit," he mumbled as she squealed.

The grump complemented his frown. She, on the other hand, couldn't hide her smile. It wasn't like him to be out of sorts.

"Are you okay?" she asked, resting a hand on his bicep.

"Yeah, I… that sweet scent…"

When his attention dropped to her bare legs, she wiggled her lilac-frosted toenails. "Are you surprised I have legs?"

"Didn't think I'd be lucky enough to see them."

In relaxing him, she melted. "Your shorts wouldn't stay up. Thanks for the tee-shirt."

"Now I regret giving it to you," Bastian said. "I might have got to see more of you if I kept it to myself."

Being around him was so easy. Right there, she wouldn't dwell on the show they put on for the outside world. This was a rare chance to chill and drop the pretense.

"We should clean this up," she said, scooping some of the fruit goop from his arm then sucking it into her mouth. "This is good."

"My secret recipe," he said. "I thought you'd like it."

"I do," she said, wiping more from him and licking her finger again.

"It tastes like you smell," he said, running a fingertip across her temple. "I use peaches with the berries now… because of you."

Whatever was in the blender tasted good. Or maybe that was enhanced by its source. She picked up a lump of peach from his wrist and sucked it into her mouth.

In apparent response, he took a long backward step.

Enjoying the new treat, she'd missed the sterner angle of his brow and the tension rippling his shoulders.

Uh… "You okay?"

"Don't do that."

Yeah, she shouldn't eat fruit straight from her exhausted host, that was kinda rude.

"I'm sorry, I—"

"Don't apologize, just—"

"Tell me about Robyn."

He faltered. His pained expression faded in lieu of confusion.

"Robyn?"

Decision made, she wouldn't beat around the bush. Bastian hosted her last night, he'd saved her from embarrassment in front of Damon and introduced her to his family. No, she was in no hurry to introduce him to her folks, but that was a whole different ball of wax she'd reserve for another time.

Friendship. Attentive friendship. That was what he deserved. And what better place to start than with his last heartache. That was the kind of thing friends talked about.

"Your ex. Your last significant ex. Were you serious?"

Stupid question. If the relationship wasn't serious, would Robyn have met the Hunt family? Although… she'd met the Hunt family and they weren't even dating. What did that tell her? Not to make assumptions, that's what. Her assumptions were almost always wrong, but they wouldn't be assumptions if they didn't just pop into her head as pseudofact, would they?

She wouldn't judge him, he'd never judged her. This was a good man. One who didn't deserve to be mistreated by anyone, certainly not by a woman entrusted with his heart. If she found out this Robyn woman hurt him, she'd wage all-out war.

Still, it appeared he didn't understand the question. In his defense, why would he expect her to ask or care when she hadn't before?

"I wouldn't say she was significant," he said. "We

went out for four, five months."

"When did you break up?" Harper asked.

"November, maybe December. Why are you asking about Robyn?"

She slid onto a nearby high stool. "You know about Damon," she said. "We've talked about our families and you made the effort to get to know me. I haven't returned that kindness. I'm sorry, Bastian. I didn't mean to be so selfish."

When his dimple peeked at her, she guessed he didn't feel the same way.

"We had to be a couple in front of your family and friends," he said. "We had to prioritize."

At the time, sure, she'd give him that. Since then, things had developed, for better or worse.

"Now we have to be a couple in front of yours," Harper said. Bastian began cleaning up. "Give me that." She took the cloth from him and rinsed it out before carrying on. "I need a pen and a piece of paper... please."

Bastian rested a hand on her hip to step in behind her, reaching for a drawer. Before he got there, she bent at the waist to pick fruit from the crossbar of a stool and—whoa. Bastian's other hand found her opposite hip and—

She froze.

Her tee-shirt had ridden up, now Bastian was behind her, holding her hips... and he wasn't letting go. But she wasn't backing off either. Should she? Should she slip free? Oh, she didn't want to.

Her heart thundered behind her ribs sending blood rushing straight to her dizzied head. Her inner muscles clenched, anticipating the forbidden. Oh, bad idea. Bad idea. Good sense understood nothing could happen, her heart wasn't so sure, whereas her libido missed the message of the myth altogether.

This wasn't a real relationship.

It wasn't any relationship.

Being in the home of a gorgeous man first thing in the morning, in a state of undress, mutual undress, didn't mean there was anything between them or that this was going anywhere.

Those strong, capable hands slid up to her waist. There was little pressure in the move, but the tee-shirt hitched up further. Her thong wouldn't hide much. Other than that scrap of fabric, she was naked from the waist down.

It should be awkward and uncomfortable. There, together in his kitchen, silent, her body bent over in front of his, it was almost inviting him in. Like a confession she'd submit to whatever his body required, she just stayed there, exposed for his visual consumption.

When one hand moved, she stopped breathing, anticipating where it might explore next.

A shrill ring wrung a gasp from her lungs. She straightened up so fast, her back bounced against his chest. His palm skimmed from her waist around to splay on her upper abdomen, steadying her, encouraging her to lean on him.

The shock subsided and... what was...Something pressed into her spine... some—that thick, powerful shaft betrayed his reaction to their... proximity.

He was hard.

Oh, God—and there was something else, his pulse raced too. So fast that it was difficult to differentiate his from her own, frantic, eager, deafening beat.

The ring came again.

Filtering the sound through the fog of increased blood pressure was a challenge.

As though he sensed her mental disarray, Bastian

kissed the top of her head, reminding her he was right there with her.

"It's the phone," he murmured, leaving her with nothing to lean on.

Bastian walked out of a sliding door into a room she hadn't seen. She couldn't follow, he needed to take that call, and she needed to get her senses back.

She finished cleaning up and opened the drawer Bastian had been aiming for before... anyway. Among other things, she found a small notepad and a pen. She wrote down her number, then went upstairs to text for a cab.

Didn't take long to jump back into last night's dress. Clutch in hand, she ran back downstairs to the kitchen just in time to see Bastian closing the sliding door behind him.

"Sneaking out on me again, Sweet?"

Smiling, she shook her head, wishing for a hair tie. "I'm not sneaking out," she said. "I have to get home and ready for the day. There's a few things I want to get done at the office."

"We could take the day off," he said, crossing to the island.

"There's no need for that," she said. "Our families think we spent the night together. We've done our duty and given ourselves cover for the week."

"I was thinking about that," he said, picking up the notepaper. "What's this?"

"My phone number," she said. "Just in case."

"Of what?"

Huh, rejection. Ouch.

It wasn't like she was asking for a dinner invitation. A way to communicate should be the minimum required for their fake relationship. That way if his mom did any more scheming, he could warn her in advance. It was too much to hope that he'd pick up the phone just to confide in her. What about practicalities? The reality of both families believing there was something between them?

"We have to coordinate our breakup. My sister and her fiancé know where you work and how to get in touch with you." To her horror. "Your mother showed up at my work, and she's met Damon. We'll have to coordinate in case any of them come across each other. Our stories have to match."

"My mother's having a dinner party on Tuesday," he said. "Would you consider joining me? Save me from being fixed up by her cronies."

Harper nodded. This was mature and sensible. Knowing what was coming up, and what was expected of them, reduced the chances they'd be caught unawares.

"Yes, I'll be there."

"You have a launch next weekend, don't you?"

Impressed that he remembered, there'd been no intention to invite him along.

"Yes, but it's Sunday night." She winced. "You'll have to work the next day."

Not deterred, little phased him. "That's okay," he said. "I'll make it work because it's my parents' anniversary the following weekend."

"You need company?"

"I have to give a speech," he said. "And the next weekend will be your birthday."

And how did he know that? Maybe it had come up while they were dancing, sometimes she zoned out when her head couldn't believe reality. That dimple was intoxicating all by itself, never mind the incredible man it belonged to. Sometimes she couldn't keep up.

"It's not a big deal. There's nothing planned," Harper said. "For my birthday. There never is, it's just another day."

He folded the paper with her number and tucked

it into his back pocket.

"One day at a time," he said, coming to join her. "Now we know we're together for at least the next month. No need to start thinking about our breakup yet."

She took a deep breath. "Okay," she said, hooking a hand around the back of his neck to pull him down for a cheek kiss. "Will you text me the details for Tuesday?"

"Let me change my tee-shirt and I'll drive you home."

The kindness thing came from his mother, had to. Carolyn would be mortified if her son wasn't a consummate gentleman.

"You don't have—"

"If we spent the night together, I'd be driving you anywhere you needed to go. We're keeping up appearances, aren't we?"

A man with an answer for everything. That quick mind of his might work with others, she wouldn't let it overwhelm her. Not with something like this. Looking after herself was second nature, something she'd have to reassert.

"I don't need a driver," she said. "You don't have to take time out of your day."

Why should he inconvenience himself for a charade?

"It's that or you pick a car. Those are your options."

Taken aback, wit deserted her. "Pick a car?"

Pride shone from the smile by his dimple, he did like surprising her. "There are a few on the premises," he said. "I take you home, or you accept one of the cars."

Independence had its limits. Something she was learning right there. Dumb as it sounded, and she couldn't really explain why, but the idea of driving

Bastian's car was a thrill, taking a part of him home with her appealed. Was that weird?

"You'd let me drive your car?"

Sometimes, if it was ever desperately needed, she'd drive her father's car. More often than not, cabs were her primary mode of transport. A car was an expense she didn't need. She much preferred to reinvest her money into the company. As a one-woman operation, only she was on the hook in success or failure.

Smiling, he stroked her upper arms. "Want to have a look?"

Though she tried to subdue her mischief, she couldn't play it coy and pouted a little when she asked, "Did your mom say something about a Porsche?"

Lacing his fingers between hers, he guided her knuckles to his lips. "I'll bring it around for you."

TWENTY-ONE

"YOU DON'T HAVE to be nervous. There's nothing to be nervous of. It's food with Carolyn, a dinner party, no big deal, easy breezy. Don't psyche yourself out."

On the phone, her gorgeous friend just couldn't identify with gnawing anxiety.

"Rox, you're never nervous."

"I'm nervous, I… I'm not the best example of how to live your life, honey. Anyone who models themselves on me will end up in hot water. I guess the mantra should really be, 'what wouldn't Roxie do?' Though, hmm, there's not a lot on that list." Her friend hummed for a pondering second, then snapped back with renewed zeal. "Talk to Bastian. If you really don't want to go…"

Except she'd agreed already. "I can't just randomly call him."

Showering, getting ready, had been autopilot. She'd had momentum and now it was time to leave, the butterflies started.

"He's your guy," Roxie said. "That's what they're

for. You can randomly call him any time. There doesn't need to be a reason."

"He's not… really my guy."

"He gave you a car. How much more does a guy need to do?"

"It's on loan. Not permanent. Driving in LA isn't fun. It's more stop than start. We don't need cars. You don't have a car."

"I have a fleet of them and a hoard of drivers. I'm happy to send someone over to yours right now if—"

"No. I've taken too many liberties already."

"Liberties? If I need a car, I take one from my BFF's boyfriend—husband. That's taking liberties. Or it would be if we cared about that shit in our group."

"Bastian's just too… kind. But I'm giving it back. Today. Now."

At his place the past Sunday, Bastian escorted her to the car in the driveway and gave her a rundown of the controls. The seat hugged her whole body, the sleek dash almost glittered. In his kitchen, she'd worried about monopolizing his time. For some reason, monopolizing his car didn't worry her. Not to the same extent. She'd been too excited about taking something so powerful for a spin.

In a testament to not losing her senses altogether, she'd looked him in the eye and asked if he was sure. Bastian was a bachelor and probably prized the sports car as much as another man would value his child. He must've spent a lot of time saving for it, or he had a massive line of credit that would take three lifetimes to pay off.

"Consider it a trade for your phone number." Those were his words after her third request for confirmation. *"Those digits mean more to me than this hunk of metal."*

Sunday and Monday were gone. Tuesday had

rushed up on her. This was the night of his mother's dinner party.

"And how will you get home?" Roxie asked. "Are you spending the night with Bastian again?"

Roxie didn't do judgment, she'd never seen it, never heard it. And right then, Roxie was the only one beyond her and Bastian, who knew the full truth. Zairn didn't count with secrets, that's what Roxie said. He was a vault of silence… or maybe didn't care enough to listen, she'd forgive him for that. Being in it, her head rattled. Sometimes she couldn't keep up.

"We didn't talk about it." They'd have work tomorrow. "Depends how late it goes, I guess."

"Bastian will have a plan. Men like him always have a plan." Would be nice if he looped her in. "If you want to go home with him, go home with him."

"My parents are back tonight."

At some point.

"Which means…?"

More people to hear her lies. "Are you close to your parents?" she asked.

"I love them, but we don't talk every day. Z might, I don't know. It's hard to keep track of him."

Yet Roxie wasn't at all fazed or concerned.

"You're really lucky to have found each other."

"If you want us to come tonight, we'll come."

"No, you have more important things to do."

And it wasn't her place to invite extra guests to a dinner party. There were only so many chairs and so much food.

"But if you'd feel better with—"

"Bastian will be there. I'll be fine."

Pathetic as it was, she'd been excited to see him again since the moment they last parted. Somehow, God only knew how, but she'd resisted getting in touch with him. Her impulse control wasn't always the best and already she brimmed with things to tell him. Crazy, right? She'd forget them all the minute they saw each other. Her brain would evaporate all rational thought and she'd just gawk. More than likely, it wasn't her brain but Bastian's proximity that did the evaporating.

Ready in her shimmering golden dress, she dug heels out the bottom of her closet. Noise rose from beyond her room, people moving around, voices.

"Keep my number handy," Roxie said. "If you need to get out of there or someone to talk to…"

"Thank you, Roxie." Feet in shoes, she took one last look in her full-length mirror. "I better get going."

"Call if you need anything."

They hung up and she tucked her phone into her clutch, then the purse under her arm to make her departure.

Running down the stairs, her mother and father were just inside the front door with the rest of the household crowded around them. Their arrival couldn't delay her, she might hold up dinner being served. Wouldn't that be mortifying?

"You're back," Harper said, coming to a halt on the bottom stair. "How was your trip?"

"There's a new Porsche in the driveway," her father, Davis, said.

No hello or hug, just an abrupt question. Though it did sound more like a statement.

"We told him it was yours," Adara said. "He doesn't believe us."

"Maybe she stole it," Charissa said though no one responded.

The poor woman spent a lot of time talking to herself. Adara cared more for her friend than Damon did his girlfriend. She knew it; she'd been there. Damon could charm a woman and be attentive when it suited him. Soon as he had the commitment, he'd go cold in a heartbeat.

"Or it's payment for services," Damon grumbled.

Trust him to come out with a hackle-raising comment.

"It isn't mine," Harper said to her father. "A friend let me borrow it. I'll be returning it."

Maybe she was supposed to have returned it already. Bastian wasn't so clear on that.

"Which friend?" her father demanded.

"Her boyfriend," Adara said with a roll of her eyes. "We told you, Daddy."

Their family wasn't exactly warm and fuzzy, but this had to be a record. Her parents hadn't even taken their jackets off and already the whole gang were picking her life apart.

"Boyfriend?" Davis asked his eldest daughter then switched to his younger one: her. "Hunt… you were serious about that?"

The question wasn't really meant for her, even though she was standing right there. She knew how their father worked as well as Adara, which was why her sister was the one to address his incredulity.

"He was at our engagement party," Adara said. "He didn't stay long, but we told you he was there."

"You're in a relationship with Bastian Hunt?" Davis said, cutting through the melee of people around him to get to her at the bottom of the stairs.

Had she ever been singled out by her father? No. Hmm. She didn't like it. The weird look in his eye made her uneasy. It was almost like this information pushed her up in his estimations. Why? One guess was good as another.

She wasn't completely haggard and hadn't quite reached spinsterhood yet. In her opinion anyway. Had her father feared he'd be left with her in his house forever? Was Bastian that much of a reprieve? Great vote of confidence from the patriarch.

What was she missing? Why was every face… something?

"He's a friend," Harper said. Everyone was watching her. Adara's smile was the widest. Carnell looked happy too, though that could just be because he was next to the fiancée he adored. Both Damon and Charissa were frowning, and her mother looked like she was ready to cry. "It's not a big deal."

"Not a big deal," her father said. "I'm so proud of you."

When he pulled her down the last stair and into his arms, she almost blacked out. Her father wasn't a hugger. She couldn't remember him ever even touching her let alone hugging her. How did she…? She was an awkward hugger at the best of times. It might help if she knew the root of this happiness.

"Proud?" Damon said. "She said they were using each other for sex!"

"She was kidding," Adara said, hitting Damon's arm.

Had her father heard Damon? No idea. He pushed her away from his embrace and turned his back to consult with Damon.

"If he could push his business our way…"

"That's a lot of business, Davis," Damon said. "Could we handle it?"

"For that amount of money? I say we'd damn well find a way."

What was she watching unfold? The men were in some kind of zone.

"He might have internal—"

"No, it'll be contracted out," Davis said, "and what better way to ensure bidding success?"

"Than to pimp out your daughter?" Adara said.

"She's happy, Daddy, shouldn't that be our first priority?"

"Yes, yes," Davis said, reaching back to pat Harper while looking at Adara. "But a billionaire, Adara! A billionaire in the family... Luck's smiling on us after all!"

TWENTY-TWO

A BILLIONAIRE.

Harper played the word around and around in her mind, struggling to find any sense in it, any concept of meaning.

Given her family thought she was in a relationship with Bastian, she couldn't exactly question them. So she'd muttered something about being late and left the house in a stupor, barely able to focus.

Before she got to the Porsche, a long city car pulled into the driveway and a driver got out.

"Harper Scott?" he asked, straightening his hat.

She probably nodded, she couldn't really remember. He ushered her into the back of the car without resistance. What was with her getting into cars with strangers these days?

Bastian had sent the car. She trusted a man she didn't know. The chauffeur might be shocking, but she preferred it over Bastian showing up without an invitation. Especially on that night. Her family were apparently counting on her for… something. More fool them, she couldn't form words let alone foster business relationships on their behalf.

A billionaire.

Still it ran through her mind, nauseating her.

The suit. The watch. All those details from that very first night she'd dismissed. Damon's reaction to Bastian made it so obvious, her ex had been threatened. What was with her blinders?

Owning not one fancy car but two... And Carolyn! The sophistication of the Hunt matriarch... Harper's chin came up. That building they'd dropped Carolyn at was the family home, wasn't it? Shit. Apartment complex? What an idiot!

Opening her mouth, she sucked in a breath and blew it out slowly.

She'd never bothered to explore Bastian's home. The size of the kitchen and the bedrooms alone should've been a hint. Everything was expensive. His home was filled with luxury from the heavy furniture and the thick carpets to the pair of cars. She'd dismissed his comment about having a few on the premises as a joke. Another clue she'd blanked out. The truth had been staring her in the face and she'd missed it. How could she have missed it?

Come on! This was her! She missed things all the time. But this... this...

Fishing her phone from her bag, she did what she should've done when all this started: searched him on Huddle Hunt. The moment the results flashed on the screen, she regretted it.

Bastian wasn't just any billionaire, he was a well-known and successful billionaire with a lot of powerful friends.

His family was old money on Carolyn's side, explained the woman's refinement. Bastian started out on his own as a young teenager. Now he owned a chain of hotels and an exclusive airline company that only the very best would use. His wealth surpassed the rest of his family's combined worth.

Grand. She read the name of the hotel chain and her eyes closed. It was his damn hotel. The night she'd met him in the basement he'd been working out in his very own hotel—hence the sales spiel.

She thought he'd come to the engagement party of his own accord to save her! She'd been so grateful that he'd ventured into the unfamiliar to support her despite his own discomfort.

Now she felt like an idiot.

Was an idiot.

Honestly, she'd gone to the charity ball and been awed by its opulence and assumed everyone else felt the same. Now she learned that kind of pretentiousness was normal for the Hunts.

Not only an idiot, she was a fraud too. She hadn't belonged there and certainly shouldn't have worried about Bastian's comfort level. He could own any room he walked into and never be concerned how people might view him. When you were that rich, other people pandered to you no matter their private opinion.

The fog lifted as fight or flight kicked in. Flight. Definitely flight. As stupid luck would have it, at that same moment, the car came to a halt. Less than a second later, the door opened, and a suited man stood ready to help her from the vehicle.

No flying now.

This was the house they'd taken Carolyn to after her ER visit. The stairway and entrance were lit again, except this time the door at the top of the stairs was wide open ready to receive people.

"Receive people," since when had statements like that been part of her life?

Three stories, eight tall windows, four on each

side flanking the central reception column of windows that towered over the front stoop. Stoop? Yeah, that wasn't the right word. How far back did the house extend? She couldn't tell and almost didn't want to know. Huge was the word.

Boy, wrong wasn't a strong enough descriptor.

Bastian grew up there. In his family home.

Bile threatened the back of her throat again. Her face flamed. She couldn't relax. Why? She was an imposter. She didn't belong there.

The stranger who helped her out of the car also escorted her up the stairs. She couldn't run away while he had a hold of her. Even if she broke free, was she supposed to run to the road? She'd probably pass out dead on the journey.

Once inside the marble floored foyer, the curve of the sleek double staircase dominated the space. She might be a fish out of water, but she couldn't deny the beauty of the architecture.

And that wasn't the only beautiful thing present.

Bastian approached. "Hi."

The man from outside left her side.

"Hi," she managed, but tensed when he bowed close to kiss her temple.

"I'm sorry, I wanted to pick you up, but there was a disaster at work and—never mind. I'm sorry."

Shaking her head quickly, she clammed up completely when he tucked her hand into his elbow. One clumsy foot in front of the other somehow kept her going.

Her focus stayed low. Shifty, that's how she'd look, but she couldn't help it. If these people got one straight look, they'd tag her a phony. Trying to relax just made it worse, her body stayed rigid.

Still walking, Bastian gathered her closer in a sort of subconscious suggestion he sensed her discomfort.

All she saw of the hall they entered was the beautiful parquet floor beneath her feet. She couldn't bring herself to lift her chin. The buzz of noise surrounding them revealed that this wasn't like any dinner party she'd attended. There were more people there than in some restaurants. Thirty people? Forty?

"What's the matter?" Bastian asked, bringing her around, face to face, using his body to block her view of the room and everyone in it.

"Nothing," she said, meek even to her own ears.

Her tone didn't matter much when she still couldn't meet his gaze.

"Sweet, talk to me," he said, grazing his finger down her temple. "Has something happened? If you're not in the mood for this, we can get out of here and—"

"I didn't know," she murmured, forcing herself to look up.

His frown fell. The blank expression that took its place became something else, something like pity. Shit.

She counted to ten. No words passed between them.

As his mouth opened, a gong sounded and he closed it again.

"That's dinner," he said on another breath. "We'll talk after, okay?"

She nodded. It wasn't like she had much of a choice.

TWENTY-THREE

THE DINNER WAS exquisite, no other word for it.

Being seated opposite Bastian, she didn't have to talk to him throughout the meal. Which worked because she still hadn't processed. Each time she sipped her wine, her eye caught on his scowl. He wasn't happy, but she wasn't sure she was either.

The meal stretched on for hours. Felt that way anyway. Only after the coffee and brandies were handed out were they allowed to leave the table. People were directed into another room to enjoy their refreshments. After consuming a seven-course meal, she didn't have space for another mouthful, even a liquid one.

The food and service were provided by the professional elite. The crème-de-la-crème. If she hadn't discovered his secret before, she would like to think she'd have figured it out from that clue alone. Was she sure? No. It had been staring her in the face since the night they'd met, and she'd missed it. Putting any money on her comprehending the obvious would be a bad bet.

None of the guests made a move to leave the

house; the party was far from over. Guests were filtered back into the parquet-floored hall they'd started in. Harper left her wine on the table and went with the herd waiting their turns to stroll through the bottleneck.

"Come here."

She heard Bastian before she saw him. Her hand was snatched, and she was tugged away from the other dinner party guests. More than a few noted her and Bastian's escape to the opposite corner.

Through a door, up some stairs to a corridor, and into a room, much homelier than the dining room. It didn't quite fit with the impression of the rest of the house. The thick, purple rug on the floor was lush, but modern. An open fireplace dominated one wall. On another was a huge television with deep, wide couches aimed its way.

"What happened?" Bastian asked, snapping her focus from the decor.

"Nothing happened," she said, admiring the dark gray fabric across his shoulders when he turned his back. Except something had happened, hadn't it? "I'm an idiot. I suppose that happened. But it's nothing new."

"You're not an idiot," he said, taking off his jacket and tossing it to the back of one of the couches.

"I didn't see it," she said. "I suppose I saw what I wanted to see. Or rather didn't see what I didn't want to see."

"What are you talking about?"

He could be exasperated, he could be angry, but both of them had to face the truth.

"I know who you are." Now, she now knew, hadn't before. Idiot. "If you deny it, Huddle Hunt will call you a liar."

"Sweet—"

"No," she said, stepping out of his reach. The conflict in his expression tore between anger and contrition. Her own thoughts produced a question as they fell into line. "What the hell do you need me for, Bastian? Do you know who you are?"

"I know who I am. My identity doesn't take away all life's worries."

"You're not worried," she said. "Coming to my sister's engagement party was a game for you, nothing more. Why in the hell did you come to the hospital?"

"I was concerned."

Fingernails digging into her palms, she wanted to scream. "About what? One of your associates could've got an update. I'm sure you can pay the hospital for information like that over the phone."

Anger brought his scowl back full-force. "You learn this one piece of information and re-write my whole character around it?"

"I shouldn't have had to learn it from someone else. I thought we were in this, whatever this is, together."

"We are."

That was an insult. "You lied to me."

"I didn't lie."

"You weren't upfront."

"This whole thing was a con from day one."

"To everyone else, not to us." Least that was what she'd believed. "I didn't know you were conning me the whole time. I've been nothing except honest, but you… What is it? Charity? Is that what I am to you?"

"No."

"You didn't need me," she said. "A man like you doesn't—you don't need charity."

"You're not charity. I haven't changed. This doesn't change anything."

He hadn't even asked what she learned or what was going on. He knew without explanation, proving he wasn't ignorant to the issue, or how she'd react to it.

Adrenaline fizzed in her veins, but at least her

breathing was evening out a little.

Still, it was like her whole existence was in shock.

"This started at Adara's engagement party," she whispered, taking herself back to the beginning.

"It started outside the gym."

Everything he said churned up confusion again.

"At the hotel? Your hotel. Why didn't you tell me it was your hotel?"

"What does that matter? Building ownership was, is, completely irrelevant."

It had to be deliberate, causing this frustrated infuriation, he had to be doing it on purpose.

"Not to me," she said, moving closer. "And that doesn't answer the question. Why didn't you tell me?"

"When?" he asked. "When was I supposed to tell you?"

Talk about a copout.

"Don't give me that, like you had no time to bring it up. We've danced alone; we've spent the night in the same bed. We've talked. All we ever do is talk when we're together. Why didn't you tell me?"

He didn't have to shout to convey his aggravation. "I didn't want this," he said, gesturing between them. "Every single time a woman I care about… if I think they…" He took a deep breath and turned his eyes to the ceiling. "Men, women, employees, friends, society, whatever." He did his half-shrug. "When people know, they… it changes things. I cease to be whoever they thought I was, and I become… a lie."

The depth of his sincerity elicited sympathy, but that didn't change anything.

"We were lying," she said, admitting that they'd both been at fault. "We were never who we said we were."

"We were to each other," he said. "We knew what was going on. There was no lie between us."

Though tension still crackled in the air, resignation settled over them.

"Bastian," she said and reached to take his hand.

He moved it before she could make contact. "Forget it," he said, straightening in a fashion she didn't recognize of him. He looked at his watch, grabbed his jacket, and started for the door. "It's not important. I'll have a car take you home."

She didn't want to leave. She wanted to forget the animosity and kick off her shoes. She wanted to dive onto one of those couches and pull Bastian down with her. Not this starched, detached Bastian, but her Bastian, the Bastian she knew.

When he opened the door and gestured for her to exit, she couldn't refuse. He led her back the way they'd come, through the dining room that was now being cleaned by various members of household staff. He didn't take her through the hall, thank goodness. It would be filled with people curious about the woman being unceremoniously ejected.

Bastian left the building with her, ran down the outer stairs and leaned in to talk to one of the valets who then disappeared.

Now what? They waited. The party was still going on. No doubt he'd rather be there than in the cool evening air with her. There was no need for him to stand there, chaperoning her, unless he wanted to be really sure she was gone. Ouch. This moment, together in silence, punctuated the end of their association. Another chapter closed. How come the chapters of her life always ended with awkward humiliation?

"I can get a taxi," she said.

"As you've discovered, I could have a chopper come pick you up and take you home if there was somewhere to land at your place," he said, draping his jacket over her shoulders before retrieving his phone from the inside pocket. "The driver is on salary anyway, it's only right he earns it."

The same car that drove her to this fate pulled up in front of them.

Bastian opened the door for her. "It was nice knowing you, Harper Scott."

The smile he aimed for didn't reach his eyes.

Lifting her hand to his face, she traced where his dimple should be. A dimple she'd never see again.

"Bastian," she whispered but couldn't say anything else.

There was nothing to say.

This was it. Over.

TWENTY-FOUR

"OVER?"

His mom had said the word five times. Every time it twisted a knife in his gut.

"Yes, Mom," Bastian said.

Without speaking to another soul, he'd suffered through another half hour of the party. Now at his limit, he was ready to leave. That meant saying goodnight to his mother.

And, of course, she'd asked to say goodnight to Harper too…

Nothing else to do but tell the truth.

Yes. It was over.

After confessing, his mother hustled him into a drawing room. Standing there alone together, witnessing her shock wasn't pleasant. Dealing with anyone else's emotions with finesse was a stretch too far. His had just been through the wringer.

Carolyn managed to close her mouth, eventually, but her eyes were still wide.

"Why? Harper was so good for you. What on earth happened?"

"It doesn't matter," he said. "Explaining the process doesn't change the outcome."

There was too much his mother didn't know. He wasn't ready to give the full story voice. He'd disappointed her enough tonight.

"She hurt you?" Carolyn said, trying to take his hand. Contact would only reignite his frustrations, so he backed off. "Did she share herself with another man?"

As if he didn't have enough going on in his head, he didn't need that picture too.

"What? No. Harper would never do that."

"Then what—"

"It doesn't matter what happened."

"It does matter," Carolyn said. "You're upset. You care for her. Whatever happened, you can fix it."

"No, I can't," he said.

"If you explain to her—"

"Explain what?" he snapped. "You don't know what went on between us."

Much as his mother didn't like him snapping, it didn't put her off interfering. Carolyn didn't have time to be offended when she was busy looking out for his best interests.

"She made you happy, sweetheart," Carolyn said. Sympathy made way for the solemn truth. "Love is not something you can buy. Happiness can't be found through mergers and acquisitions. You're good at business, you always were, you've got a good head for it. But every woman you've brought to us has been sub-par and you know it. That's why you get frustrated. Other successful men are happy with their models and trophy wives; you are not one of those men. You want a connection with your partner, you have to feel something more than a physical attraction. Something like what you felt for Harper."

That she was right only enhanced his dejection.

"I appreciate your insight. But she's gone so—"

"You let her go?"

"Sven's taking her home."

"You got your driver to take her home?" Carolyn asked. "Why didn't you take her?"

"One car ride wouldn't have made a difference. We can't talk ourselves into caring for each other more than we do."

"I don't think it's possible you could care for her more than you do," Carolyn said, sitting down and flattening her hands on her lap. "I think you're in love with her."

"Mom…" he said with caution. "Where do you get that from?"

Though he chastised, there was a good chance his mother was right. Something in him sat uneasy since he'd welcomed Harper into the house. The second he'd laid eyes on her, he'd known something was wrong. That unease still swirled within him.

"For a man so relentless in business, you are very easily defeated in love," Carolyn said. "Would you have been so successful in business if you adopted the same attitude? If you walked away when things got tough? Your perseverance is an asset in business, perhaps if you applied that—"

"I get it, Mom," he said already formulating how he might approach this unfamiliar situation.

He'd never wanted a woman in his life as much as he wanted Harper, in whatever capacity he could have her.

"You're thinking." Carolyn smiled. "You're going to do it, aren't you?"

"Go back to your party, Mom," he said, sitting on the chair next to hers. "I need a plan."

TWENTY-FIVE

"YOU DIDN'T CALL last night."

Raising her eyes from the work on her desk, the view of Roxie Kyst darkening her doorway was like a mirage.

"You never look real," Harper said as Roxie strode in, swinging her arms in time with the sway of her hips. "You're like a movie star."

"Plenty of that going around in this city." Roxie descended into the chair opposite. "Why are you still working this late?"

"Nothing better to do." She re-angled her laptop. "And it's not that late."

"It's after ten."

Was it? She didn't know the—ah, wait.

"You didn't go by my house, did you?"

"Me? No," Roxie dismissed her. "I sent Zairn over there."

"Oh my God." She sprang to her feet. "You didn't—you couldn't—he—"

"Relax." Roxie laughed. "I'm kidding. Think I'd

leave him alone with your ex? My man can get along with anyone, if he chooses to."

And Damon wasn't the kind of man anyone would choose to get along with.

"Have you spoken to Carolyn?"

Made sense that was how Roxie found her office.

"Long enough to know you and Bastian are over." Oh, good news traveled fast. "That's amazing. Being over with a guy you were never with."

"Yep, pretty special."

"So…" Roxie continued, "do you want to go home and change or will I have someone meet us?"

And she was lost. "Meet us for…?"

"I have clothes at the club." Roxie rose, arm outstretched, seeking her hand. "We can grab something there."

"Grab something at—the club? What club?"

"My club."

The broad pride on Roxie's face didn't invoke calm.

"Your—Crimson. You want me to go to Crimson?"

"It's what we do," Roxie said, her arm dropping. "Break up with the guy, wash him out of our systems."

Her lips barely moved when she asked, "How would I do that?"

"Any way you want to. Crimson is your playground. We drink. We dance. And if anyone catches your eye…"

"Oh, I don't want… anything."

"You'll be completely safe. I have security. Fantastic security. If you don't want a guy near you, no one will get close." Inspiration raised Roxie's chin. "We can have a girls-only night in the club!" She squinted. "Hmm, why isn't that a regular thing in Manhattan?" Her tongue slid across her lips. "Bet Casanova had a few nights like that in the penthouse. We really should remodel."

"Isn't the club already open?"

"In Manhattan?"

"LA."

"Right, LA. Yeah, but that doesn't matter. If I choose to herd every one out, they'll go. Fantastic security, remember?"

"That's Zairn's business—"

"And my eccentricities turn him on. We can kick him out too or keep him around to mix drinks. Gives us something pretty to look at. Z won't hit on you… unless you want him to. Do you want him to? He knows how to make a woman feel good."

"You're pimping out your husband?"

"He's a beautiful man with an incredible heart. Unfortunately, when it comes to performing for women who aren't wearing his ring, he lacks, but he'll still make you feel good, just without the cherry on top."

And that was the sweetest thing she'd probably ever heard.

"He loves you so much."

"He does. And the wedding cost a huge fortune, he needs to bulk up the coffers before we divorce."

It wasn't always easy to tell when Roxie was joking. That was a joke… wasn't it?

"Aren't newlyweds supposed to be…"

"Horny?" Not what she was going for, but okay. "That's one marital duty he takes very seriously." Blowing out a breath, Roxie fanned her face. "No other reason to marry a playboy. I get a workout every night. It's cheaper than the gym."

Sex every night. Hmm, she couldn't even remember the last time she'd had sex. The last time she'd slept with a man, on the other hand…

"I can't take you away from him."

"Nothing takes me away from him. We're together whether we're together or not. That's one of the best things about us, we find our way back to each other. Worrying about Z is my job. His happiness comes from mine. And I'm never happier than when I'm dancing and drinking in the club surrounded by family."

She wasn't family.

"Would Bastian be there?"

"Doubt it. I have no idea if he's ever been in Crimson… on days other than our wedding day."

Wedding day. Roxie's wedding day was… "You got married in the Grand."

"Yep."

"Bastian's hotel."

"We paid for it… I think. I don't see many bills or invoices these days… or for a lot of days. You know what? These billion-dollar guys have people for everything. Like everything. We even have a guy employed purely to switch the toilet roll before we run out. Billion-dollar guys know how to take care of people."

It was one of those billion-dollar guys who'd put her in a mood.

"I can believe that," she said.

"You have a problem with the money? Is that why it's over? Because I have a lot of experience to share and stories to tell."

"It's not the money. I guess I just feel stupid. It was right there in my face and I—we met in one of his hotels and I had no idea he was him. My goddamn ex knew it before… I'm the first to admit I'm not always the most perceptive. It's something I've had—it's a spectrum thing my parents don't like me to talk about."

Since she was young, she remembered being told to be more like Adara. Her sister didn't put that pressure on her. If anything, Adara did her a favor by giving her an example to follow. She mimicked her sister in social situations. Unfortunately, as they grew, they weren't always together. At those times, Harper didn't have an example on hand to follow.

Yes, her impulse control was never much attuned and she was often confused by practices others took for granted, but it was things like this that hurt her inside. She missed things. She didn't pick up on social cues and said things she didn't know she shouldn't. Sometimes it was easier just to be quiet or wrong than to assert herself.

Roxie came around the desk to take both her hands. "Don't ever apologize for who you are, Harper. Not to me, mine, or yours. And corny as it is, you're in a safe space with me. At Crimson. With my guy. You're part of our circle now."

"I can't do that to Bastian, he was your friend first."

"We can be friends with people who used to date," Roxie said. "Believe it or not, I'm a good mediator."

"Oh, God, I would never want anyone to feel—"

"Okay, that was kind of a lie. Z's a good mediator. He is also good at pointing me in a certain direction and telling me when to shoot. This is one of those situations. He keeps me sane… me and a whole helluva lot of other people. If it wasn't for his distracting hotness, I'd send him to these come to Jesus things."

Is that what she was doing?

"I should've known, shouldn't I? As soon as Carolyn brought you to lunch…"

"Why? I'm not a billionaire. I wasn't—forget that." Her friend cleared her throat. "The money means nothing to you." Roxie raised a gentle hand to her chin. "You're upset because you think you don't know him as well as you thought."

"I don't know him. And it doesn't matter. I just—why would he do that? Fake date me? A man like him, he doesn't…"

"A man like him is no different to any other man." The strength in Roxie's hand gave her head a little more height. "Your first mistake is thinking there's anything different about him. Though with your guy, according to the world, the only thing different about him is his amazing need to take care of people."

"Like me? Like charity?"

Roxie shook her head and smiled. "The things you told me about Bastian, about how you are together, I promise he doesn't see you as charity. If he did, he'd have re-directed you to a Breckenridge." Her frown showed she didn't follow. "Never mind. Bastian was how he was with you, did what he did, because you brought it out in him."

"A man like him doesn't need someone like me in his life."

"Really?" Roxie asked, her shoulders going back as she peered closer. "Doesn't it then follow that Zairn doesn't need someone like me in his life?" Oh, God, she'd insulted her. "I'm no different to you. Hell, I'm nowhere near as good as you. You run a business. All I did was read and send an invoice."

She didn't know Roxie's history. Maybe that deserved another trip to Huddle Hunt.

"Zairn fell in love with you."

"Because I gave him the chance to fall in love with me."

"Bastian isn't in love with me."

"Who cares if it's love, friendship, or a fling? If you're done with him, you're done with him. Life has to be allowed to unfold."

"It's too big."

"All we're doing tonight is putting on our pretty

dresses and dancing our troubles away. There's no rest of the world at Crimson."

"It's late. It's a weeknight, my family will ask questions."

"When we're done, you can come back home with Z and I. We have plenty of space. We'll have a sleepover."

"You have a house in California?"

"Well our house is… uh…"

Roxie wasn't the type to hesitate.

Suspicion prickled. "What is it?"

"The house isn't exactly ready. We're staying in a hotel…"

Right. Now she got it. "The Grand?"

"We can stay anywhere. It doesn't have to be the hotel. We have a bunch of friends here. Or, hey, we can fly to Vegas."

The thrill of that unexpected suggestion bubbled laughter from her gut. "Vegas? No notice? Just go?"

"Honey…" Roxie said, cocking a hip to land her hand on it. "There ain't nowhere in the world I can't go with no notice."

The beauty's bold attitude was infectious. Already her cells were awakening, enlivened by the boundless possibilities. Even living them vicariously was a thrill. Her potential may not be limitless, but Roxie held the universe in the palm of her hand. And she was offering to share it, for a while, at least.

"Zairn wouldn't worry?"

"Nah, we're pretty good at phone sex." Roxie linked their arms and started for the door. "We'll start in LA and see where the night takes us. We can always send someone over to your place for your passport."

Her passport? Yeah, Roxie was used to no constraints. Nothing could go wrong… could it?

TWENTY-SIX

ANOTHER SMILE, another handshake. She made it all the way to her product launch that weekend. In spite of Roxie or because of her? Minute to minute, it wasn't always clear, but at least she was still in LA. No passport required... yet.

Any event that went off without a hitch was a win. The launch wasn't big or flashy, but it was functions like this that paid her bills. With everything in full swing, she could relax. Not completely, but enough.

Attendees mulled around, networking before the launch presentation. Music played. Canapes were distributed. Every cog moved as planned.

The product was some kind of smart device. Everything was smart these days. So much so that the "smart" part was almost redundant. If it didn't plug in and sync with everything in a person's house, they didn't want it. God forbid anything ever went wrong with the electricity powering their lives.

The young geniuses who created these products wanted nightclubs and light shows to complement their launches. Flash and pizzaz were ubiquitous these days.

She didn't have to stay all night but probably would in case of hitches. And, who knew? Maybe she'd drum up more business for herself… if she was in the mood to schmooze. Which she wasn't.

Numb sickness still plagued her whenever Bastian came to mind, which was a lot. Though with Roxie taking her for dinner and drinks and dancing every night, all week, she at least didn't have time to dwell on it.

Her father hadn't taken the news of her breakup well. Adara offered sympathy, while Damon enjoyed her misfortune. Him, always him, being him. Honestly? She couldn't get far enough away. No big surprise. God love Roxie for providing the perfect excuse to avoid the family home, or any building that might contain Damon.

Her family didn't attend her functions. There was no need to. This was business. Her job. It didn't require an audience, her part didn't anyway. That would just complicate things and she'd never get a pat on the back, so what would be the point?

Every once in a while, like that night, she brought a date. Men liked the glitz of these situations. It was LA. Glamor was required. Typically, her dates would get bored with her working. More often than not, they left early or with someone, anyone, other than her.

Michael, that night's date, had disappeared a while ago. Maybe about twenty minutes ago. Might've been half an hour… ish. It was anyone's guess if he was still there or not. No, it wasn't exactly nice, but she was in no rush to locate him.

The presentation would start in around fifteen minutes. And where would she rather be…? Home alone? With Bastian? Lost in the mists of Crimson hedonism? The middle one. Always the middle one, and the one she'd never be again. Damnit. Why did he still occupy so much room in her head?

Hubbub near an internal doorway drew her attention. A distraction. Good. Given it was her job to maintain the integrity of the guest list, and defuse problems, she started over there to do her job. Any incident should be taken care of before it affected the client's guests.

The chatter got louder as she got nearer and camera flashes were going crazy. One of the security guards on the internal door side stepped and… Roxie and Zairn.

The red carpet, that had been all but abandoned moments ago, was now swarming with security and paparazzi. They must've brought that with them. She'd never get that many cameras by herself. Hmm, well, the client would be happy.

People rushed past her from inside and more security came from… somewhere. Everyone wanted a piece of this and if it was going to be—she hadn't invited Roxie, hadn't thought she'd be interested. Her friend knew it was happening but—

"Quite a show."

Brought around fast, she didn't expect…

"Bastian?"

"Got a minute?"

A minute? She loosely nodded and took his proffered hand to guide him into a short corridor parallel to the hall.

"What are you doing here?" she asked, touching his tie.

"Who's this?" Oh, so Michael hadn't gone home. There he was at the end of the corridor. Scowling. "Huh?"

"This is, uh…" She swallowed to moisten her throat, fingers curling around Bastian's tie. "This is Bastian Hunt."

Michael frowned. "Yeah, I know who he is."

"Then why did you ask?" Bastian said. "Who are you?"

"I'm her date," Michael said.

Bastian's eyebrow slid up. "Is that who you think you are?"

"You've been MIA most of the night," she said to Michael. "I figured our date was over."

"So you called him?" Michael asked. "Damon said you two were history."

"Not anymore," Bastian said, his arm strengthening around her waist.

In his petulance, Michael huffed and stormed off. She never had luck with any man who knew Damon before they knew her. Though, in this case, that was a good thing. She'd rather be free for Bastian. Oh, and Michael would take this news directly back to her ex, the storyteller. Saved her the trouble of filling anyone else in.

"You're dating other men?" Bastian asked, dimple on show as he angled her back to the wall.

Just like that, the numb sickness drained from her body. "Bastian," she exhaled.

Instinct coiled her arms around him until she was pressed close. After less than a second of hesitation, his embrace wrapped tight around her.

"Did you miss me?" he asked, stroking her hair.

Heart racing, skin clammy, excitement and adrenaline mixed with sorrow and anticipation. Being with him again was overwhelming. She had to look up to check this was real, it was really him.

"I didn't think I'd see you again. I thought… I thought we were over."

"So did I," he said, his dimple deepening. "For about thirty minutes."

She didn't get it. "What?"

"I'm good at what I do because I'm relentless.

You and I had an agreement. I need company, you need dates, you scratch mine and I'll scratch yours. Is there any reason for us to go back on that?"

Was it that simple? Maybe. No, it couldn't be that straightforward.

"But you're... my family will hound you. They knew who you were before I did..."

"Is the money the only obstacle?"

"It's not the money." Not exclusively. "For them, it's your influence, your reach—"

"I don't care about them, I'm asking you. Only you. Is money the single obstacle?"

"It's not the money."

"Give me a chance to show you I'm not as shallow as the money might suggest."

Shallow? Bastian? Maybe in Topsy-Turvy Land.

"You've worked hard for your money," she said. "I know you're not superficial."

His calm contrasted her internal mania. His open hands moved down her hair to her back.

"No pressure. If it's something you can't surmount I'll respect that and leave you alone. Break up with me any time."

She smiled. "Fake break up with you," she said, running her hands up and down his lapel then taking his tie in both hands. "It was never the money, Bastian. A man as incredible and successful as you... You don't need a fake relationship, you don't need me. Millions of women would line up to be with you. It's embarrassing that I'm so pitiful—"

"Only one I want in that line is you," he said. "Think of me like any other guy. Like the guy you've been with whenever we're together. Do you want to break up with him?" After a long breath, she shook her head. "Good."

Clinging tighter to his tie, she pulled just slightly,

and that was enough of a signal. He bowed to rest his mouth on hers. It lingered for a beat before pushing harder, demanding more. Oh, he could have it. All of it. Mmm… She sighed into him and stretched her arms, looping them around his neck.

The only other time they'd done this, they were completely surrounded by those at the ball. Right then, they had no audience. Bastian urged her flat against the wall. Parting her lips for his slick, hungry tongue, she groaned and locked her fingers in his hair, angling for a deeper connection.

His chest rumbled with a reverberation that went through them both.

Work was forgotten. It was him. All him. Life. Earth. Sanity. None of it existed without him.

A nearby clatter forced them apart. Not far, just enough for her to see the fog in Bastian's eyes. Another sound startled him into action. Getting in front of her, Bastian blocked her view.

"Do you have a comment for—"

"Get out of here!" Bastian demanded.

Two security guards ran into the corridor as she peeked around her shield. A man with a camera was wrestled away by their protectors. When they were gone, Bastian turned with an apology in his eyes.

"Our families won't need much convincing now," she said, threading her fingers between his. "Will they?"

"That'll be on the internet within the hour," he said with regret. "I'm sorry, Sweet. I can call my lawyer. He'll do what he can. These things have a way of getting out there anyway. Zairn and Roxie deal with situations like this every day. Sometimes fighting makes it a bigger story. If you want me to use our resources—"

"No." She shook her head. "Who hasn't had a picture of themselves making out with a billionaire plastered all over the internet?" Widening her smile, she wanted to reassure him. "So if you're my date, do you want to buy me a drink?"

His dimple brought him back to life. "I do."

He hooked her under his arm and led her out to the launch. This would be one corporate event she wouldn't soon forget.

TWENTY-SEVEN

"YOU MUST GIVE hundreds of speeches," Harper said into the phone the next Friday afternoon. "You're not really nervous about speaking at your parents' anniversary."

"No," Bastian admitted with humor. "Sharing my anxiety is just an excuse to talk to you."

Sitting in her office, she sank back in her seat, admiring the covered window.

"You've called at least twice a day all week. You should know by now, you don't need an excuse to speak to me."

"I like having your phone number," Bastian said. "I prove that by using it."

Talking to him was the highlight of her day, every day. "You've had my phone number for a while."

"Yeah, but I came too close to losing you."

An experience she didn't want to repeat any time soon. Just thinking about it returned the weight of sickness to her gut.

"So now you have to phone me twice a day from

work to prove I'm still here?"

"I didn't call twice from work yesterday," he said. "I phoned once from work and once from home."

Playing with him brought more than satisfaction. She couldn't explain why the delighted ease relaxed and comforted her in equal measure. Maybe it was almost losing each other or having their relationship scrutinized on the internet that brought them closer. Thankfully, the press were far more interested in why Roxie and Zairn had gone to such a low-level event.

Ah, how nice, her insignificance turned out to be a bonus. She didn't know how her friend coped with such attention.

Though she had dealt with some of it herself. Calls about new business had skyrocketed. Wasn't a bad thing, but she didn't have an assistant, she'd never needed one. Since the picture, she spent vast portions of her day making appointments and discussing packages. More than she spent actually planning anything.

In some ways, that part of her job was becoming easier. One new client asked about having an event at a Grand Hotel. The chain was notoriously difficult to reserve for functions, especially at short notice. To satisfy an adamant customer, she called the hotel to request they send her an email confirming they were unable to accommodate the event. To her surprise, the staff wouldn't do that and in fact did the opposite. She got that date and offered several others. Life was getting expensive.

Bastian swore he hadn't sent out any memos on her behalf. Grand staff were choosing to elevate her company all on their own. The picture of them kissing was out there for all to see. Everyone and their dog had seen it. Pandering, Bastian explained to her, was an unfortunate side effect of notoriety.

As great as it was to be in professional demand,

it didn't compare to the excitement brought on by Bastian's number flashing on her phone screen.

"There's something kinky about you phoning me when I'm in bed," she said, sitting up to doodle circles on her headed notepad.

"We should have phone sex tonight," he said. "You never know what element of our relationship will be tested."

"Phone sex!" She laughed. "It's okay for you, you live in an empty house. I don't."

"I'd tell you to come over to mine, but then I wouldn't be in an empty house." The grin in his voice transferred to her lips. She closed her eyes, imagining his dimple. "And the phone part would become redundant."

He loved to tease, and she could give it right back.

"You know for a big important businessman, you don't seem to do a lot of work."

His smile was still in his voice, though he seemed to be playing dumb. "I don't?"

"I've had to return four of your calls this week. Every time I phone, Tina puts me straight through," Harper said. "Do you just sit around all day waiting for women to call you?"

"Believe it or not, I'm not an easy guy to get on the phone."

She laughed. "Could've fooled me."

"You get special privileges," he said. "You're a rung above my mother on the calls ladder."

"Wow," Harper said, connecting her doodle circles. "That throws the phone sex thing into a completely different light."

His single burst of laughter fired through her heart, awakening her hormones.

"Not the phone sex," he asserted. "You're the only one Tina will pull me from a meeting for."

Whether they were dancing together or just talking on the phone, he flattered her. With words, with the look in his eye, with the way he admired her. His tone. His depth. His… everything.

"Is that why sometimes it takes you a minute to speak?"

"Don't knock it, it's more than my previous girlfriends got, believe me."

"Which maybe explains the 'previous' in that sentence." Pressing the point of her pen into her notebook, she winced when confessing, "My father wants you to come to dinner with us next week."

"For your birthday?"

"No," she said, returning to her doodling. "He's desperate to meet you and wants to take you to a restaurant. If we eat at home, you won't be suitably impressed."

"Why not?"

Upon learning she and Bastian were back together, her father almost whooped. Davis didn't bother to ask what happened, that was irrelevant to the picture he painted his clients. She'd never been his favorite anything and wasn't sure she liked the new status.

Still, he was her father, she couldn't refute that fact.

"I don't know," she said. "It's something my father's constructed in his mind, who knows where it came from."

"Are your family cat people? That could be a reason."

"No," she said, wishing for a view of his dimple. "Would that be a deal breaker?"

"Definitely," he said. "I could never have a cat loving girlfriend. No one would believe that."

Sometimes he could be such a goof. CEOs the world over might quake in their boots when he strode into their boardrooms, they weren't on the receiving end of his sense of humor. So much of him the world didn't see.

"Much better we should be in a serious, long-term relationship after having met for just a few seconds in a hotel corridor. People would totally buy that."

"Obviously," he said on a comic scoff. "Isn't that how most people get together?"

Pushing back in her chair, she could stay right there on the phone all day. Yes, she had piles of work to do, but she wasn't ready to give up his voice yet. She may never be, though she should be wary of his responsibilities.

"Do you have work to do?"

"That's the good thing about getting to the top," he said. "Everyone underneath takes care of business. I delegate and prioritize what's important."

Her?

The Grand empire was a massive operation with hundreds, possibly thousands, of employees spread across the world. The hotels and airline were just the tip of the iceberg, Bastian had interests in industries beyond her understanding.

"Honestly…" she said, "I struggle to imagine it."

"Imagine what?"

She could tell him anything, he'd told her that numerous times, that didn't mean she wanted another fight.

"You'll be offended."

"I won't. Trust me," he said. "You struggle to imagine what?"

She took a deep breath. "I struggle to imagine you in your big fancy office with your minions scurrying around trying foolishly to please you."

"I don't own a Dickensian company. I made the conscious decision when I started out that I wouldn't stand over them with a whip while the foreman stoked the fire."

She laughed again. "You know what I mean. All that stuff on the internet…"

"I apologized for that, and I'll keep apologizing, for as long as you need me to."

Bloggers and the business media loved to comment on his life. The kiss picture fueled another wave of commentary. For the most part, people were complimentary. From what she'd read, Bastian had a good reputation. He was generous with his people, which wasn't exactly a surprise, though he didn't always extend that kindness to competitors. To succeed, sometimes he had to be ruthless.

In truth, the sheer volume of what was written about him took her breath away.

"I don't want you to apologize." She wasn't ashamed to be seen with him, even as a hussy enraptured by his mouth. "We have nothing to be ashamed of, I just… I wonder why people should care, you're just a person."

"You say that now," he said. "But when you found out—"

"I was surprised. I felt foolish for not noticing the obvious when it was right in front of me. And you were right, I did construct a new image wholly unrelated to our time together. But… I knew almost straight away that I'd been an idiot."

"You did?"

Breathing in, she prepared herself. "At your mom's… after dinner when… when we argued upstairs… I didn't want to leave," she admitted. "I wanted to sink into one of those couches with you… that big TV, the fire… Maybe for a minute we might've forgotten everything else, our lives, our business, our families…" Silence. No response. Had they been cut off?

"Bastian, are you still there?"

"I have to tell you something," he said after a longer pause. "I want to tell you, but I don't want you to get upset. We've never argued over the phone before so if you hang up on me…"

Her heart raced, what had she missed this time? "I won't."

"I'm saying if you do, I'll come over there right now. No respectable distance. I'll be in the car in a minute."

"You won't have to come here."

"If we're not communicating, I will be at your door," he said. "Whatever happens with us, with this, whatever we are, we stay in touch, okay, Sweet?"

Maybe sometimes that ruthless edge trickled into his personal life too.

"Okay," she said, but wasn't going to let him forget that he'd piqued her curiosity. "What did you want to tell me?"

"The house, my house where you spent the night."

She stopped doodling as dread crept in. "What about it?"

"That isn't my bedroom." It sounded like he braced for… something. "You didn't sleep in a guest room."

"I don't understand what—"

"Technically, we've been sleeping in staff quarters. Though I don't have residential staff at the house anymore."

"Staff?"

At the top of a staircase that led from the kitchen, yeah, that wasn't the master suite. She hadn't been thinking, what a surprise. In her defense, the bedroom she'd used was huge. Except given the size of the kitchen, she probably should've figured out it was more than a regular two-bedroom house.

"Don't get upset," he said quickly. "Don't think I was trying to deceive you. After your accident, it was just easier. I didn't want to overwhelm you. You'd had a tough night and were reluctant to come to mine. I didn't want you to have an excuse to leave, and—"

"Bastian," she cut him off, he'd keep going until she forgave him. No need to open old wounds and fight about the same issue over again. "Next time, can I see your bedroom?"

Another silence. Why did he do that? Where was his head?

"Want to see it right now?" She laughed more with him than anyone else. "I can come over there, pick you up. I've got some very fast cars and—"

"Do you have a big TV?"

"In the foot of the bed," he said. "No open fire in the master bedroom, yet. If it'll get you in there, I'll build you one."

"With your own bare hands?" she teased.

"Sure, but that would take longer than writing a check," he said. "I'm not sure I can wait. I'd have to be trained and—"

"Bastian," she said. "You can show me tomorrow, after your parents' party."

"That a promise?"

"If we have time to watch a movie."

No better treat than relaxing with Bastian in comfort and forgetting the world for a while.

"We'll make time," he said. "That'll give me something to think about instead of my speech."

As previously established, he wasn't worried about talking at his parents' party.

"Glad I can help."

"Bring some things," he said.

She frowned at her doodle. "What things?"

"Whatever you need to make yourself comfortable overnight, for a few days, leave it at mine."

Her lips circled in understanding. Guy would be sick of her plundering his wardrobe. No chance of his shorts falling off if she wasn't wearing them in the first place.

"Okay."

"I'll pick you up tomorrow—no arguments. No one would believe we're together if I don't pick you up. I won't have your family, or mine, thinking I'd disrespect you like that."

No big deal that a date wanted to pick her up. Except that left her with one rather large, expensive problem.

"Okay," she said. "But I still have your car."

"What car?"

"What car?" It was just crazy he could forget something so extravagant. "The Porsche."

"Oh yeah…" he said like he really hadn't remembered. "Keep it."

She almost swallowed her tongue. "Keep it?" she said. "Why would I do that?"

"All part of my plan to make you beholden to me," he teased. "It's just a car, Sweet. I have more of them."

Though there was no way in hell she'd keep the car, it did make sense to take one vehicle to his parents' party rather than two.

"I'll keep it for now, but not permanently. I can drop it off to you."

"Good. That gives you a second excuse to come to my place. Bring it back to me on Sunday night. I'll take you to work on Monday."

This was getting out of hand. Every plan they made begat another plan.

"We're already spending tomorrow night

together, now you want to add Sunday too? Is two nights in a row believable?"

He sighed. "Sweet, you should be staying at my place full-time by now."

That suggestion was almost offensive. "I'm not your other girlfriends," she said, hackles rising. "I'm not interested in your money."

"That's not what I meant, Sweet, but I'll give you time to figure it out. Pack a bag, we'll leave it in the car during the party… unless you want to sleep naked at mine."

"You wouldn't give me a tee-shirt?"

"Nope."

"Such a gentleman," she said to his tease. "Okay, I'll throw some things in a bag. If I have clean clothes, I'll be able to shower at yours."

"Bring your scented stuff."

Odd request, but a kind of flattering one too. "A man who wants me for my body lotion, how romantic."

"Do you want to get dinner?"

"Tonight?" she asked, flabbergasted by the whiplash. "Now?"

"Yes."

With the amount of time they'd spent on the phone, she'd probably be in the office until midnight making up the lost time. That aside, they would be distracting each other all weekend.

"We've just discussed spending Saturday night at your parents and Sunday night together. Next week we'll be eating with my family."

Bastian didn't miss a beat but missed her point entirely. "What do you want to do for your birthday?" he asked. "What's your wildest dream? You've got a boyfriend who can make it happen."

Reining him in when he was on a role was impossible, so she just went with it.

"I'm not sure I should tell you," she whispered, restraining her humor. "This isn't a secure line."

"Now I'm interested."

A knock on her door interrupted them. Her next appointment.

"I have to go, Knight. I have a client."

"Okay," he murmured. "I won't let this one go."

"Color me surprised," she said. "We'll talk later."

The minute she signed off and hung up, she wanted to pick up the phone and start over.

Smart and funny, Bastian understood her crazy talk and gave it straight back. They were on for a busy week. They'd pull it off. He was the best fake boyfriend anyone could ever have.

TWENTY-EIGHT

THE FRONT DOORBELL sounded, Bastian had arrived. Her burnt orange dress was tight and stopped just above her knee. Moving fast wasn't really an option. Though neither was loitering when her family were in the mix.

The front door was already open when she got to the stairs.

Darnit.

As she descended, her father shook Bastian's hand, trying to draw him inside. Talk about calamity waiting to happen.

Only one person could save Bastian from that fate: her.

Running down the remaining stairs, she dashed across the lobby, passing Damon as he materialized from the dining room. Squeezing between her father and the door, she flattened herself against Bastian, urging him back onto the outer stair.

"We've got to go, Knight," she said. "We're late."

Bastian followed her lead and didn't resist. "Nice

to finally meet you," he called to her father, taking Harper's hand to lead her to the car. "Are we in a hurry?"

"Just get in."

He laughed and helped her into the car. She didn't think it was so funny but didn't care so long as they were heading away from her parents' house.

On that trip, though the car was exactly the same size, it didn't feel oppressive. Rather than anxiety, it was excitement that joined her. Maybe it was being alone. Just the two of them. Without his mother. She hadn't been this eager with him before. Her stomach did flippy-flops around him, sure, but—that kiss. Why was she thinking about his mouth? Hers? Unity and—oh, she'd drive herself mad.

They knew each other now. Better anyway. Every word they shared brought them closer together. He captivated her. There was no other word. The ease of his smile, that dimple, the glow in his eyes when they briefly met hers.

When they arrived at the Hunt house, Bastian handed his car off to a valet as another helped her out. A breath later, Bastian hooked her hand into his elbow. Like clockwork.

There would be people. Lots of people. Far more than dinner party night. The number of strangers at the charity ball unsettled her with their volume, but there, in that place, these guests meant something to the family, to Bastian, they weren't strangers.

"Oh, there are people here, lots of your friends," she muttered as they ascended the stairs. "Do your parents know everyone in California?"

"Probably."

A nod here, a smile there, Bastian kept them moving into the house. If they stopped, she guessed they'd get no further for the rest of the night. It wasn't just that the people existed, it was who they were that made them different.

"These people mean something to you. Last time we were at an event like this, I embarrassed you."

"How did you do that?"

Had he really forgotten? "I kissed you."

"I remember the kiss. I don't remember being embarrassed."

"Don't encourage me."

"To kiss me?" he asked. "Tell me the trick and I'll do it every day. Every hour."

On glancing up, she caught his eye. That smile. Oh, he delighted her. This man was beyond a catch. Whoever landed him would lead a happy life. So, so happy.

"I promise not to assault you. I'll sit quietly, smile, I won't talk to anyone."

"That's a shame," he said as they crossed the buzzing, bustling hall.

"A shame?"

A group moved aside as they approached the bar she hadn't noticed before. Was it...? No, there were sliding doors that opened to reveal the bar. It hadn't been there the last time. She didn't think but—

As others made way for Bastian's determined step, a woman at the bar turned and...

"Roxie," she said, practically ignoring the men with them to accept Roxie's embrace. "What are you doing here?"

That was a stupid question. Roxie and her husband must've known the Hunt family longer than her.

"Never say no to a good party," Roxie said, perched on her stool, leaning back against Zairn. "And it's always a good party if I'm around."

Whether the three had known each other longer or not, the way Bastian brought her in and came immediately to the bar suggested this may have been orchestrated. He'd guided her to friends. That was pretty much confirmed when Roxie pushed a glass down the bar to her.

One quick sip and, "Gin and It."

"That's it, baby," Roxie said. "You'll need a lot of fuel to get through tonight."

Uh oh. With their friends present, she thought they'd bypassed the need for social anxiety. Couldn't she just stay there, at the bar, and let others pass her by. Her? Maybe. Roxie? Not so much. Her friend was a butterfly in these situations.

"Why will I need fuel?"

Without leaving the stool, Roxie took her arm, angling her to face the room.

"There are a lot of people out there you should get to know." Her friend's lips came closer to her ear. "A lot of prospective customers. Super rich prospective customers."

"She's lying," Zairn said. His words tipped her head back, but he was scanning the same space. "Roxanna wants the people out there to share Bastian stories."

"Embarrassing ones, ideally." No contrition from Ms. Kyst. "And they can be both, Casanova, sources for stories and prospective customers, though that reminds me." The beauty whipped her around fast. "How come none of your parties are at Crimson, Harper, honey?"

"My clients can't afford Crimson. And it's got to be something special to even be considered."

Crimson, LA. Crimson, anywhere, was an exclusive get. Yeah, she knew the owners now, but she wouldn't exploit that friendship.

As always, Roxie remained enthusiastic. "You can plan our next big event."

"Be careful," Zairn added. "The last person Lola

asked to plan an event for us ended up getting married at that event."

Now that had to be a joke.

"No chance of me getting married. Anywhere. Probably ever."

"You don't believe in marriage?"

"I don't believe in relationships working out, no offense. For me, I should add. I don't believe in relationships working out for me."

As did her family and maybe every person she'd ever known.

"I don't believe in that," Roxie said. "In fact, I guarantee I can find you the man of your dreams in this very room."

"Good plan, Lola. Set her up on a date while her date for the night is standing beside us."

"He's a faker, Casanova." Roxie waved over her head as though Zairn was an irritating bug. "Not the real deal."

Zairn caught his wife's hand and pressed his lips to her palm. "You know better than that, Lo," he said, trailing his fingertips down Roxie's arm. Her friend flinched and she guessed it wasn't the cold. "Who do you think you'd set her up with?"

"Rourke is in the room."

"He's married. And what woman in her right mind would choose that?"

"Good point. Roux had to be the right kind of nutty… and maybe a little high. Never really got to the bottom of that one. Maybe he's blackmailing her… Hmm…" Roxie reflected for a second then snapped out of it. "Kintyre's the most stand-up guy you know, Scroogey, but he's married too. Wow, your single friends are dropping like flies. Soon there'll be no way to get my friends laid."

"There are Breckenridges," Zairn offered.

"Right, Tripp, of course, sex on tap. He can work them on a conveyor belt."

"Sexy," Zairn murmured, kissing the inside of Roxie's wrist. "And I've often wondered what you two talk about."

"Innovation, Lover Man. Innovation. That boy models himself on you in your heyday, Casanova. The legend that no longer exists."

"A previous lifetime."

"Yes, just a teeny, tiny blip in your rearview that marriage will never allow you to experience again. You're stuck now. For good. One pussy, no waiting."

"I spend half my life waiting for you, Lo."

"You're lucky to get it at all, Husband. Honestly, one of us will end up permanently damaged if we don't stop all this newlywed sex stuff." With her lower lip just a little out, Roxie pouted toward her husband. "What kind of mileage we get out of this newlywed stuff anyway?"

"You mean how long can we completely neglect our grown-up duties before we start hearing hostile takeover?" Zairn asked and half shrugged. "I don't know. I'm getting laid, what do I care?"

Roxie scoffed. "Like that's ever been a problem for my big, handsome billionaire. I'd be more worried about how long Ogilvie can be without you before we have to institutionalize him."

"You'd institutionalize him in a heartbeat."

"Yeah, I'm already in negotiations with the therapist Tripp's screwing. She'll handle the paperwork to have Ogilvie committed providing Tripp keeps her coming… if you know what I mean."

In that drawled deep voice, Roxie could almost be channeling Elvis. She was some woman.

"Lola says the therapist thing for effect," Zairn told them, for the first time breaking the volley with his wife… kind of. "But don't bet on it being untrue."

"Tripp sleeping with a therapist?" Roxie asked. "Why do you think he's so well balanced?"

"He's a Breckenridge," Zairn said like it was obvious.

"Yeah, but come on, Tripp talking to a woman, other than me, who'd believe that?" Roxie's lips went to the side for a second. "Where is your protégé anyway? On the hunt?"

"If he's a real pro, he'll be onto his third or fourth course by now."

"Ah, romance, Casanova, so smooth." Roxie fake swooned, gathering her hands by her cleavage. "Lickety-split in the ladies' room then on to the next one."

"Sharing your proclivities there, Lo?"

"We could be in a cesspool, and you'd still expect to get yours. Never heard you say no."

"Never will, Lola Bunny. Never will."

Without looking, Roxie tapped Zairn's hand that now rested flat on the bar. "But you're missing the point."

"Baby, I'd be amazed if you had one."

"Love," Roxie said. "Comes after we get the sex part right. We have to get that part right for Harper first."

"There is more than one Breckenridge present," Zairn said.

"Yes! Breckenridges!" Roxie straightened fast and reached up behind her, catching the back of Zairn's neck. "Grown up ones? Not the babies. Caber's not here."

"Axon is."

"He's too serious. We need someone fun. Caspian's here."

"Not a Breckenridge, and Caspian's your go to for fun?" Zairn asked, almost deadpan though his fingertips went further south, tickling their way to Roxie's waist. "Hell if I know when you saw Caspian's fun side. Does Caspian have a fun side?"

"Never seen it either," Bastian said. "You can introduce Harper to anyone you want, but the only guy she's getting set up with is me."

And when he opened his hand to her, she took it. "Caspian's one of your good friends?"

"He is. Breck's somewhere around with Sequoia too. You should meet her."

"Sequoia is amazing," Roxie said, exaggerating the last word. "But Breck's too serious too." Her friend frowned at the man curving an arm around her. "How come all your friends are boring and serious, Mr. Hunt?"

"Comes from prioritizing success," Bastian said, the warmth of the words proved he wasn't offended. "We build up our businesses—"

"At the cost of your personal lives. I've heard it, you break your mother's heart," Roxie said. "Maybe we need a man makeover too."

"You can't get more gorgeous than Bastian."

"Not in looks, honey, he has that in spades. Just a few tweaks, here and there. Change his priorities. Wash out some of that starch, loosen him up."

Except the Bastian she knew was loose. He smiled. He laughed. There weren't words for how much she adored him.

Maybe Caspian and Breck weren't as rigid and boring as Roxie thought. It was all in the eye of the beholder, right?

She wouldn't mind meeting Bastian's friends though, the men he'd chosen to be close to, they meant something.

Roxie picked up Harper's drink to hand it over before raising her own.

"Girl, we have a room to work."

The beauty tapped a manicured fingernail on her

cheek. Zairn bowed to dutifully kiss the spot. Then Roxie kicked out a leg to hop off her stool.

A room to work. Oh, boy. This wasn't a professional event where everything was under her control. She couldn't distract and busy herself with tasks, even ones she'd made up. Still, Roxie wouldn't abandon her and meeting Bastian's friends…? She was too curious not to take advantage of the opportunity.

TWENTY-NINE

"CALL ME IN the morning," Roxie said, hugging her again. "As soon as you're awake."

Zairn eased his wife from the embrace. "Leave the woman alone or she'll press charges."

"She would not in—" Roxie faltered, loosening a little. "We're still in LA, right?"

"Still in LA," Zairn confirmed, offering a warm smile. "You're welcome at the club any time, Harper."

"Next time we'll bring rubies," Roxie said like that meant something and dropped her head against her guy. "We still have a shift at the club tonight, Casanova?"

"Yes, Lola. We do."

Roxie exhaled a kind of mutter. "Okay, well, sex in the car it is." Snagging her hand, Roxie gave her another squeeze. "You want us to take you to Bastian?"

"No, he's with people at the bar. I'll be fine." For the ten or fifteen seconds it would take her to walk over there. "You have a good night. And thank you."

Another squeeze, another smile, and the couple disappeared from the room. She was done for the day. Zonked. Exhausted and ready for bed. Roxie and Zairn were on their way to another party. Unimaginable. They were true champions of their lives.

As they'd gone around the room meeting this person and that, Roxie exuded an interesting mix of professional and personal. Her new friend knew most of the people, not that familiarity mattered, somehow Roxie walked away pals with everyone.

Maybe it was easier being in a room of friends. She didn't imagine Carolyn would invite enemies to celebrate with her. Though this was LA, truths were often hidden behind façades, which made her work a whole lot harder.

The number of revelers had thinned, though not by so much that there was a clear route to Bastian. Last she'd seen him was by the bar with a group. That wasn't as intimidating as it might've been at the start of the party.

Throughout the night, she'd kept one eye on him, as he did on her. They'd danced, and not just together, she'd danced with more men that night than she'd probably met in her life. Bastian had some attractive and curious friends. As each song ended, Roxie was there to whisk her off to meet someone else, or to provide another dance partner.

The Hunt family were well loved. They deserved to be. People in that room cared about each other, the ones she met anyway. There was safety, a security that surrounded them all. Could be a money thing. Could people really have serious worries when their financial futures were guaranteed?

There she went jumping to conclusions. Again.

Of course, no one else's attention was as absolute as Bastian's. Even when they weren't together, he was always right there, just on the periphery, ready to step in. It was a thrill when he did, when his arm held her to him or their fingers interlaced. Having him near was so flattering that she had to remind herself not to get too used to it, he wouldn't always be there.

And don't think the saving was only for her. It wasn't. More than once, he'd used her as an excuse to leave a conversation, whether to dance or get another drink. Sometimes he needed the reprieve and she was happy to give it. Wasn't that her whole reason for being there? Singletons sticking together? Saving each other.

Before his congratulatory speech, he kissed the end of her nose and went to do his sonly duty. Smiling through his address, she loved not only the sound of his voice, but the response of the crowd. Some of the guests would be pandering no doubt, but there was a real affection in the air.

After his speech, Bastian descended the dais to be swallowed by the horde. She hadn't seen him for a while after that. She and Roxie talked with another half dozen people before he emerged from the fracas of adorers doing their best to waylay him.

The second he spotted her, he came to her, everyone else seemed to become irrelevant. And she knew the feeling. With him at the end of the bar, back almost to her, Bastian didn't notice her approach.

"It's ten days, not two weeks," Carolyn was saying to her son.

"Mom, if you're trying to manipulate—"

"I'm not trying to manipulate anything. I'm offended by your accusation."

Wrapping an arm around him, Harper smiled at his quick surprise that accepted her in a heartbeat. "Am I interrupting?"

His strong hand pressed her lower back. "You're never interrupting, Sweet."

Pushing up a little, she kissed his jaw. "I'm not sure those you talk to would feel the same."

"We do," Carolyn said. "You look wonderful

together." Was that a hint toward their mended breakup? "Have you enjoyed yourself tonight, Harper?"

"Bastian's proud of his family and his friends. You're lucky to have each other."

"Sometimes," he said, stroking her hair from her face. "Mom is thrilled you're here."

She'd just assumed that the family knew they were back together and that they'd be over any excitement about the couple reconnecting.

"I would have thought that after the picture—"

"Pictures don't always tell the full story."

Harper couldn't deny that. Half of what had been written about them on the internet was nonsense.

"No, I suppose they don't," she said, flattening her hand on his tie, sliding it down and curling her fingers around the smooth fabric.

"Are you okay?" he asked. "Tired?"

"A little."

Concern erased his dimple. "We can go if you want to—"

"No, the party is still going—"

"I was the headliner," he said. "Now I'm done, nothing else will measure up."

"I could do with taking my shoes off though." She raised one foot, then the other. "They're new."

"You should never be uncomfortable in this house," Carolyn said. "There are dozens, maybe hundreds of shoes in this house."

"There are hundreds in one section of Keely's closet," Bastian said, backing her up to perch her on a stool. "She wouldn't even know they were gone. Take your shoes off."

She toed off one and then the other. "I won't raid your sister's closet."

"Then home it is."

"No." She tucked her head against his chest. "We

should stay."

"Whatever you want, Sweet."

The rhythm of his hand moving from her hair, down her body loosened every muscle. On a yawn, her eyes closed. Forget the shoes, this was by far the most comfortable she had ever been, and she already regretted the minute they'd have to part.

Staying like that, curled against him, wouldn't last, but for just a minute, she wanted to live in the illusion.

"Bastian…"

His name passed her lips in a whisper of its own volition.

"You are tired, Sweet."

Somehow, he knew that. Was it the sound of her voice? Her breathing? The way her body begged his to keep it upright?

May not be tiredness, not entirely. Being near to him intoxicated her mind, her heart, every cell of her being.

"If we stand here much longer," she murmured. "I'll fall asleep."

As a joke, it was meant to be a joke. Though she'd be the first to admit she hadn't sold it.

Bastian stroked her hair. "Time for us to say goodnight."

"And you can rest right here," Carolyn announced. "You don't need to go traipsing out into the night. Bastian's bedroom is upstairs, get comfortable there. No one else shares that hallway, you'll be alone."

That piqued her trepidation.

"We're staying here?" Harper asked before she'd fully processed Carolyn's wily smile.

Carolyn had a way of conning her and Bastian into intimate situations. In her sleepy haze, had she walked into another of those setups?

"Do you want to stay here?" Bastian asked. "I can just as easily get the car—"

"Nonsense," Carolyn said as Thomas joined them. "You pair go up to bed. We'll see you at breakfast."

"Mother," Bastian warned.

Harper's feet slid from the stool's crossbar. She was too tired to fight the matriarch. Carolyn was a strong woman who didn't give up easily. And if there was no one else in that hallway, Bastian wouldn't have to share space with her.

"Someone give me directions," she mumbled.

"Son," Thomas said, "be a gentleman."

Harper yawned, not expecting to be suddenly plucked from the stool into Bastian's arms.

"Oh my God, you don't have to…"

He didn't flinch as he carried her across the room. Other guests were interested, she couldn't blame them. No one could've predicted that spectacle. Including her. Socialites cleared a path but watched as long as they could. Resting her head against him, sure that she was safe in his control, she relaxed.

If people wanted to watch, they could watch, she wasn't about to cause a scene. More of a scene. Sometimes the unexpected wasn't so bad.

After he maneuvered them through a couple of doors and up a set of stairs, Bastian opened a final door. A breath later he bowed, laying her down on a deep duvet that smelled of Bastian and sunshine.

He returned to the open door and a distant murmur of conversation. Had someone followed them upstairs? Had that person brought her shoes?

She sat up in sync with Bastian closing the door.

"Close your eyes," he said. "You can sleep now. There's no one around."

Another yawn. Man, where were they coming from?

"I should get changed," she said, stroking the delicate blood-red cotton that adorned the four-poster bed. "Where's your car key?"

"Someone will bring your things up."

No, she wasn't used to this lifestyle, though it made sense someone could be sent to fetch her things, otherwise what was the point of Bastian carrying her up the stairs?

She hadn't seen another bag in the trunk. "What about you?"

"This is my room," he said, opening the closest drawer to show his clothes in it.

"Oh," she said, lying down while reaching under her arm to unzip her dress. "We're supposed to have sex, aren't we?"

"If you insist."

A grin spread on her face before she laughed. "I meant that's what people will think we're doing."

He smiled and opened a door on the far wall. A spark of light revealed a bathroom. Bastian went in, leaving the door open a crack.

"My shoes are downstairs," she called, listening to the water in the bathroom as she wriggled out of her dress and tossed it aside.

Ideally, she wanted to lose her thong too. That wouldn't be polite, given that, by the looks of things, she and Bastian would be sharing a bed.

The water went off.

"They'll be fine," he said. "I can have someone bring them up if you're worried."

"No. I just thought I should say in case someone asks."

"Who would ask?" he asked with that smile in his voice again.

She didn't know the practices of a house like this, or what was acceptable of its guests. Presumably when the party was over and everyone was gone, staff would clean up. They'd find a random pair of shoes… and hopefully not get rid of them. Maybe they'd end up in Keely's closet. If she was going to be leaving her shoes lying around the place, she should start writing her name in them. The last thing she'd want to do was accidentally pilfer a billion-dollar pair belonging to someone else.

"Whoever."

A knock drew her attention to the hallway door.

"Yeah," Bastian shouted from the bathroom.

Her silent inhale was almost a gasp; she had just enough time to clamp her hands under her arms to cover her naked breasts before the door opened. At the same time, Bastian stepped out of the bathroom.

The uniformed man in the doorway lost his stoicism to a flash of surprise.

Bastian's double-take was fast. "Out," he shouted at the steward.

Drawing her lips into her mouth, the horror on the steward's face almost warranted a laugh. The employee didn't have to be told twice, he dropped her bag and literally fell out of the room.

When the door closed again, she looked to Bastian. "Oops."

"What the hell do you think you're doing?"

Her humor faded under the heat of his anger. "I'm sorry, I didn't—I wasn't… I'm sorry I wanted to—"

"What?" he demanded, marching to the side of the bed. "Don't cheapen what's going on here! He'll tell every man on the staff exactly what he saw. Those men want you. They've thought about you—"

"Bastian," she said, kneeling up in front of him. "I'm sorry."

He closed his eyes and turned his back, bringing his hand up to his forehead.

"Cover yourself up," he commanded and marched back into the bathroom.

THIRTY

TEARS NIPPED HER EYES. Sealing her mouth, she feared opening it would dislodge the sob locked in her throat.

Upsetting him wasn't the point, she didn't want to upset anyone. It was late, her mind was foggy and she just wanted to rest. Sleep. Bed. That was it, all she'd wanted. And she couldn't dial it back enough to do the right thing. The smart, sensible, polite thing.

That look on his face. Oh, she couldn't get it out of her head even with her eyes squeezed shut. The glower as he blatantly refused her. She wasn't offering, it wasn't...

She was getting comfortable, expecting her nightdress would turn up with her bag. It wasn't like she wanted to seduce him or anything. Though if she had, his rejection couldn't have been more clear. It hadn't been her intention, but knowing how he felt about her body...

Surely Bastian must have seen thousands of breasts in his time. Why were hers so offensive? Did he think she was throwing herself at him? Being inappropriate? Expecting something? The sex thing was a joke, he got that… Did he get that?

It didn't matter.

Leaving the bed to go get her bag abandoned by the steward, she crouched to unzip it and retrieved a sweater and a pair of jeans. Sweater first, she scooped her hair out of the neck, swiping at the tears on her cheeks.

She couldn't stay. Knowing his true opinion, being faced with it—he'd be embarrassed, by what he'd seen, what she'd shown. Even his carrying her upstairs took on a different tone. It wasn't romantic, it was necessary. Almost falling asleep on him at the bar was ridiculous. Why did she keep forgetting this was fake? Why did she keep embarrassing him?

It didn't matter.

Nothing mattered.

All she could see was the ferocity of his disgust. That was a memory she'd never erase.

Zipping her bag, she wiped her nose with the sleeve of her sweater. Hold on. Hold back the emotion, Harper. Getting upset would only compound the humiliation. She fought to contain the grief. She had to. Just a little longer. Just until she could get out of there.

Goddamn her. They'd been getting along so well. The night had been a dream. Friends, laughter, a night she'd hoped to remember with happiness. Until she ruined it. What a surprise. It was always her. People often said they were their own worst enemy. And there was her, proving the adage true every day.

Angering and repulsing him weren't the goal of her stupid, selfish act. Why couldn't she be more aware? Everyone else managed it. What the hell was wrong with her?

Throwing the bag backward onto the bed, she

stood up, jeans in hand, and took a minute to unwind the legs before stepping into them. Once they were up, she fumbled with the zipper, struggling to see through her blurred vision.

"What are you doing?"

Instinct tempted her to turn in the direction of his voice, but she couldn't. If she looked at him, the last thread of her composure would snap. Besides, her face would be a mess too, he didn't need to see that. Please. Hang on to the last frayed shred of dignity.

"I'll hail a cab from the street," she said, hoping the vibration wasn't as audible as it felt.

"Like hell you will," he said. "If you want to leave, we'll leave. But I'll fire the guy if—"

"It wasn't his fault," she said, still unable to turn around.

Idiot. Again. Why had she thrown the bag to the bed? Another example of her stupidity. Think things through. Think then act. It didn't matter how many times she told herself that…

The exit was right there in front of her, just a few feet away, if she had her bag, she could leave this minute.

"You don't have to leave," he said. "I don't want you to leave."

Like a gentleman, raised to display every courtesy, could say any different. His tone was softer, but she couldn't take his pity.

"I need to go," she said, fighting to clear her throat and strengthen her timbre. "It's not your fault, it was me. I'm sorry, I didn't think about—" He touched her shoulder and her whole body clenched. After a silent breath, she tried to step away, but his fingertips curved around the ball of her shoulder, holding her there. "Please let me go, Bastian."

"I hurt you." When his chest met her shoulder blades, she wanted to lean, she so desperately wanted to draw strength from him, but she couldn't. "I didn't mean to shout. I'm sorry."

"You have nothing to apologize for," she said, attempting a smile, hoping it would carry to her words. What a futile hope, she wasn't fooling anyone. "You can't help your honest reaction. Could you pass me my bag, please?"

That request was a full-page ad announcing her humiliation. Now she did want him to take pity on her. It was plain as day, she couldn't even look at him. Turning around wouldn't change anything. Meeting his eye wouldn't make this any better. She had to get out of there. Away. Free. Into the open to breathe.

"Sweet," he murmured. His lips met the top of her head. That was meant to be a comfort, to soothe her, but it didn't relax her rigid body. "I'm sorry. Don't walk out. We made a deal to communicate."

Yes, they had a deal, but declaring her feelings wouldn't erase any of the embarrassment. At least she couldn't imagine it was possible to feel worse. Maybe honesty would be cathartic. Seemed it was the price of freedom either way.

"You couldn't even look at me," she whispered the stinging confession. "I wasn't trying to make you angry. I didn't think you'd notice enough to care but… you couldn't even look at me."

"This is about Twaddle," he said, withdrawing. "You honestly still think—"

"Just hand me my bag, Bastian, please," she beseeched and held her hand out backwards.

She couldn't do this. She couldn't fight. She was too tired to explain herself. He'd never convince her that anything other than his initial reaction to her nudity was genuine. Anyone could make up excuses and reasons later; the kneejerk reaction was always the most honest.

Instead of her bag, her hand came into contact

with skin, hot sculpted skin. His hand spread over hers, pressing it against his abdomen.

Pull away. Walk out. To hell with the bag. Why wasn't she moving?

He slid her hand downwards over the soft cotton of his underwear. Immediately, she felt the width of him, the length of him; hot, hard, and ready to fill the void inside her.

Without thought for tears, her head snapped around to meet his eye. She didn't steal her hand away. In fact, when he averted his gaze, she curled her fingers around his cock through his underwear, shrouding his darkening focus. Tension gathered in his shoulders until his body was as taut as hers.

"Bastian…" she whispered.

Jaw clenched, he reached for the hem of her sweater, baring her body again. Releasing him was a torture she endured as pain. The second her jeans and panties were gone, she grabbed for his length again. If she was going to wake up any second, she had to make the most of each moment.

Bastian scooped her from the floor fulfilling their mutual desire when her legs twined around his hips. With a single step, he pinned her spine against the post at the bottom corner of the bed and just held her there, making love to her with his gaze.

Bastian was sure. Always. She couldn't say the same about herself. This could be a huge mistake. They were friends. They weren't supposed to be intimate. Not like this. They hadn't talked about it; there were no rules for the physical. If they gave in to whatever was going on here and now, they may not be able to go back to the way things were later.

Answers were distant. Intangible and irrelevant the instant his lips met hers. She locked her arms around his neck and arched against him, desperate to be closer, driven to be a part of him.

Bastian slid a strong arm under her ass, boosting her high, freeing a hand to go exploring. Caressing her hip, her waist, her breast, he squeezed her. All she could do was squirm against the ridge in his underwear.

Any uncertainty she had flew out of the window when he lowered his mouth to her breast and breathed her in. With a gratified yelp, she secured her ankles at his back and grabbed his hair to pull his mouth to hers. She needed him. She needed his mouth. Needed his body. Needed him to occupy her, all of her.

Sucking his tongue from his mouth, her hands clamored with his underwear, shoving them down his legs out of the way. She released his mouth, but caught his lower lip in her teeth, overwhelmed by a need to keep him.

The glitter that shone in his eye braced her for what might come next. Yet, there was still a question in him. Was it her he doubted or himself?

He kissed her again, slow this time. On his release of her mouth, he guided himself into her, watching her so intently that one advance matched the other. As he went deeper, she grabbed for his shoulders, stalling him.

Stalling? Oh, no, that wasn't right.

Shaking her head, her nails dug deep into him. "No," she murmured. "White Knight, don't dare stop."

Doing as told, he kissed her again and continued to ease in. Ah, she couldn't help herself, her whole body moved, arching and writhing, wringing a moan from her deepest depths. His tormenting mouth kissed wherever it could reach. She couldn't let him get away with that and tossed her own head forward to land her mouth on his throat. With a growl of approval, he surrendered all restraint and plunged into her pliant body.

Engulfed in the surging torrent of desire and

emotion, his generous girth stretched her in a painful pleasure. Oh, she had to be calm, hold on, breathe. All sense flew away when he drew out and thrust in again. Moving with him, all she could do was surrender and let this heaven happen.

His strength was impressive, he kept her pinned, piercing into her with every new breath, building the pressure of desire and gratification behind a dam eager to crack. In a single blast, her scream of climax clamped her around him, once, twice, squeezing and pulling him deeper, begging him to remain within her always.

A dark rumble blackened his throat. He didn't relax, he didn't give her up, not yet. With each advance, she got louder, until emotion clashed with the physical and she cried out again. Bastian echoed her plea and with another thrust, froze within her, spilling his seed deep.

Neither said a word.

His forearm hooked under her, he supported her while they both fought to breathe in a normal rhythm. Nope, wasn't possible. It just wasn't. He leaned back and looked into her eyes. What was that? What was looking back at her? Something different. Something inside him wasn't the same. She didn't know what it was. She didn't even know if it was a good change or a bad one.

"You're incredible in bed," he said with a twitch of a smile.

Her whole body sagged in relief and amusement. "We're not in bed," she said, freeing a grin and nudging his shoulder.

He took half a step to the side and fell forward, landing them on the mattress.

"Now we are, and you're still incredible," he said, bracing himself over her on his elbows. "Let's see what else you can do."

Only with him could she go from being in tears ready to flee to laying in bed laughing. Then again, what were friends for?

THIRTY-ONE

THE NEXT MORNING she was getting dressed when Bastian came out of the bathroom fastening his watch.

"We can spend the day here," he said, coming up behind her to scoop her hair from her neck to taste her still sensitive flesh.

Excitement and arousal zipped and zapped. As it had all night.

"We're in your mother's house."

"Do you have a thing for the kitchen?" he asked, sneaking his hands up her sweater to cup her breasts.

"The kitchen?" she asked, hitching her head his way. "Where did that—"

"We can't do it in the kitchen here because there are people around," he said. "We can do it in the kitchen at home."

She laughed. This smart, respectable gentleman was horny as a teenager. God, he made her feel good.

"No, we can't," she said, trying to push his hands out of her top. As he fought to keep playing, she laughed. "I don't have a thing for kitchens. I don't have a thing for anywhere. Until last night I'd never done it outside of a bed."

"Really?" he asked. "Now you've got the bedpost, the floor, and the shower checked off your list. There are plenty of other places to acquaint you with."

It was nice to be bathed in the morning afterglow. These feelings were new. Invincible. Worshiped. Bastian gave her so much.

"Oh, how generous," she said. "It's already ten a.m. I've never slept so long in my life."

"We didn't do much sleeping to be fair."

"Bastian," she whimpered.

"Okay. Okay," he said, concluding playtime with her breasts. "I don't want to go downstairs, I might see that bastard from last night."

She sighed. "Bastian, it wasn't his fault. Technically, it was yours for granting him entry when we weren't in the same room."

"I didn't think you'd be naked," he said. "Do you think if I'd thought you were going to be any kind of naked I'd have been in a different room?"

"Yes, you've certainly mastered making your point. And to think I thought you were repulsed by my body."

She grabbed her bag from the floor, and he immediately seized it.

"Your body is beautiful."

"You snapped at me."

"Because I wanted to make love to you so badly. Do you know what it's like to want something so damn bad? God, I thought I'd explode."

"Charmer," she said and tried to grab her bag back.

He held it away from her. "You don't carry the bags, I carry the bags."

"What are you? My valet?" she asked. "I can

carry a bag."

"We're rich, sweetheart, you never have to lift a finger again."

Ah, dry wit. Good thing she could read it in him or that would've been offensive.

"I have to go home," she said when his gaze slithered down her body. "I have to go home. I have a car to return tonight, remember? If I don't leave your company, how can I return to it?"

"Keep the car," he said, tossing her bag aside to bear down on her.

Her hands rose but he kept on coming until she was flush against the bedpost, palms flat on his chest.

She screeched. "Bastian!"

"I can be quick," he said, caressing her hips and ass until he had the latter in his grip.

He squeezed her closer until her eyes flared. It didn't matter how many times she saw it, or had it inside her, he always felt overwhelming. Rather than fear, the anxiety of accepting him made her mouth water. She'd never been sex hungry before, never in her life. She wriggled closer, lifting one leg to his hip. He grabbed it to balance her, granting her access to rub her clit against the stimulation he offered.

"You're so hot," he muttered. Eyes closed, head back, she writhed, literally using him as a sex toy. Shit, what was wrong with her? Straightening, she tried to take her leg back but he held it higher. "Don't be embarrassed. I want to share this with you."

"It's not much fun for you."

His grin slid up slowly. "You'd be surprised, Sweet."

She nudged his chest and he relented. "We're late for breakfast."

Somehow, it could only have been divine intervention, but they managed to separate and get downstairs to the Hunt breakfast table. Greetings were exchanged, coffee was poured. All civilized. She could do normal, respectful, social. Could she? There had been points in the night the whole damn world was topsy-turvy. It wasn't quite right on its axis yet.

"Did you decide?" Carolyn asked over the breakfast table. "Bastian?"

Bastian was frowning at her. Frowning wasn't good. What did she do wrong? His parents and sister awaited his response, but his focus remained intent on her.

"Knight," Harper said putting down her knife to cover his hand with hers.

"Hmm?" He snapped out of his daze and checked the faces around the circular table. "What?"

"Mom asked about August," Keely said to him.

"Have you made a decision?" Carolyn asked.

"No," Bastian said.

"We take a family vacation in August," Carolyn explained. "By this time of the year we've usually decided on where. Do you have a preference?"

"Me?" Harper asked. "Why would I—"

"You're family now," Carolyn said. "Where in the world would you—"

"I voted for the Caribbean," Keely said. "I know it's been done, but there's a reason it's so popular."

"Bastian and Harper may want to holiday alone this year," Thomas said, picking up a folded newspaper.

"They can holiday together whenever," Keely said. "This is family time, we have to get to know Harper too. Bastian can't keep her all to himself forever."

"We'll do dinner together next weekend," Thomas said, opening the paper to read.

"That's very kind," Harper said. "You'll all be sick of the sight of me."

"No, no, we love spending time as a family,"

Carolyn said. "It's the most important thing in the world."

"We could go to Crimson Isle," Keely said. "You'll love it there. It's Roxie's island, so you can be totally in charge."

"That's not why we enjoy going there," Carolyn added. "Though knowing the owner does have its advantages. Roxie is a wonderful hostess, I'm sorry I didn't see her and Zairn leave last night."

"They had to get to the club," Harper said. "She's so careful about taking care of people and makes them feel so important." Even nobodies like her. "It's a gift. She asked me to call her later."

Everyone stalled. Instantly. Like she'd just admitted to murder or mayhem. Even Thomas peeked over the top of his newspaper. Trouble was, none of the faces hinted at the reason for the dramatic response.

"Did Roxie give you her phone number?" Carolyn asked.

"Yes. Why would that be strange?"

"The only time Roxie gives out her number is if she has no interest in speaking to you."

She didn't quite—

"Let me see," Keely said, wiping her hands before extending one toward her.

She opened the contact and handed it over.

"I wouldn't take it personally," Carolyn said. "Sometimes that girl doesn't know if she's coming or going."

Keely held the phone out to give it back. "You're okay. It's Zairn's number."

"That's a good sign." Carolyn's lips curled. "You'll get through to him, or Tibbs, at least. He'll get you to Roxie."

Tibbs, great! Whoever that was. She couldn't wait.

"Where's your phone?" Bastian asked his sister.

"Upstairs," Keely said, "I think. Why? Forget to pay your bill? Need me to spot you?"

The brother's mind was on a different track. "You know Zairn Lomond's number by heart?"

A gleeful Keely chose that moment to grin. "Is there a woman on the planet who doesn't? Much as we love Roxie, every one of us is waiting on that call."

Though Bastian didn't appear amused, it was pretty funny. Especially when Keely bobbed her brows upward and tossed a berry in her mouth.

Carolyn laughed. "Keely, sweetheart."

"Do you know my number by heart?" Bastian asked.

"Nope," Keely said. "Know Tripp Breckenridge's though."

"Gets better and better," Bastian muttered.

"She's playing with you," Carolyn said. "Neither of those men would take advantage of your sister."

"Know who would?" Keely asked, switching her focus to Harper. "Ricardo Whey."

"Don't go there," Bastian said quickly.

"What did he say to you at the charity ball, Harper?" Keely ignored her brother. "I never get that close to him, he's a total creep."

"For those unprepared. He hides his true nature behind his money," Carolyn added. "Yes, I have to say, that's a man every young woman should avoid at any cost."

"And his wife. She should avoid him too, she should run away. Fast." Keely nodded. "I don't know why that woman stays with him."

"Money," the Hunt parents said in unison.

A ringtone buzzed.

Bastian was the only one who didn't hear it.

Harper squeezed his hand again. "Knight?"

"Hmm?" He sat up, grabbing his phone. "Hunt," he answered and kissed her hand before getting up to pace out of the room.

Thomas smiled at his wife and disappeared through a different door.

"Do you want to come shopping with us today?" Keely asked.

"I have work to do today," Harper said. "But thank you for the offer."

Keely grinned at her mother. "Have you ever seen Bastian so out of it?"

"He knows what I think," Carolyn said. "I hope you're over your spat."

Heat gathered in Harper's cheeks. "Yes."

"They had sex in his parents' house." Keely giggled. "I think they're over it."

"Keely," Carolyn warned. "Don't pry into your brother's private life."

"You reserve that right for yourself, Mom? Harper's going to be my sister," Keely said. "I don't think it's a surprise they're crazy for each other."

Bastian returned. "What's going on?"

"I have to get to work," Harper said, leaving the table.

"Two minutes alone with the family and she's running for the hills," Bastian said, coming to her side.

"I'm not running," Harper said, tugging his tie lightly, which prompted him to kiss her. "I'll call you about tonight."

"We'll talk about it in the car," Bastian said.

"If you're coming with me…" Harper smiled. "Why did you kiss me goodbye?"

Bastian gathered her up, holding her tight against his chest.

"Kissing you doesn't need a reason, just an opportunity," he said, kissing the top of her head. "Phone if you need anything and happy anniversary again, Mom."

"Thank you for your hospitality," Harper said.

"I'll phone you in the week and we'll do lunch, just us girls together," Carolyn said. "And we'll insist about next weekend."

Before she could get a word in, Bastian answered, "We're busy next weekend."

"All weekend?" Keely asked. "Dirty vacation?"

"She hasn't decided yet," Bastian said. "It's her birthday."

Keely squealed. "Your birthday!"

"What have you got planned?" Carolyn asked.

"Nothing," Harper said.

Keely gasped. "You haven't arranged anything for your girlfriend's birthday? You're a sucky boyfriend."

"I'm disappointed, son."

"I told her anything she wants," Bastian said, "she hasn't decided yet."

"I'm happy with dinner," Harper said.

"A big dinner party." Keely had zeal in spades. "I'm in."

"She may have meant privately," Carolyn said. "But we can arrange a party if you would like."

"We'll talk about it in the week," Bastian said. "Don't pressure her, now we have to go."

After the last goodbye, Bastian led her through the house to the large front door. His car sat waiting for them, as did the man who opened her door, tres formal.

"We can't have a party," Harper said when they were alone inside. "That would mean bringing our families together."

"So?" he asked, driving toward the gates.

"We can't bring them together, our families are too different."

"They'll have to get used to each other," Bastian said.

"What if our stories don't match?"

"We'll talk about it in the week," he said. "Gives me an excuse to phone you. About tonight—"

"Bastian I'm serious," she said. "We can't bring them together."

"Everything will be fine, Sweet. I've got it under control."

"They'll embarrass me. Damon will show up, I

don't want him mouthing off in front of your parents."

"They won't think less of you for his behavior. Trust me, Sweet, it will be fine."

She didn't share his confidence but when he moved the conversation along, she didn't persist. He'd get it after they did dinner with her family. That experience would teach him a lot, and maybe send him running for the hills.

THIRTY-TWO

THE PHONE RANG and rang. It felt sort of rude calling knowing that she wouldn't get through to the person she actually wanted to talk to, but there were no alternatives.

"Hello?"

Okay, a male, definitely not Roxie, but without the smooth charm of Zairn.

"Hi, uh, my name is Harper Scott and—"

"She's with Astrid," he said. "Hold on, I'll put you through."

The line went quiet then beeped. One beep. Another. Roxie? He meant Roxie, right? If Roxie was busy, she didn't want to interrupt whatever was going on. And Astrid. Who was Astrid? A friend? An employee? Those two probably weren't mutually exclusive with Roxie.

"Hey! Harper!"

Yes, this was good. This was Roxie.

"Your parents aren't rich, are they?"

"My parents?"

"They're just like regular folks, no billions in the bank?"

"No, why? If you need money, I can hit up my guy. I've paid him plenty in sex. Hell, what am I saying? I have access to the accounts. No sex required. Let's clear him out and fly to Tahiti."

Damn, she wished she was in the mood to enjoy that joke.

"How did you introduce your parents to Zairn? Were they cool? How was Zairn afterward, pissed off? Were you mortified?"

"I don't really do mortified. Though I guess I did that first day, my dad is so... First time they talked, I wasn't sleeping with Zairn. It was more... business. Now they talk to each other more than I talk to either of them. God knows *what* they talk about. Men things? Oh, no, I don't want them talking about men things. Sport? No. Hobbies? Zairn's hobby is screwing me, so hopefully not that either. The weather...?"

She exhaled. Yeah, that was her luck. Of course she was the only one with embarrassing parents.

"Fantastic," she said, flat, frustrated.

"Your folks want to meet Bastian, huh?"

"They want to have dinner this week. And Bastian's talking about it like it will really happen."

"Dinner's not a bad first parent date. Go out though. You don't want to cook or be stuck at home all night with no escape. Or worse, at Bastian's place and you can't get them to leave."

"Yeah, we'll go out.

"Bastian will get you a reservation somewhere real impressive. Me and Z can—hey! Wait a second, Harper, honey. The emperor just walked in." Roxie's voice got louder. "Yo, Skippy! What do you and my dad talk about?"

"How much we love you." Quick answer from

Zairn there in the background. "What else is there to talk about?"

"Good point," Roxie said like she totally believed it.

"They'll say things to him," she whispered, unable to shake the chills. "My parents will say things to Bastian."

"He can say things back," Roxie said. "Want me and Z to come with you? I can single-handedly fill an entire conversation for the duration of a dinner. No problem! I'm great at monologuing. No one else will get a word in."

"She's not kidding," Zairn said, closer, but still in the background. "Who are we joining for dinner?"

"Harper and Bastian. And Harper's parents."

"We have the thing downstairs later."

"It's not tonight," Roxie said to Zairn then switched to her. "It's not tonight, right, Harper?"

"No, and thank you, but no. You don't have to come. No way. I'm terrified enough of them meeting Bastian, if I was to bring you and Zairn Lomond too…" Her head moved slow as it shook. "I'd never be able to look any of you in the eye again."

"I'm just a regular Joe, no one cares about me." That wasn't her experience. "And Zairn can switch it all off, he does brooding and boring every night at the club, he won't say a word." So Roxie wouldn't shut up and Zairn wouldn't speak? A match made in heaven. "And don't think of him as the legend, Z's just… another guy at the table you're not sleeping with."

Her mouth opened because she'd intended to say something. What? She couldn't remember. No, her lips slowly met again because… how did she—should she… Oh, boy.

"Uh…"

"Uh…?" Roxie asked then gasped. "Oh my God!

You slept with him!" This time she had to tuck her lips in her mouth, squeezing them closed in her teeth. "You had sex with—good for you, girl—Z, Bastian had sex last night!"

"I'll call Reuters and AP," Zairn muttered.

"Ignore him, oh my God, was it good?" Roxie asked. "Is he good? What does it mean? Are you together for real now? Was it a one-night thing? Do you regret it? I guess you only regret it if it sucked. It would have to really suck. Did it suck? Because you can come back from that. If you want to. Do you want to?"

"Breathe, Lola," Zairn said. "Shit, give the woman a damn chance."

"Oh, hush, Skippy," Roxie huffed. "It's your fault I don't get to live the thrill of a new guy. Won't ever again. Proud of that?"

"Yeah, actually," Zairn said with obvious swagger. "You're welcome."

"If you want to keep that smug smile of yours, I have to live vicariously through my friends."

"I don't really know how..." Harper started. Details? What should she share? What did it mean? Damn, that was a good question. "It happened at his mom's, we stayed there last night."

"Wow, right there in the Hunt mansion? Phew, that screams urgent. I love urgent sex."

"We didn't mean to—I didn't mean to—it was just... I don't know what it means."

"Did you ask him?"

"No, we... I don't know, we just..."

"Lived in the moment. That's okay. Do you want it to mean anything? I've got to say, you look good together and Bastian was... obsessed last night."She tsked. "He was not."

"You didn't see it, the rest of us saw it. He barely took his eyes off you all night. He's into you. I've seen husbands less interested in their wives. Mine included."

"If I stared at you all night, Lola, you'd blindfold me again."

Again?

"Only to have my fun, and you do stare at me all night, Casanova," Roxie said. "Checking out how many of your spondoolies I'm frittering away."

Except they owned the club and she'd never seen money change hands.

"Gotta keep an eye on my investment," Zairn said. "And you want faithful? It's your fault I don't get to live the thrill of a new gal, Empress. Can't let that pussy get too far when it's the only one I'm allowed to play with."

"We're talking about Harper's pussy right now, Skippy. Get in line. I'm sorry, honey. Z's pussy-obsessed."

"Always worked for you before, Lola."

"Ignore my guy. We're talking about yours. Bastian. How was he?"

"Good. Amazing."

"You don't have to be polite," Roxie said. "Bastian's a nice guy. Sometimes it's like that, you know, they do their best, and you don't want to be rude—"

"Not something you've ever worried about, babe."

"What do you know about women, Skippy? Sometimes we do that, sometimes we lay there, we smile—"

"You don't smile when we're having sex."

"And what does that tell you, Casanova? Anyway, you never see anything during sex, you're too cross-eyed because I feel so good."

"Why do you think I married you? I don't care if it's good for you, just need a good woman to do her part."

"What? Lay there? Open her legs?"

"Qualities you excel in, dear."

"Why are you part of this conversation anyway? This is girl talk. Aren't you the same guy I kicked out of bed this morning? Sex pest. You're stalking me."

"Finally she figures it out."

On a sigh, Harper murmured, "You're incredible together."

The pressure of drama and anxiety eased in the aura of the newlyweds' love.

"So people keep telling me, I don't see it myself."

But she did. Roxie was great at flirting and laughter, great with sass and banter. Underneath that, it was impossible not to notice how the couple tracked each other in every room. Love looked like them together. They lived the fantasy.

"I'm sorry I called to unload on you."

"I'm exactly who you call," Roxie said. "Tibbs knew to put you right through, he's good that way. Keeps the defenses high when we need him and ducks out the way when we don't. Somehow, he divines it."

"Helps he has no life," Zairn said, coming and going in whatever he was doing.

"Tibbs has a life, in spite of your attempts to stifle him. Poor boy."

"He's only got another couple of years to worry about, then we'll set him free. Maybe then he'll get laid."

"Oh, that boy gets laid. Don't you be worrying about that."

"He gets—who?"

"He didn't violate your sister." Roxie's voice came closer. "Which I know for sure because Z doesn't have a sister."

"Lo…"

"What? Stop looking at me like that," Roxie said, enjoying her superior position. "I'm not talking to you about the sex lives of other men. What kind of husband asks his wife to talk about other men's sex lives?"

"You brought it up."

"I did not! You said the thing about him getting laid."

"Which was a joke, and you knew that, which means you want to tell me this secret."

"It's not a secret. I tell you when I have secrets."

"Like walking in on Knox and Jane together."

"Yes, like that. See, I didn't tell you the secret, only that I had one, so you couldn't be mad when you found out."

"We both keep people's confidences."

"There you go, ha, topic concluded."

"Not topic concluded. You said this wasn't a secret."

"And you said we keep people's confidences. Is this one of those situations where I need to distract you with sex?"

"I'd say yes, but I have ten guys waiting downstairs for me."

"Oh, Casanova, I have them queuing around the block."

"I know, we sell tee-shirts and Crimson-branded condoms. Rouge Rubbers."

"Ha, funny, I see what you did there. Are they actually rouge? That's a missed opportunity."

"Roxie's Rouge Rubbers?"

"Bam, man, there's your winner. Can they be Gin & It flavored?"

"Ah, baby," Zairn drawled, "we make a helluva team."

"My inspired ideas make you so much dough, it's a wonder Ogilvie ever had a problem with me."

"Triple-R, not triple-X."

"To go with our Triple Seven," Roxie declared on

a brief laugh.

"They'll be put into production immediately."

"Don't I need to approve the flavor first? Does it have to be done in a factory setting?"

Zairn's snicker was almost a groan. "Alone in the dark, you and me."

"It's a date—ah, uh-uh—" Roxie interrupted herself to exclaim, "I don't think so!"

Didn't make sense to her, or Zairn either. "Don't think so—"

"You kiss me goodbye before you walk out on me, Casanova," Roxie said, affronted. A few seconds past. "There see, thank you."

"Happy wife," he murmured. "Happy life."

"And don't you forget it. Good, thank you. Now you can go," Roxie said. "Don't know what he was thinking." Her friend's volume rose. "What if your elevator plummets to the lobby, Casanova? That kiss might be our last!"

"Am I interrupting?" she asked after a couple of beats. "I should've just text. I'll text next time."

"No, call, always call. Texting is complicated because it goes to Z's phone and Tibbs has to filter it. Sending it to Astrid is more—just call."

"Okay, thank you."

"And I meant what I said, Z and I will come if you want. He doesn't have to do the brooding thing. It wouldn't be the first time we've trotted out Z's charm to win over parents. I'm not even talking my parents, I mean for other people in our circle. He doesn't have to be getting laid to go on the offensive for you or Bastian."

"Bastian thinks it's no big deal," she said. "But I know what my parents are like."

"We judge the world based on our perception of it. You've got to look at this as a good thing. If Bastian can handle your parents, he can handle anything."

Except they had no future. This wasn't the start of something. In fact, they should be thinking about winding it up. It had already gone too far. Far too far. Did that mean she'd get out of the dinner? No. Probably not.

THIRTY-THREE

THURSDAY.

She'd pushed the dinner, back and back every day until Thursday. This was as far as anyone allowed her to go. Next Thursday? The week after? No. This one. It had to be now.

No matter how many times she tried to cancel, no one got the hint that this was a bad idea. Bastian didn't help. He actually seemed eager to spend time with her family. How nice it must be to go through life oblivious to the perils hurtling toward you. Other families weren't quite as tolerant of each other as his, Bastian was in for a treat.

Didn't matter now. Not while riding along in Carnell's car with Adara on the way to the restaurant. Her sister chattered about her nuptials. Weddings were so... pointless. Each to their own, but why were flowers so important? More to the point, why were they so expensive? Still, she'd forgive Adara's excitement if she could be equally excused for her lack of it.

One tiny reprieve? Damon and Charissa were

travelling with her parents.

Short lived though it may be, she appreciated the breathing space.

When they stopped, a valet was there ready to take Carnell's keys.

Azame, what kind of name was that for a restaurant? Wait, was this the place in… Shit. A salad in this place cost three figures. Wow, talk about eager to please. How did her father get a reservation at an exclusive place like this?

Her party congregated, straightening skirts and cuffs, exchanging mumbles about the journey. Okay, maybe not mumbles, but she had no interest in listening to Damon more than was absolutely necessary. Blah, blah, blah. Her father could shoulder that burden. Charissa and Adara were clearly excited about the exclusive location, and her mother wasn't far behind in joining their glee.

And she was—whoa, brother.

Forget the family.

There was the yummiest prize she'd ever seen: Bastian. He emerged from inside and she went to meet him halfway.

Her eyes drifted shut when he kissed her and traced a fingertip down her temple.

"You're here," she whispered. He looked amazing. So him, so cool, so exactly what she needed. "I didn't know you'd be here waiting. You're a nice surprise."

"I had to be early," he said. "No need for you to enter alone."

"Bastian," Davis announced from their side. Where had he appeared from? Almost petulant, she resented her father shattering their private moment. "I must introduce you to the family. This is my wife Bea, my daughter Adara and her fiancé Carnell."

"We've met before," Adara said. "Let's get inside, it's freezing out here."

So inside they went. Table, seats, order, all went like clockwork. The staff were more attentive and informative than she'd ever known. And she knew exactly why. Her father would like to think it was for his benefit. It wasn't. Bastian was the one they fell over themselves for. *"Yes, Mr. Hunt." "No, Mr. Hunt." "Whatever you want, Mr. Hunt."* She couldn't blame them, pleasing him gave her a buzz too.

As her father explained something to Adara and Charissa, Harper leaned in closer to Bastian, locking their fingers together on the table.

"I'm coming home with you tonight," she whispered, grazing her lips on his jaw. "Will you let me come home with you?"

When their eyes met, his shimmered with a carnal heat she wanted to bathe in. His fingers slid beneath the table to rest on her thigh for a single heartbeat before they snuck under the hem of her dress.

"If I made the rules, you'd spend all your nights in my bed."

Boosting up, she touched her lips to his. "Who makes the rules?"

"It's all you, baby," he answered. "All you."

Her laugh silenced the table. Was she that interesting? Her head fell to his shoulder and he kissed her hair, joining their hands beneath the table again.

"I'm glad we have this opportunity to get together," Davis said. "I suppose we'll have many chances now that you and Harper are an item."

"You're very handsome," Charissa said. "Do you carry a lot of cash?"

Adara and Carnell laughed like it was a joke.

Damon frowned. "Do you always buy your way into people's lives, Mr. Hunt?"

"We're family. This is family," Davis said on a gruff laugh. For the first time, her father would want Damon to shut the hell up. Welcome to the club, Daddio. "We would be very interested to hear about your recent partnership with Sporta."

Bastian shook his head while sipping water. "It's not a partnership," he said. "We've got them treading water, so now we can bail them out."

"It's a takeover?" Damon asked.

"That's what they wanted in the beginning," Bastian said. "They approached us about the acquisition fourteen months ago."

"You refused?"

"Grand Holdings isn't a charity," he said. "Fourteen months gave our finance division time to carry out a complete historical audit. I know what I'm doing. And this is small potatoes. Sporta only blipped on my radar because my aunt knows their CFO."

"You didn't take it on faith?" Bea asked.

Bastian smiled. "Faith doesn't have much of a place in business. Trust is precarious enough in personal situations. You play at my level, facts and figures are the only faith we have. Even they can lie sometimes. This deal is eight figures. Peanuts in the bigger picture, but you look after the pennies…"

"This from the guy with nine cars," Adara said.

How did her sister know that?

"There's nine at the house," Bastian said but didn't add a qualifier.

"Is it true you own a theme park?" Charissa asked.

"Sold it," he said. "Didn't fit my portfolio."

"How many hotels do you own?"

"There are five twenty-five in the chain worldwide," he said. "Give or take, we offer franchise options if you're interested."

"Harper must have told you what we do," Davis said.

No way she'd let that axe drop.

"We shouldn't monopolize the meal with business," Harper said. "You boys can talk shop another time," or never as far as she was concerned.

"Where did you two meet?" Bea asked. "This is a very unusual situation, isn't it?"

"Sure is," Bastian said. "I can't believe I was so lucky as to meet the most incredible woman in the world. How I got her interest, I'll never know. Still not sure how I swung that."

"You can be difficult," Harper said, following her words with a faux sigh.

Bastian kissed her temple. "I'm a lucky guy."

"You must have women knocking down your door," Charissa said.

"It's double locked," Bastian replied. "There's only one girl for me."

Her date smiled at her and, damn, she believed it. This guy was a helluva salesman. Talk about hyperbole. She shouldn't laugh. Wouldn't. He was being sweet again.

Trust Damon to ruin the mood with his scoff.

Bastian's smile fell in the second he turned to the sound. "Do you have a problem, Twaddle?"

"No," Davis said. "He has no problem."

"It's OTT," Damon said, him and Bastian locking eyes. "Harper's not the type of woman guys shoot their load for like that."

"Damon," Charissa chastised him. "Your mom is right there."

Bastian's next words were cool, measured. "I assure you, Twaddle, mine shoots just fine. For Harper, and only for Harper."

A laugh busted out of Adara. "Sorry…" Her sister's eyes watered in their hilarity. "That was a good comeback. Guess some men work a little better than others. Carnell's healthy as a horse and he has no trouble with me." Adara wrinkled her nose to patronize Damon, just as he deserved. "Maybe you should go to a doctor."

The way Damon's scowl flipped to Charissa led her to believe, huh, there could be something in that. Had the friends been talking?

But, typically, Damon dug his heels in when drawing his eyes off Charissa. "Men like blondes," he asserted. "Sophisticated and cultured. Not too much work. You've got to admit, Harpy, one thing you are is hard work."

Lovely. Wasn't that nice. It wouldn't be a family get-together without a dose of Harper bashing, next time she'd wear a helmet.

"Not all men want the same thing," Adara said. "Not all women want the same thing either. You want a quiet little trophy wife to trail along behind you and do as she's told. Maybe Bastian doesn't want that. There are four couples at the table, do you think if we mixed and matched our qualities that we would be as happy?"

Four couples. Harper was used to being the singleton. For the first time, she was actually happy and it was all down to the man at her side.

The food arrived and the conversation moved on but the contentment remained. Unfamiliar, but not unwelcome, she'd never be able to repay his kindness.

THIRTY-FOUR

"THAT WASN'T SO BAD," Bastian said as they drove home later that night. "Was it?"

"Which part? When my mother asked for your social security number or when my dad started going on about seeking new investment? Oh no, was it when Adara asked you to be groomsmen or when Charissa wanted you to admire her necklace? The cleavage was totally incidental."

"They're people. People are people." Whatever that meant. "What were you and Damon talking about outside?"

At the restaurant while they were waiting for the cars. Hmm, she'd caught Bastian's scrutiny but hoped he wouldn't ask.

Hope extinguished.

"Nothing."

"It was something."

"Damon being Damon," she said. "Don't worry about it."

"There's something on your mind that wasn't

there when I met you tonight."

How did he know that? He wasn't wrong, but how did he know?

Her troubles, and meandering thoughts, weren't his to shoulder. "I'm fine."

"Your family are your family," he said. "You can't do anything about that. I don't judge—"

"No, it's not—you were incredible. Way more patient than I would've been."

"You've tolerated plenty from my family. What did Damon want? I'll turn right around and ask him if you don't tell me how he upset you."

"He didn't upset me."

"You're lucky. Guy upsets me whenever he breathes."

Another grievance she'd introduced into Bastian's life. Rather than sadden her, it infuriated her.

"I'm so exhausted with it all. I'll never be free of him." She tucked her purse by her leg. "My father needs Damon and will always pick him over me. I should move."

Planet, if possible.

"Yeah, you should. I can talk to your father, tell him to get rid of the guy."

Given her father's veneration of him, Bastian may be the only one with a shot of getting through. Still…

"I would never ask you to do that."

"I'm offering. Hell, I'm begging. I want that guy out of your life for good."

"And what happens when you're out of my life?" There would be nothing stopping Damon from swanning back in. "Besides Charissa and Adara are best friends." Meaning as long as he was with Charissa, Damon would be a part of her life. She exhaled. "Sorry. I'm sorry."

"Don't apologize."

"Let's talk about how amazing you were tonight. You really impressed my family." He did that just by being him. Impressed everyone with that trick. "You impressed me. I don't even know how to… My family were ready to write me off. This could buy them another year or two of hope that I may not be a lost cause."

Her father was thrilled, her mom, her sister, finally had proof someone else might take the burden of her from them.

"We'll have to date for another couple of years before my family think that of me."

"Your family know you're pure gold. Keely was talking you up to the travel agent we met last week. I think she was trying to make me jealous."

"I'm sorry about the vacation talk, she gets excited about it."

"She should, it's fun to travel." That wasn't why he was apologizing though. She read it in the way his hand tightened on the gear shift. "I don't mind that she gets excited." Sliding a hand over his, their fingers found their way between each other. "She's an amazing person. All your friends and family are."

"They like you."

Which in itself was newsworthy.

"I was clear in not committing myself to anything," she said. "We'll have to put an end to this before, you know…"

"Before what?"

"Money changes hands."

"I don't care about money."

"If there was a cost for any vacation, I'd pay my way. I don't want anyone to put down a deposit…" The corner of his mouth twitched. "What?"

"That's not how it works, Sweet."

"How what works? Vacations? Don't you talk to

someone, pick a package—"

"Not exactly."

She didn't get it. "How else could it work? You can't just show up at the airport."

"Want to go to the airport right now and see how far we get?"

"Bastian."

"Forgetting for a second that we actually own an airline, we can show up at the airport any time we want."

"And kick other people out of their seats?"

This time, he laughed. "Baby, we own planes. We don't fly commercial."

Oh. Right. Duh. "And how do you know there'll be a—" Sort of stupid to wonder about accommodation given he also owned a chain of hotels. "It's a whole different life."

"Yep," he admitted. "And I don't tell you this to boast. I tell you so you know it's taken care of."

"I wouldn't be able to afford that."

"You wouldn't pay a penny."

"Bastian, I don't—"

"It's something I'd do for any…" Why did he trail off like that? "Keely goes nuts with her own accounts whenever she wants to."

"She's your sister."

"You don't think Zairn does the same for Roxie?"

"They're married."

"Recently married," he said. "We've never talked about it, but I'd bet our fortune Z opened his means to her a long time ago." They were in love. Together. The forever type of forever. "He's a generous guy, I'd bet her friends and family are taken care of too."

Roxie and Zairn had been nothing but wonderful; all Bastian's friends were welcoming.

"Did you know they met on a talk show?"

"I did."

"Have you seen it? It's on the internet," she said. "They didn't interact much, but the look Rox gave him just before winning…" She laughed. "Let's just say it wasn't love at first sight."

"Sometimes it works that way."

"They argued the first time they interacted."

"I'd heard."

The legend must've traveled far.

"You don't strike me as the type to gossip. Let me guess, Keely?"

He shrugged one shoulder. "Her and it came up at the wedding."

Another duh moment. "That must've been a sight. Them at the altar. A real fairytale. I'm sorry I missed it. Not that I'd have been invited if—"

"There were more than a thousand people there."

"So they invited everyone they know? Increases my chances, I guess."

"Actually, no, there was some drama about people being left off the guest list."

Something Roxie hadn't mentioned. "Oh…" She made a sound of intrigue and twisted to rest a shoulder on the backrest, transfixed. "Tell me."

"Oh, no, I don't—Keely's your bet for that." So she was right about him absorbing rumors by osmosis. "Or Mom. I almost didn't go to the wedding at all."

"Why wouldn't you go?" she asked. "Roxie loves you, she's just… particular about sizing people up." Men more than women in her limited experience. "You've known Zairn a long time. You didn't want to support him?"

"Yeah, but it's a wedding…"

"In your hotel." Her cheeks plumped. "Were you worried about complaints?"

His dimple joined them. "No such thing at a Grand Hotel."

"I believe you."

"You ever have a complaint?"

"About the hotel? No. About the people you let in it…"

"Something I'm willing to change with your permission. Nothing would give me greater pleasure than to see your ex stopped on the threshold."

"I wouldn't give him the satisfaction. He's the kind of man who should never cross your path. I'm sorry for putting him on it."

"Forget about me. He's not worthy of being near you, let alone…" His hand tightened under hers. "I struggle to see it. What in him appealed to you?"

"I struggle too. Maybe it was more of a situationship than anything emotional… I was never caught up in him."

Never excited. Never sped her heart. Never touched every corner of her body with a single glance. Not like Bastian. He was more, a perfect man. A dangerous way to think; no one could live up to that, but, really, how could any woman not fall for him?

"Good. That's something. I thought my family were bad, but…"

He glanced her way, their eyes lingered longer than they should.

"Yeah, you won the family lottery. You should be proud of your family. They want to embrace…"

"Embrace…? Women who mean something to me."

She licked her lips on a smile. "Women they *think* mean something to you."

"Think?"

"It's not… This. It's not believable," she said. "Our families have accepted this, us, together but I don't get it. It's just not believable."

"Us?"

"Why would we ever have reason to meet?"

"We did meet."

"Yeah," she said, "but socially meet. Even if we did, we'd have no reason to converse. We'd never be attracted to each other. Not in any actionable way." Because who could look at Bastian and not admit his hotness? Her point was... "This would just never happen."

"Is that what's been bothering you?"

"No," she said. "It's not bothering me. It's odd that our families have accepted it so easily when we're from completely different stratospheres."

His hand slid out from under hers to rest on the wheel. "Yeah," he said not entirely convinced. "It's a complete shock."

"Have I upset you?"

"No," he said, his shoulders moving in... something. "What do you want for your birthday? We're down to the wire now."

"Adara guilted you?"

"She mentioned it was coming up."

"Right. Okay." Yes, her sister would assume her boyfriend knew her birthday. "Nothing, it's not a huge deal."

"Nothing's not an option."

She edged a little closer to tease. "You could sleep with me."

"Sex? That's your request?" he asked. "Tough to gift wrap and present at a party."

That would be a birthday for the books.

"Do you think that's taking our attempt to be convincing too far?"

"It might make your guests a little uncomfortable, but it'll be a helluva show... I'll hire a posse."

She pinched his shoulder. "Are you going to stay in the audience?"

"To watch a string of men parade on stage and make love to my woman? No, I'll be somewhere off-site arranging a hit on each male who touches you."

"I want sex from you," she said, enjoying the warmth surrounding them.

"Tell me what you want for your birthday," he said. "And I'll promise to satisfy you tonight."

That was a given. "Just once?"

"As many times as you want."

"I don't know."

"If you don't tell me, I'll buy you one of everything."

"Everything?" Hilarious. "Why not just take me out for dinner? I don't want a fuss."

"A meal? That's it? For how many? Where?"

"I don't care about where."

"My mother will recommend somewhere," he said. "You want to keep it small, or have a larger group?"

"You'd never get a reservation for—"

"Sweet, I'd get a reservation."

"Two," she said.

"Two what?"

"A table for two," she said. "You and me. I don't want to put up a front for our families."

"Yeah, that's a big stretch for you on your birthday," he said, reaching for her hand to put it under his again.

Admiring the width and strength of his body, she had to be impressed with his work-out regime when he was so in demand socially and professionally. His business was spread across the world and, as he'd said, it was always business hours somewhere.

And that gave her an idea.

"There's one thing," she said.

"Name it."

"I've never spent a night in a Grand."

His smile stretched. "You want a hotel for your birthday? We have plenty of those. We'll name one for you—no, we'll start a division for you."

"Not a hotel, or a division," she said. "A night in a hotel, we could eat in, room service."

"That's it? A meal and a reservation?"

"And your company," she said. "You're a man in demand; I wouldn't be able to afford you if it wasn't a gift."

"You got it, Sweet."

Bastian carried himself with an authority, an innate confidence that filled her with pride. In security and safety, he could fulfill any wish or desire. And somehow, at his side, she could do no wrong. No one would harm her under the umbrella of his protection.

One jarring fact… the security wouldn't last. Soon, his companionship would be lost. Her family would be devastated. And what about her? Bastian had become a part of her life, he was her friend. Would that friendship endure after they cast off their deceit?

They drove into his garage and he turned off the engine. They just sat there, in silence, sharing a moment that would soon be lost.

Time was limited, she had to make the most of it. Leaving the car, she went to the kitchen without waiting. The light came on, as it was programmed to do, and his car door closed.

Good. She walked across the kitchen.

"Sweet," he said from further behind her.

She paused at the sliding door to the den and turned to see him still on the other side of the room. His concern remained, but it was tinged with a tenderness she tried to ignore. In times like this, when they were alone, they didn't have to be worried about anyone but themselves.

She unzipped her dress and pulled the slide from her hair. "I want to go to bed."

Stepping out of the puddle of fabric, she walked away, confident he'd follow her to the bedroom, if he didn't get there first.

THIRTY-FIVE

"I LOVE BIRTHDAYS," Roxie said.

Zairn filled his wife's wineglass. "Everybody's got one."

She and Bastian had left their suite to join Roxie and Zairn in theirs. The suite? Yeah, Bastian hadn't just provided a room for her birthday, they'd been in a Grand suite for three nights. Work, family, it was all still out there, though Roxie and Zairn were the first people they'd seen, or talked to, since before they arrived on Friday.

"Know who sucks at birthdays?" Roxie asked, electing to snag her husband's brandy. "Zairn sucks at birthdays."

"Your birthday was a smash hit," Zairn said. "People are still talking about it. We'll have to kick it up a gear this year." He swiped the glass back just as it touched Roxie's lower lip. "Brandy gets you giggly and we're in company."

Angled against her husband, chairs so close they had to be touching, Roxie returned to her wine. "He's not worried I'll embarrass him, he's worried I'll turn him on."

"Around you, Lo, I'm always at eleven."

"What were we talking about?" Roxie asked. "Birthdays, yes. Your birthday was a non-event, Casanova. Bo-ring."

"I had you, Wife. At my beck and call. What else do I want, Lo? We party every night. We can party any time."

"We have sex every night too, just the same as we did on your birthday. What made it so special?"

Zairn leaned in, burying his mouth in Roxie's hair. "Want me to remind you?"

"It wasn't that kinky," Roxie said, patting his cheek over her shoulder as he sat back, smirking in his bold arrogance.

"Sex was my birthday request too," Harper said, drawing some amusement. Bastian raised her hand to his lips. "Maybe I shouldn't have said that."

"Hey, you get it, girl." Roxie raised her glass in a silent toast, though then crooked a suspicious brow at Bastian. "Providing he delivered. And I don't mean just for himself. Showing up gets no reward, it's all about satisfaction."

"Lola grades me."

Bastian's laugh clashed with her horror. "You grade him?"

"He passes…" Roxie folded an arm under her breasts while swinging the glass to her mouth. "Most of the time."

"Ha," Zairn said, his hand dropping beneath the table, most probably onto his wife. "Would anyone believe you'd let me leave the room if you weren't satisfied?"

"No," Bastian said. "No one would believe that."

Almost strutting, Roxie's shoulders went back. "I'm glad my reputation proceeds me."

"So other guys hear it?" Zairn slid his arm along the back of Roxie's chair. "Me too, keeps them far, far away. Talk about taking one for the team."

"It's no dent in your reputation that your wife won't free you from our marital bed." Roxie's grin flashed. "Almost two months in and this wedding thing is still going. Still weird though."

"You mean marriage?"

"Oh, marriage is a way bigger slog," Roxie said. "After the wedding, it shouldn't feel different…"

"But it does," Zairn finished for her and kissed her head. "This gorgeous fucking creature…"

"You're still attracted to each other…" the whispered words weren't meant to come out. They had, which she knew because the couple's focus quickly switched to her. "Sorry, I… I didn't mean…"

"Harper has a theory that everyone ends up settling," Bastian said. "That love is an anomaly—"

"That's not what I—I only said it's not as common as people think."

"She said most people settle with respect and cohabitation."

"Wow," Roxie said, something saucy curving her lips. "That kind of turned me on."

"My Lola loves a cynic."

"Also known as a realist."

Zairn let that one slide. "There's all kinds of people out there, some do settle. That's an unrefuted fact."

"Thank you, Mr. Patronizing." Roxie leaned a little closer. "Harper, honey, I was you. I still am you. Sometimes. People do settle. I believe that a hundred percent."

"That's exactly what I just said."

Roxie ignored her husband. "Not everyone. Some. Not all. I was settling with my ex before Z. I didn't know it at the time, not exactly. He's an amazing guy. Smart. Funny. On the fast track, or some kind of track, I don't know."

"And that's the first time Lola didn't lead with his penchant for suicide."

"His penchant for—"

"Porter does have a penchant for suicide—given he's a prosecutor going after a mob boss—but that's beside the point."

"What is your point, Lola? That no guy measures up to me? That's public knowledge, babe. Why'd you think you have so much security?"

"Your many, many admirers are my posse now, friend. My Delights, my Crimsettes—"

"My Crimsettes—"

"Formerly," Roxie said, nudging him with a shoulder when he got closer. Her friend still leaned across the table. "The wheels turn in his world because I power the engine."

"You power something." Zairn nipped his wife's waist, bringing her body backward into his embrace. "My Empress."

"It's been almost two years, right? Since you got together."

"Since we met."

"I've never met a couple who…"

"Still want each other?" Roxie asked. "It's why some of us have to look so long. It does happen, and not just with us."

Some of the people she'd met at the Hunt anniversary party were more than just settling.

"I didn't really think about it, not until… I don't think you're settling."

"You don't have to settle either, honey. You deserve the real thing. Honestly? I'd say unless it's real, there's just no point. I'd definitely rather have lived my life alone than spent the whole thing with Porter."

"Sure about that, Lo? Could've got you all the way to the White House."

"If I wanted the White House, Skippy, I'd have the White House. I wouldn't need a man to get me there."

"If any woman is capable," Bastian said. "Roxie's probably our best bet."

"I'd have no problem serving under her," Zairn drawled with such innuendo that Roxie laughed.

"You could be First Lord."

"I'll be your first anything, baby."

It wasn't just that they weren't settling, they still had fun. Someone could be forgiven for thinking they were in the early throes of a new relationship. If this was what they were like now, what were they before?

"I suppose it's important to appreciate each other in private," she said. "It must be difficult to have the whole world watching."

"Oh, we're used to that. When Roxiverse airs, the scrutiny will only grow."

"And you're okay with that?"

"It's what we signed up for. Now with the wedding out of the way, we don't have to worry about faking it so often."

"Faking it?"

"Z and my problem was the opposite to yours and Bastian's. You're faking being together… with sex. Z and I had to fake not being together… with sex."

"With sex makes a big difference," Zairn said.

Roxie half rolled her eyes. "You don't know the difference between together and not together."

"Not when it comes with sex."

"Casanova tends to progress things in his own way, his own time. To hell with the rest of us."

"If I didn't do what I did, we'd still be playing phone tag, Lo."

Roxie raised one concessionary shoulder. "I'll give you that."

"When it's love, you forgive," Zairn said, bowing to kiss Roxie's shoulder. "There are knocks, but when it's forgive or walk away forever…"

"We don't do too well with the walk away part." Roxie sighed on a whole body bump against her husband. "He's only being nice to me because he's leaving me."

"Leaving you?"

"I'm going back to New York tomorrow," Zairn said. "Alone."

"Why alone?"

Bemoaned, Roxie sighed. "I have an appointment with a global audience."

"Roxiverse is picking up the pace. Lo's in LA for another week, then off to Boston," Zairn said. "Preliminaries are out of the way—"

"So, hey, Harper, you want to come with me to CollCom tomorrow?"

CollCom was—"The CollCom Complex?" Owned by the massive global-dominating media conglomerate? "I don't—I never…"

"It's not as scary as it sounds. There are so many people you should meet."

Glancing over her shoulder, Bastian smiled at her. "Could be fun."

Yeah, or terrifying. "I have work. Calls to make and—"

"You can do that from CollCom, or we have a whole squad of people geared up to do whatever you need. It's no problem."

But she… Could be fun… terrifying… informative.

A door closed elsewhere in the suite.

Roxie sprang upright like a meerkat on alert. "Are

we being robbed? My husband's too pretty for jail, so I'll be the one kicking your asses!"

"Since we lifted the embargo, this place is like Times Square," Zairn murmured.

Bastian laughed. "That why you're going back to Manhattan?"

"For a break?" In one of the most densely populated cities on earth? "Could be."

"It's just us," a disembodied female called.

Roxie gasped and leaped to her feet just as that female entered the dining room.

"Oh, Jane!" Rushing over, she pulled the woman into her arms. "Oh, Janey-Jane. Jane. Jane! Oh, I've missed you!" Leaning back, Roxie stroked Jane's hair. "Oh, you're so pretty." She yanked her into another hug. "You are what I need! Here, on time, perfect, as always. I missed you! I love you! My Jane!"

"This could go on a while," Zairn informed them.

A blond guy came in behind the hugging women. Whoa, now that was a Hollywood pinup for sure. The epitome of LA personified stood right there with them. Would be great if his name was Oscar. Nah, that didn't suit him… Adonis would be a better fit.

"Come in and sit with us," Roxie said, releasing her friend to hurry back to the wine on the table. "We have so much catching up to do!"

Pouring another glass, it was serendipitous that they had spare. Though maybe that was by design if they had so many visitors.

"Good to see you, man," Zairn said to the pinup guy. "You look rested."

"You don't," the guy said.

"Yeah, well, marital duties, etc."

"Pulled that shift too, buddy," the guy said, "and I got a tan."

"Harder to screw outside around here. What with the buildings and masses of people hanging around."

The pinup's smile actually stole her breath. "Try harder next time."

"There's still a mile or two in this first wife," Zairn said. "So I'm told."

It was definitely getting hotter. With so many of these gorgeous guys around, they created their own tropical ecosystem.

"People keep asking how you're doing, honey," Roxie said, still pouring, ignoring the men. "I keep telling them, there's no way Jane lets Knox off that island before—" Roxie stopped, raised her head and slowly twisted to look back over her shoulder at the couple. "Oh my God."

"Don't…" Jane said, holding up a flat, horizontal hand to block Roxie as she squeezed her eyes shut. "Don't look at me."

The wine bottle went to the table. "Oh my God."

Pinup was intent. "Don't look at her."

"Oh My God."

Harper rested on Bastian to whisper, "Why does she keep saying that?"

"Because she knows something we don't know," Zairn answered and picked up the freshly poured wine to tip it into his wife's glass.

"Knows something that—"

"You're pregnant," Roxie's words were a rushed breath. "Oh my God, Jane—"

"Don't look at me! Stop looking at me!"

Roxie screamed, startling the room, and rushed back to hug her friend again. "Oh my God, honey, I am so happy for you!"

"I said if she looked at me she'd know," Jane whined to the guy at her shoulder. "She knows!"

"You are. You're pregnant!" Roxie squealed again and grabbed her friend's upper arms to match their eyes. "You did it? You peed on the stick!"

Jane nodded. "It's super early, we're not telling people."

"Of course we're not telling people," Roxie said, ushering her friend over to settle her in a chair. "No, this is just for us right now."

"Us?" Pinup asked, raising a brow.

"Yes, Knox," Roxie said, stroking Jane's hair again. "Us. You haven't been waiting years and years and years for this day. Jane and I have been waiting years and years and years." Roxie cupped the new beauty's face. "Oh, honey, you should've called me. We would've been there with you."

"We did just fine without an audience," Pinup said.

Uh, Knox, right, not Pinup.

Jane whispered, "We're not telling people."

"I love that it happened on the island," Roxie squeed. "It happened on the island, right?"

Jane nodded. "We thought about staying until… we got past the twelve weeks, you know, but…"

"Collier children get the best from conception to the grave."

"So Knox wanted you to see a doctor. Okay, maybe he gets points for that."

Knox. Wait… Knox Collier? Holy hell!

"You went on vacation with pregnancy tests?" Harper asked.

Roxie tipped back. "Jane barely goes from one room to the other without pregnancy tests. We've been waiting a long time for this!" Another squeal and Roxie sat by Jane to hug her again. "We need soft seats for baby names. And we need a birthing plan." Roxie pulled Jane onto her feet. "Harper, come around here…" The brunette blew a kiss to her husband. "We need virgin cocktails for the new momma, Casanova. Oh, this is so exciting!"

As the others filtered out, she stood with Bastian. "Should we go?"

"Do you want to go?"

"They're your friends. I wouldn't want to…"

"Sweet, when Roxie Kyst wants rid of you, you know." He linked their fingers. "And they're your friends too."

New friends on a new adventure. This was her most interesting birthday weekend yet.

THIRTY-SIX

Bastian

BASTIAN TOSSED HIS pager to his desk and took his phone from the top drawer. At the end of the week, he was more than ready to submerge himself in Sweet Harper again.

She'd forced them out of their suite Tuesday morning. Much against his will. Those four nights with her meant more to him than any of his own birthdays. Given his own way, they'd still be there. Maybe he'd sneak her back tonight and see how long she'd let him keep her this time.

That day, he'd tried to get her on the phone but she'd been unavailable. Unavailable? No one was unavailable for him. Except Harper. Typical that the person he wanted to speak to most didn't reciprocate his need. Business was important, but not more important than her. Though he had a squad of people to take care of his, Harper was on her own. In that way, her responsibility was greater than his.

Friday night meant they'd made it through

another week. As soon as he finished up, he'd go to her place. All week she'd resisted getting together. He was no stranger to a hectic schedule, sustaining that took a lot of effort and dedication. Good thing he was the right guy to ease her burden.

"You have a visitor," Tina's voice came through the intercom.

"I'm on my way out. You should get going too."

His office door opened and his mother came in. No saying no to Carolyn Hunt.

"What happened?" Carolyn demanded.

That didn't narrow the field of possibilities. "Give me a clue, Mom."

"I thought you were going to marry that girl."

"That girl?" he asked, retrieving his wallet from the drawer to slide it into his pocket.

"Harper! She was beside herself. She's a strong one—"

"What's wrong with Harper?"

Urgency drove him around the desk to bear down on his mother.

"I knew something was wrong at lunch on Tuesday, Harper wasn't herself. If there was a problem, you should've told us. Your sister cried! She's beside herself. It took me an hour to calm her down."

"Tell me what happened!"

A knock interrupted.

Harper peeked around the door. He'd never seen such an incredible, and relieving, sight.

"Tina told me to come in," Harper said. "She's heading out."

"Thank goodness you're here," Carolyn said. "Yes, you two should talk."

"Mom…"

Ignoring his warning, Carolyn pulled him down to kiss his cheek. "Please talk."

His mom crossed the room to kiss Harper and say something in her ear. God, the woman didn't know when to stop. The door couldn't close behind the matriarch quickly enough. Though he wouldn't put it past her to be loitering in his executive foyer.

"Saved me a trip," Bastian said. "I was on my way to yours."

"This office is bigger than my father's house," Harper said going to the vast windows. "I bet you can see my office from here."

"You had lunch with my mother?"

His mother wasn't known for overreacting. The fact she'd raced over to berate him didn't bode well.

"On Tuesday," she said over her shoulder. "I told you that on the phone."

"And today?"

"We met for a drink a couple of hours ago." All exuberance, Harper bounded across the room to drop into his chair. "I should've come here sooner, we could've added your desk to the list of places you've acquainted me with."

"What's wrong with right now?" he said. "Come here."

"If only," she said. "I've got somewhere to be."

"We have a function tonight? Thank God I'm free."

So sad that even if he wasn't, he'd clear the calendar for her.

But she wasn't teasing.

She pulled herself in at the desk and spread her hands on it. "You are free. Completely free," she said. "You're officially off the clock. Permanently."

Alarm tightened his gut. "Meaning?"

"We should've spoken about it at the hotel, but it was my birthday and I... suppose I enjoyed the illusion."

"Illusion?"

"I love spending time with your mom, and your sister, they're incredible people. We can't lie to them anymore, Bastian. It's not fair. My mother wants you over at the house. Adara's talking about you in the wedding party like it's a done deal. We've filled our allotted time."

"Our allotted time?"

"We've done everything we said we would. My birthday was a cherry on top. I appreciate everything you've done for me. Everything."

"What are you saying?"

"You're off the hook. We're done."

"We're done?"

"We said we were together for a month. A month is over. It's pumpkin time."

"Over?"

"Your mom and Keely wanted to make arrangements for the vacation in August. I had to tell them we were done. I would've anyway, but… I couldn't let them make arrangements with me, or for me, when I knew I wouldn't be around."

She got up to come join him.

"Just like that?" he asked. "We're done?"

"You're free, Bastian," she said, widening her smile. "Go out there free and single, have some fun. Get back to your life without the crazy chick you met in a basement." She held out her hand. "Thank you, Bastian. I've had the time of my life. You're an incredible human being and the best man I've ever known. Thank you."

He bypassed her hand to touch her temple and ducked to kiss the top of her head.

"Thank you, Harper."

What else could he do but accept her position? Superficially at least. Done didn't mean done. Not to him.

"We want different things." They want—"That's what I told your mother." Slowly she lifted her hand to his face. "Show me," she whispered.

The smiling, bouncing woman revealed a flicker of something behind the impervious exterior.

If he pushed, she'd run a mile. His instinct was to grab hold and tell her every truth within him. It wouldn't help. This was the long game. And he'd play it through, even if she didn't know it.

Obliging her, he smiled, and her thumb moved against his cheek. "Goodbye, Bastian."

"Call me if you need anything," he said, taking her hand from his face to kiss her knuckles.

She nodded but her smile faltered. Immediately she turned away as if to hide it. Too late, he'd seen it. Never one to draw out discomfort, she went straight to the door and... though she paused, she didn't look back, just slipped out of his life.

THIRTY-SEVEN

DAVIS SCOTT NEVER missed a chance to promote his own self-importance. Hence why they were in the midst of a party celebrating Scott Solutions turning thirty. Yep, it was the business's birthday… Was there going to be cake?

Every client, past and present, had been invited to the hotel ballroom, hired to accommodate them and every contact in their proverbial rolodexes. Not as flashy as a Grand Hotel ballroom, but it did the job.

Adara and Carnell were on the dance floor, her mother and father networked with every new face. Damon and Charissa had disappeared somewhere a while ago. Judging by how they'd been recently, they were either screaming in each other's faces or ripping their clothes off.

Life ticked along.

Harper put her empty glass aside.

"Would you like another drink?" her date, Donald, asked.

"Yes, thank you."

And keep 'em coming. How was she back here again so soon? Life teased her with happiness only to remind her of the true order. She was the woman who couldn't keep a man, yep, that had been proven once again.

"Wait here," Donald said. "I'll be right back."

They'd seen each other a couple of times that week. Donald was a pleasant enough man to spend time with but standing there examining the smiling, glamorous faces present, her thoughts returned to the man she hadn't seen for two weeks. Memory had tormented her with him over and over. She couldn't catch a break.

Time to distract herself. Marcie Weathers wore a salmon dress that was four sizes too large. The woman had successful gastric band surgery, yet hadn't sprung for the wardrobe to match.

Matthew Huggett was here. The youngster couldn't be more than fourteen but he stood there rigid, struggling to project the image of a suave businessman in a designer suit. Had Bastian been the same at that age? Had Bastian always been discerning? Always been astute and perceptive? Or was it something he'd made a conscious choice to work on?

So much for distraction.

"Harper?"

She turned with the expectation of facing another of her father's clients. The fact that he sounded like Bastian was nothing unusual. She often heard his voice for no reason.

Except this time there was a reason. It was him. It was actually...

"Bastian, hi. I didn't think... What are you doing here?"

"I got an invite," he said.

No surprise, damnit, she should've considered

the possibility.

"You did?" Harper smiled. There were so many people in this room. So many people watching. Just like the night they met. Though she hadn't understood his confidence then. "You didn't have to accept it."

That wasn't bitchy just, relevant. What had he been thinking?

"I didn't have anything else to do tonight," he said. "It's important to support local business."

"Ah! Bastian!"

Adara rushed up to kiss both of Bastian's cheeks.

"It's good to see you," he said, shaking Carnell's hand.

"We've missed you," Adara said. "Did Harper tell you about her award?"

"Award?"

"For charitable services," Adara said. "There's an award ceremony next month."

"Congratulations," Bastian said.

During the Bastian drought, she kept telling herself that her mental picture of him was exaggerated. That she was making him a big deal when he wasn't a big deal. He was a man. Like any man. But, boy, she'd been low balling it.

He was taller, broader, prouder than she remembered. Had she really shared a bed with this guy? No way. A guy like that wouldn't look her way twice. Their brief time together seemed surreal. Like a dream she'd conjured to placate her ego.

Adara was talking about trouble with her wedding venue. Bastian listened intently, his focus absolute on Adara. See, they were strangers, they didn't have time together, they had a scheme. Cooked up as some kind of charity to combat her pitiful life.

The reality of what they were slapped her right across the face when a stunning five eleven blonde joined their group by sliding her hand inside Bastian's elbow.

"Everyone this is Audine Slivinski," Bastian said. "These are my friends, Adara and her fiancé Carnell, and her sister Harper."

Audine shook hands with them. Polite. Personable.

Adara's sister. Is that how he'd just introduced her? Adara's sister? They'd got naked together but she'd been slotted into a social space beneath her sister? They only knew each other because of her.

"What do you do?" Adara asked Audine.

"Can't you tell by looking at her," Carnell mumbled, earning himself a not-so-discreet shove from his fiancée.

"I'm a model," Audine said.

"Drink." Donald joined the group and handed her a glass. Ah, redemption. She downed half the contents. "Donald," he introduced himself to Bastian and Audine.

"Donald's an insurance broker," Adara said. "A successful one."

Bless her.

Her sister was trying to help yet somehow managed to make her feel worse. Luckily that was the moment Damon started gesturing for her attention from across the room. Luckily? Had she ever thought that word would precede Damon's name?

"Excuse me," she said, putting her glass into Adara's hand and leaving the group to get to Damon. "What's up?"

"I need to talk to you," he said, grabbing her arm.

She stayed put. "What's wrong?"

Damon sighed. "It's over."

"I don't understand what—"

"It's over, Charissa and me, it's over."

"What? Oh my God." Her hands fell to his chest

when she stepped closer. "Are you okay? What happened?"

Damon took hold of her other arm too. "I couldn't do it anymore. We've not been happy for a while."

"I'm so sorry," Harper said. "You have to do what's right for you both. Is she okay?"

"I don't know," Damon said. "I'm pretty shaken up."

"Sure," she said. "Of course you are."

"Harper," Bastian's voice came from behind her again.

Though she turned, Damon didn't let go.

Damon's expression hardened. "What's he doing here?" he demanded. "I thought you were with Don."

"I am," Harper said. "Bastian was invited." And not by her, so what was she doing? "Bastian this isn't the best time."

"Can I tempt you into a dance?"

"We're busy," Damon said.

"Go upstairs to the lounge," Harper said. They'd used this hall so often that they'd had cause to use the offices upstairs too. "I'll come up in a minute."

"Alone?"

"Yes," she said. "Go."

Damon lingered long enough to glare at Bastian again. Okay, yes, everyone saw it. Grumpy. Grumpy. A moment later he did as told and disappeared into the stairwell.

Folding her arms, she turned to Bastian. "What's up?"

He tried to take her hand, but she tucked it out of the way. Contact would not make this moment any easier.

"You don't want to dance?"

"You should dance with Audine," she said. "I

have to help a friend."

"A friend? You're being sucked back into Damon's orbit again?"

"I'm with Donnie now."

"With him?" Bastian said. "How long have you been seeing him?"

"A week."

Though not really, to say "*seeing him*" was kind of a stretch.

"Are you sleeping with him?"

Who in the hell did this guy think he was? What gave this gorgeous billionaire the right to ask Adara's sister questions?

The demand provoked her frown. "You want to know if I'm having sex with Donnie? What would Audine think about that? She's dazzling, she suits you."

In her aim to be amiable, she won herself a shot of his scowl.

"She suits me?"

"Yes," Harper said, dropping her arms to her sides. Bastian was a handsome man, which made it oddly easy to resign herself to their differences. "You make a beautiful, sophisticated couple. Your kids will be gorgeous."

"Our kids?"

"I'm just playing," Harper said, smoothing his lapel. "I know you don't have time for those things yet."

"What things?"

"Getting too invested. Your priority is your business, and, believe me, I can understand that."

"You look beautiful."

Her black linen dress hung on a boat neck and grazed her mid-thigh. The compliment was a formality, she got that.

"Thank you."

"You always look beautiful," he said.

Okay, he didn't have to lay it on thick. "Charmer." She smiled. "I should get upstairs to—"

"You didn't answer my question."

"Your question?"

"Are you sleeping with Donald?"

She couldn't understand the origin or purpose of his dark edge.

"Is that relevant?"

In public, Bastian tended to be subdued. Until then anyway.

Tension radiated off him with such ferocity, it was concerning.

"I need to know."

She rested a hand on his forearm. "What's the matter? Has something happened? Is it Carolyn, or Keely? Is your father okay?"

"This is not about my blood family."

"Good," she said. "I'm glad they're okay. Tell them I said hello."

She left Bastian to enter the stairwell. Less than three stairs up, her arm was grabbed, she was yanked back and pinned flush against the wall, the perpetrator's forearms planted either side of her head.

Bastian.

"Look at me, Sweet," he growled, his breath fogging her forehead.

She blinked up. Darkness hovered around him, closing in, somehow shrinking the world. He lowered himself within reach of her mouth, eyes probing hers just before he joined their lips.

Visceral memory flooded her body with a rush of heat.

This.

Him.

Bastian kissed her with an urgency that slammed her with another memory. Walking out of his office had been the longest, most difficult trek of her life.

Leaving was right. Ending their agreement was the logical, honorable thing to do.

His arms swept around her, stretching her to the very tips of her toes to hold her close, trapping her between him and the wall with a grip so strong, her ribs hurt. When his tongue touched her lip, she opened to welcome its arrival. Her own urgency translated to her fists locking in his hair, holding him right where she needed him. She wasn't done. This could be the last chance she had to do this. Not kissing him goodbye in his office was one of her biggest regrets.

And why hadn't she?

Because that kiss would've become this: desperation.

THIRTY-EIGHT

PANTING, SHE TORE her hands from his hair to urge his mouth from hers. "Wait…"

How did they fall back into this without skipping a beat?

He kissed her again. "No."

She pushed back. "Knight—"

"I missed you," he groaned. "I've missed you so goddamn much, Sweet."

"What is happening? We can't—we can't do this," she whispered, ducking away from his approaching mouth again. "We broke up."

"We didn't," he said, relaxing a little to stroke her hair.

"We did. Let go."

"We didn't get started," he said. "I want to, we need to… We're starting now."

"What are you talking about?" Had he fallen and hit his head? Was this a time warp? "Our lives have moved on. I have Donnie and will never measure up to Audine."

"This is our first date."

"See," Harper said. "Give her a chance. This could be the real thing for you, no more pretending."

"Have you slept with him?" he asked. "Answer me."

"No," she said, hands dropping to his shoulders. "Of course not."

"Don't."

"What?"

"Don't let him into your bed."

"You don't have to worry about me," she said, stroking his jacket.

He backed away. "I do worry about you. I've been worried for two weeks."

A chill crept across her shoulders. "You didn't call."

"You needed time to miss me," Bastian said. "I thought you'd reach out."

"Didn't we…" she said. "You're a popular, successful man. We both said it was over."

"We both didn't."

The darkness returned. What did that mean? With a meter between them, the ice of awareness crept higher.

Damon appeared at the top of the first flight of stairs. "Harpy!"

"Sorry," she said and glanced at Bastian.

He took a last look then went back to the party. Their conversation didn't seem finished, though it was probably for the best.

"What's going on?" Damon asked.

From one ex to another. At least there wouldn't be kissing with the second one. Ick. That was a hard no. She should think the same about Bastian, except…

"Nothing," she said, choosing not to dwell. "I'm coming."

She ascended the stairs, following Damon into a room more like a lounge than an office.

"That bastard giving you a hard time?" Damon asked.

"No," she said, sinking into one of the couches. "What happened with you and Charissa?"

He sat beside her. "She's talking to Adara, I don't know where we go from here."

"If you love her," Harper said, "fight for her."

"It's not that easy."

"It is. If you love her, nothing else matters. Work it out."

"She wants to get married."

And that surprised him?

"That's good," she said. "You should commit to each other."

"She wants to get married because Adara is getting married."

"Maybe that was the catalyst, but most women share that dream."

"You never wanted it."

Them? He was thinking about them?

"We never discussed it," she said, grateful for that.

"Did you want to?"

"I didn't think about it," she answered.

Almost repulsed by the reminder they'd ever been a thing, she certainly hadn't imagined a wedding with him.

"You don't even care that Adara's getting married. Most sisters would freak without their own serious relationship."

Ignoring her meltdown at the engagement party, she chose strength over vulnerability now. And where did that strength come from? Not her. From the man who'd saved her.

"You were always a straight shooter," Damon said, resting his hand on her knee.

"Charissa's being a straight shooter. She wants to get married, she's made that clear. You can't ask her to be any plainer than that."

"Yeah."

"You don't want to marry her?"

"Come on," Damon said. "Charissa's hot but it's a whole different ballgame living with her."

"Then breaking up is for the best," Harper said. "If the relationship isn't going the way both of you want, you should move on."

"Like you and Hunt," he said. "Was he a prick?"

And it was his business, how? "I don't want to talk about Bastian."

"Guys like that think they own the world. You'd never be happy with a man so overbearing."

Ha! Pot? Hello, Kettle.

Though that was hardly the time to point it out.

"We were good together," he said. "Where did we go wrong?"

Finally, an easy question. "You slept with another woman."

Damon smiled. "Always so straight talking."

His hand slid up her thigh. Oh, uh, no, this was—no way.

"Don't," she said, pushing it down.

"We were good together, Harpy," he said, leaning closer. "No expectation, no disappointment."

"Indifference," she said, using Bastian's word. "We weren't good together, we were just together."

"We were a team," he said, reaching for her face but she ducked back. "We were good."

On alert, caution tingled. "Damon…"

He lunged, putting his weight over hers. One problem at a time. She had her work cut out trying to avoid his mouth.

A scream startled him up. And there was Charissa and Adara in the doorway. Of course.

"You're having sex with your ex!" Charissa exclaimed.

Uh, no, glancing down confirmed they were both fully clothed.

"We're not," Harper said. "He's not."

"How long has it been going on?" Charissa demanded as though Harper hadn't spoken at all. "I should've known! This is why you broke up with Bastian, isn't it?"

"No," Harper said, finding her feet.

Someone took her hand. Damon. Damn Damon right there on his feet next to her.

"I'm sorry you had to see this," Damon said.

Inverted déjà vu. The last time she and Charissa's positions were switched. The view from this side was not welcome.

"Nope. Nope. Nope," Harper said, fighting Damon for control of her hand. "I'm tagging out."

Except the jerk wouldn't let her go.

"I can't believe this," Charissa howled and spun on her heels.

Adara, and her outrage, went after her friend.

Why would no one hear her?

"What are you doing?" Harper hissed at Damon, snatching her hand away.

Didn't matter now they'd lost their audience.

"You've got me back," he said as though she should be grateful.

Ew. No. Definitely not.

"I don't want you back. I will swear to the highest heaven that the one thing I don't want now, or ever, is you back."

"I know I hurt you. You've struggled without me,

I've seen that but that's over now. I'm yours again."

"No!" Harper said. "I'm not interested. Stay away from me."

"Is this about Donald?"

"No," she said, forgetting for a moment who the hell that was. "This is about me."

"You've got me." And he couldn't be more proud of himself. "I'm all yours now. I'll talk to Donnie. Explain about us."

When he tried to get closer, she backed away. "There is no us."

"We can talk about this at home," he said. "In your bedroom, we—"

"Charissa lives with Adara," she said of the woman who'd been sharing his bed less than a day ago. "You're not creeping back into my bed."

"Davis will understand."

Her father was not the problem. He was so far, far away from the problem.

"There's nothing to understand," she said. "We're not together."

"Davis went nuts when we split. Do you want to tell him you've lost a second business interest this month? We walk into that house together and—"

"Everyone will assume you and Charissa split because of me."

He shrugged. "Maybe."

"This is nuts! Your relationship falls apart and now it's my fault?"

All she'd done was get out of bed and somehow this had become her day.

"Davis—"

"Enough," Harper said, retreating. "I'm not walking in there and covering you. I'm sick of these games."

She was done with this. With him. With family.

With drama. She would not let her life careen out of control again. The wheel was hers and Damon was not close to the kind of man she wanted riding at her side.

"Where are you going?" Damon called. "What are you doing?"

"Moving out," she exclaimed and got the hell out of there.

Charissa must've made an entrance because when she opened the party door, more than a few people were whispering.

She didn't care.

Honestly, she was done.

At the coat check, she handed the slip to the attendant. She'd travelled in her father's car, and hadn't packed a house key. Backing up to peek into the party, she could see her parents, Adara, and Carnell comforting a sobbing Charissa. Yeah, that was a scene to avoid.

"Harper?"

Ah, Donald, where had he come from? Good thing he had, she'd forgotten about him.

"Sorry, something's come up and I have to go."

"What's going on?"

"It's not important," she said. "Look, Donnie, you're a great guy but this was never going to be serious. Go and enjoy the party."

"Are you sure?" he asked. "We could be good together."

"I just don't have the time, and I've been more than burned by men this year. I'm taking a break from romance, from all of it."

"Give me a call when your break's over," he said then kissed her cheek before returning to the party.

"Ms. Scott."

Ah, she went back to the counter and wrapped her shawl around her shoulders.

Now what?

The only one who might be willing and able to bail her out—

"Sweet?"

Right on time.

Striding toward her from the party, he might as well have been on a noble steed.

"Bastian," she said, the corners of her lips rising.

He frowned. "Is it true?"

"I have no idea what you've heard but I'll go with no. How much money do you have on you?"

"Money?"

"Give me your wallet."

He handed it over the moment he was within reach. "What happened? What do you need?"

"I don't have any money on me," she said, opening his wallet. "Just a lip gloss and a cellphone."

"It's an open bar. Why do you need money?"

"I need to get out of here and I can't go home."

Before she could slip any bills from his wallet, he snagged it back, replacing it with his valet ticket.

"Get the car, I'll be right back."

"But…" she said.

He brushed his fingertip through her hair, flashed his dimple, and disappeared back into the party.

Okay. So that was…

Despite being clueless, she didn't have a whole lot of options, and it was Bastian.

Bastian!

She'd do as told.

THIRTY-NINE

"THAT GUY'S A piece of work," Bastian said after her recitation of the evening's events.

In Bastian's den, on his big, deep couch, the pressures of life and drama of the night seeped from her bones. Shoes off, feet tucked under her, she could finally be herself again.

"I want to say he's hurting," Harper said. They'd made love on this couch. Whoa, what? That memory came out of nowhere. "But I'm not sure he's capable."

"He's scum and using you to excuse that."

"Was Audine upset? I can call her and apologize if—"

"Audine's nothing," he said. "I didn't want to come alone to your father's event because it would've been too obvious."

"Too obvious that what?"

"That I came to see you," he said. She inhaled to respond but he carried on. "I'm not coming on to you. We won't have sex. We're friends and I'm here because you need support, that's it..." Well, that was clear.

"Though I guess if you really want to have sex, I could probably—"

She threw a cushion at his head. "Thank you for bailing me out. Again."

"There's no time limit on you staying here," he said. "No pressure. We can be roommates until you get settled. Do you plan to go back to your father's?"

She shook her head. "I'm tired of playing the same game and putting up with all the dramas that are never instigated by me. Adara and Carnell will be moving after they're married. God knows what will happen with Damon and Charissa now. I don't want any part of it."

"It's Sunday tomorrow," he said. "Sleep in, then I'll cook you breakfast."

"I'll pick up my things on Monday while they're all at work. I should be able to find something temporary but I have back-to-back meetings Monday afternoon—"

"You're staying here," he said. "We can have your office transferred to my building too."

"Transfer my office?"

"It's an option."

And an appealing one. Imagine a clean break. And no chance of Damon wandering in at will. The idea kind of sold itself.

Except… "I can't monopolize your home and your business."

"You're at my home because you're my friend. And I'll lease you the office space, it's business."

"For what? Like a dollar?" His pure heart shone right on through. "You're a good man, Bastian, but I won't take advantage of you like that."

"You can work from here, until you're ready to agree to the lease. And I'll take fifty cents."

"You drive a hard bargain." She wouldn't do that, but this was a big house, there'd be room for an office, a temporary one at least. "Won't I dent your social life?"

"Women?" he said. "I never bring women back here."

"Why not?"

"This is my space," he said. "It's private."

That was honest, yet, somehow, he missed the contradiction.

She smiled. "I'm here."

"You're my space too," he said. "And just as private."

"If I'm staying here, I'll need a safe space as well."

"From me?"

From her white knight? No.

"Not from you." Bolster that honesty. "I'm leaving my parents because I want to move on. I want a quiet life. Only my own drama and no one else's… This is me trying to find a nice way of saying 'don't let my family in here.' Am I a horrible person?"

"No and done," he said, standing up. "Pick a bedroom and I'll get you something to wear. Some of your things are still here."

"My body lotion," she said, taking his hand when he offered to pull her from the couch.

"You're not getting that," he said. "That stays in my room. I've looked everywhere, you can't buy that stuff—"

"I make it," she said, following him through the house and up the stairs.

On the mezzanine, he stopped. "Do you want the master?"

He had no cause to be this generous. Being so altruistic, it was a wonder he had any money left. He'd swooped in and saved her at the engagement party, and done the same that night, offering his bed to his own detriment.

She touched his face, grazing her thumb across

his dimple. Even that couldn't convince her he was real.

"I'll take next door."

"Okay," he said. "On the far side, my room before yours."

She nodded. "It's your house, roomie."

He took her hand and kissed her knuckles. "Our house. Feel free to consider this place yours. You'll be authorized for the house, the company, and the vehicles immediately."

"Knight…" she said. "Stop trying so hard. You are always my knight in shining armor."

He kept her hand when she tried to back away.

"I've lost you once," he said, kissing her knuckles then releasing her.

What did that mean? She could never figure men out. In the shadow of this hallway, her skin quaked. Never in her life had she felt so safe with a person, or in a location. There, with him, was home. It felt good to be back.

"Thank you, Bastian, for everything."

On her final word, she left him before she did something audacious, like follow him into the master. Was this out of the frying pan? The temperature was definitely rising.

FORTY

"DAMON THE DICKWAD." Ah, trust Roxie to get right to the point. "You should kick his ass. No, I'm sending Ballard to kick his ass. That's what he's paid for, kicking ass."

Working in Bastian's house was easy. In anticipation of her needs, he'd had an office set up for her. It wasn't there in the morning and then just was when she got home on Tuesday afternoon. Just like that. Poof. It materialized from nowhere in an invisible plume of imaginary smoke. There was no telling the room had once been a bedroom. In a few short hours, it had been completely transformed, decorated and everything, given renewed purpose. If only it was that straightforward for humans.

Yes, it was Saturday, but she should be working. This was a quick break. A short one. Except... this was Roxie. Ignoring a call from Roxie just wasn't possible. Neither was cutting any conversation short. That was okay, she'd go with it, they had some catching up to do.

"Thank you, but it's okay. This week has been...

It's strangely invigorating to change everything about your routine."

Roxie laughed. "Are you hyperventilating?"

"Only three or four times a day."

"That's an improvement."

"It helps to hold onto a constant." Which right then was Bastian. "How's your sanity?"

"On a different continent. He's fine, we make it work," Roxie said. "No skipping the important stuff, what gave Dickwad Damon the right to kiss you?"

"He didn't make contact." Not for lack of trying. "He just threw himself on me."

"Without finesse, like it was a done deal? Would that have made a difference?"

Her friend's flat tone betrayed the obvious answer.

"No. God, no. How could he even think…? It's just wrong. It's disgusting. I feel violated and he didn't even make contact."

"Men like that believe they're God's gift. Guarantee he doesn't even see what he did wrong. As soon as you uttered a word to him, he assumed all was forgiven and you wanted him again."

That couldn't be further from the truth.

"I don't think my mom believes me."

"That there was nothing going on between you and Damon?"

"My dad appeared in my office first thing Monday. He actually came to the ground floor to talk to me."

"To check you were okay? That's something. He cares."

"To let me know it would be okay if me and Damon got back together."

"What a treat." Sarcasm alert. "Just what you needed, his blessing."

"It gets better. He said it's okay for me to get back with Damon, providing Bastian isn't still an option. Bastian would be a good fit for the family and whatever I could do…"

"Oh, wow."

"Right?"

"Did you tell your dad Bastian is an option?"

"No," she said, pushing back in her plush leather chair, rocking side to side. "Bastian's not an option. Not like that."

"Please, the guy took care of you, towed you home, gave you safety. And he's a good lay. You said he was a good lay."

"Before," she said, licking her lips. "Not now. It's not like that this time. This time is purely platonic."

"Are you sharing a room?"

"No."

"Adjoining rooms?"

"No," she said and had to laugh.

"You sleep…"

"In the next room."

"The room next to his? So one night, you're really tired, you accidentally wander into the wrong—"

"Roxie!" This woman was all kinds of crazy, each endearing in itself. "We're not sleeping together. We're friends."

"Friends who live together."

"Yes."

"You're working in his house too?"

"My father showing on Monday was bad enough. When Damon came to my office on the Tuesday, I couldn't stand any more. I grabbed everything and came home."

"To the office Bastian set up for you, like he knew."

"That Damon wouldn't stay away?" she asked.

"Am I asking too much of Bastian? It is kind of rude. I've just moved into his life and taken over."

"No! You're friends, right? That's what friends do for each other. I'd do the same. If you want to live somewhere else, work somewhere else, pick a city and I'll make it happen. You don't have to rely on him if you don't want to."

"Oh, God, I'm an awful friend."

"What kind of friend would Bastian and I be if we left you in that mess? Have you talked to your sister?"

That dropped her shoulders a little. "I think she believes me. She said Charissa never will."

"Oh no, whatever will you do?" Roxie droned with flat humor.

"I'm not losing any sleep over Charissa."

"Adara is stuck in the middle. Not your fault."

No, it wasn't the fault of any Scott. Damon and Charissa's affair kicked off this drama a year ago. Adara was in the middle then too, but at least the couple were considerate enough to leave the continent for a while after the discovery of their indiscretion. This time Damon caused the drama all on his own, yet she was a guilty party? How was that fair? She'd done nothing wrong.

Except kiss Bastian in the stairwell. Yeah. They hadn't talked about that yet. Yet? When would be a good time to bring it up? Uh… never was the most appealing option.

"They're both still staying at the house, Adara will be hearing from them every day." Which wasn't fair. "And all she wants to talk about is wedding stuff, but…"

"This is taking precedence. She'll want you involved, but want Charissa involved too."

Right then, the two women couldn't be in the same place at once.

What a mess.

Personally? She had no beef with Charissa. The affair mess that ended her and Damon's relationship last year barely flickered. Harper was so over that. If anything, she should thank the woman for taking Dickwad Damon off her hands. Unfortunately, just because *she* wouldn't start fights didn't mean there wouldn't be any. Somehow her presence incited them without her uttering a word. Would this end well? There was just no way.

"I won't make it difficult for her. She's innocent in all of this."

People brought drama to the Scott house. Boy, was she glad to be out of it. Yes, she wanted to help her sister, to embrace this happy time, but her and Charissa in the same place wouldn't end happy.

"What did you say about Bastian?"

"To Adara? Nothing."

"She didn't ask where you were staying?"

"I said I was with a friend. He is a friend. He's dating…" What was her name? "Audine."

"He is not dating Audine. That wasn't a thing. It's nothing. Guys like him get dates like that, it just happens. It looks good. They're networking, they don't actually know each other. Not like you and Bastian know each other. Shit, Zairn is surrounded by women like her all the time and he's married."

"They were on a date."

Still, Roxie wasn't buying it. "You've been there a week, have you seen her? Heard him talking to her? About her?"

"No, but the guy owns a million hotels, I don't know where he is every minute."

"So you think they're having sex? Because sex is not love. Checked and verified by me, honey. Even if he's screwing her—he's not screwing her. I'll find out."

Panic came in a gasp. "What? No! Don't do that."

"I can be discreet. I'm discreet." That wasn't the first word that came to mind when considering Roxie's qualities. "Tina will know."

"Tina his—his assistant? No, who he has sex with is his business. It's not my business."

"I won't find out for you. I want to know for me and if I happen to share that information with you…"

She exhaled. "This is complicated enough. Please. Let Bastian live his life his way."

"Have you been spending time together?"

"We eat dinner. Talk about business. He's having red tape issues with ambiguous regulations, and an even more ambiguous regulations officer."

"Sounds about right. Red tape. Red tape. Do you just talk about his stuff?"

"No, he's had some great ideas about a charity concert I'm organizing and wants me to use a Grand location for a team building thing I have coming up."

They ate together, they laughed together, and every night they said good night between their bedroom doors. Sleeping wasn't as easy this time as it had been before.

Beyond anything else, he was the best friend she'd ever had. That didn't erase her memory of the pleasure, but that was in the past. Now they were roommates and that's how it would stay.

"What are you doing today?"

"Work," she said. "You?"

"My definition of work is different to yours."

That was true. "It is great having the office so close to my bedroom. I'll never have to see another soul again."

"No, no, no, you are not going to become a recluse. The club's open door for you. It doesn't have to be loud and busy, you're in LA, you can use our private pods. Take Bastian along or Keely."

"I don't think they know I'm…"

"Shacked up with Bastian?"

Roxie sure didn't make this easy. "My family don't know, why should his?"

"You have nothing to be ashamed of."

"It's not shame, we just don't need everyone in our business." And she didn't want them getting the wrong idea. Like Roxie's idea this was something more. "We're friends. That's it."

"Friends," Roxie stated though whether she agreed was dubious. "Friends is good."

"I am going downstairs to make some food, then I'll spend the day working. Bastian's still asleep." Or so she thought. "We won't even have to see each other."

"Friends," Roxie said again. "Friends is good."

FORTY-ONE

ROXIE WAS RIGHT, friendship was good. It was. Although her female friend hadn't sounded so convinced. Had she missed sarcasm? Was it just placation? Maybe she'd had other things to do and needed to get on with her day. That would be no surprise, Roxie had so much going on in her life all the time, it must be difficult to keep track of people. Major respect that the billionairess hadn't dropped her simply because she was working out of state.

Breakfast. What did she want for breakfast?

It was the weekend so something nice, indulgent. Maybe there was some of their fresh fruit mousse leftover from dessert last night.

They'd cooked two nights that week. One night each. On the other nights when Bastian called dinnertime, she'd go downstairs to a set table and exquisite food just there, waiting for them.

What about after breakfast?

Maybe in the afternoon she'd use Bastian's gym in the basement. It was the basement, kind of because it should be below ground level yet it was half glazed to wells of light trapped in the sort of moat around it. Where did rich people get their ideas for architecture from? It was incredible.

Another great thing about working from home? She could do it in her jammies. After getting up, she'd brushed her teeth and hippity-hopped through to the office to check email. She could stop in the bedroom and change, but she was only going downstairs to forage, then she'd be back in her seclusion. And it was the weekend, why shouldn't she have a slouchy day?

She slid open the kitchen door and stopped. Dead. The room, which should've been empty, was not. Three women at the island and four men at the table all landed their focus right on her. Strangers. All of them. Unloading ingredients from boxes, it looked like.

Huh.

Okay.

Not good.

Bastian hadn't mentioned anything about guests.

The garage door to the kitchen opened and two more women appeared. Were they having a party? Everyone stared at her in her vest top and boy shorts; she hadn't so much as run a brush through her hair. Demanding an explanation wasn't her purview, this wasn't her house. As far as she knew, Bastian was still snoring upstairs. Did he know the kitchen was full of people? He could've given her a heads up that she'd wake to this.

"Hurry, hurry now, what's the delay?"

Oh, that was a voice she knew. The women in the doorway shifted and, yep, that was Carolyn Hunt. And, of course, Keely was right there behind her mother. Carolyn's jaw fell and the quiet of the tense moment was pierced by Keely's screech.

Keely ran across the room to hug her. "You're

back! You're back! You're back!" Keely chanted. "I'm so happy you're back! Back to having bags of sex with my devoted big brother! You're back!"

"Uh, excuse me," Harper managed to say and actually sounded calm.

How had she pulled off the miracle of composure?

She extricated herself from Keely's embrace and spun on the spot to hurry back the way she'd come. Picking up the pace, she took the stairs two at a time and ran straight into Bastian's bedroom, closing the door only to fall against it. And there he was, sleeping away. How could he be sleeping? Rushing across the room, she climbed onto the bed to kneel beside him and give him a shake.

"Bastian," she hissed. "Knight, wake up, please, Bastian."

"Mm, Sweet," he mumbled without opening his eyes. "Lie down."

His arm flopped around her, urging her onto her side. "Bastian."

He rolled back, pulling her to his chest. "Always what I want to wake up to."

Despite the growing storm in the kitchen, she laughed at just how tied up an unconscious Bastian could get her. There was nothing funny about the conspicuous lump pressing into her hip. To her shame, she enjoyed feeling it again, even if it was just a morning thing and nothing to do with her.

"Bastian—"

Keely flew into the room with Carolyn behind her. "Separate yourselves for like thirty seconds," Keely said, rushing to the end of the bed.

Carolyn joined her daughter, and the others from downstairs? Yeah, they were crowded on the threshold, not missing a thing.

This could not get any worse.

Okay, did she have to tempt fate like that? Stupid thoughts.

Bastian's hand slid under her vest and closed around her naked breast.

Keely laughed while no one else said a word, they were too busy grinning ear-to-ear. Wrestling with his hand could be a show, so she pinched his ribs and snagged his lower lip in her teeth because her other hand was sandwich meat.

He blinked open his eyes. Barely, but, yeah, there was movement, her teeth had done their work.

A lazy smile spread on his face. "Sweet—"

"Ah, stop, don't say any—we have an audience."

"An audience?"

He frowned and rolled only pausing when he figured out the location of his hand. Never one to miss an opportunity, he gave her a squeeze before withdrawing.

Bastian absorbed the scene as she sat up. "Why are my family watching us in bed?"

"The Keyes event is tomorrow, sweetheart," Carolyn said.

Scrubbing his hands over his face and into his hair, Bastian sat up. "I forgot."

"We see why," Keely said. "You're back together! This is great! You can be happy again!"

In vain, Bastian tried to temper expectations. "Keely don't get ahead of yourself."

"You're having sex," Keely said. "How can you have sex with the woman you love and not be back together?"

And the beauty truly meant that. Oh, boy.

Bastian tried to say something. "Keely—"

"We're taking it slowly," Harper said, snatching his hand. "We didn't expect to be outed so soon."

"We'll respect that," Carolyn said, putting an arm around a smiling Keely. "We'll leave you alone to get ready and see you downstairs."

Carolyn herded everyone out and closed the door leaving her and Bastian alone. In bed.

Bastian drew in a long breath. "Good morning."

As he lay back down, she collapsed with him, burying her face against his chest. "I'm sorry."

His fingers caught in her hair. "You didn't do anything wrong."

"It's my fault we've been dragged back into this charade."

"And mine for forgetting the event."

"I walked into the kitchen dressed like this, I froze."

"It's another one of my mom's charities. Everyone cooks, there are donations. Mom's remodeling her kitchen. When she asked to do it here, I didn't have a roommate. I would've asked you if—"

"You don't have to explain anything to me. I shouldn't have come up here. I panicked."

"It's okay."

The rhythm of his stroking hand calmed her. "It's not okay," she said. "We ended our charade so our families wouldn't be hurt; now we're back in it."

"What was the alternative?" he asked. "Do you want to tell them your ex sleazed on you thus forcing you from your family home?"

"No," she muttered.

"What's the harm? Hold my hand at dinner, that's all you have to do."

"It involved more than that the last time," she said, finding his eyes.

"I'll never pressure you."

Why was her heart beating so fast?

"I know," she answered. "But you saw how

excited Keely was—I don't want to hurt her."

"I'll worry about Keely."

"I don't want to disappoint her."

"Okay, then the only solution is marriage."

More laughter. In the moment, she pulled the covers down from his chest and spread her hand against him.

"I'd forgotten how incredible you are."

"A week with me reminded you?"

"Your body," she said. "Your personality's no picnic."

"Feel free to reacquaint yourself with any part of it."

"So gracious," she said, kissing his pec before rolling off the bed.

On a yawn, Bastian stretched and ran his hands into his hair as he sat up. "I'll grab a shower then join you downstairs."

"I had a day planned."

Stretching again, he got out of bed and tossed the duvet back, unconcerned about the obvious tent in his underwear.

Hmm, she might be drooling. Stop looking. Stop looking. Every experience she'd had with that particularly proud member replayed in the blink of her mind's eye. Over and over with a sweet, delectable, mouthwatering—

"Do you want to come with me?" he asked, crossing, arms open, herding her toward his ensuite.

"Bastian," she said, resting her fingertips on his chest when his hands landed on the bathroom doorframe, penning her in.

She leaned forward, pressing her nose to the center of his chest, inhaling the cozy, comfy, sleepy cocoon that still enveloped him. From her crown, his hand slid to the base of her skull, angling her face up.

"Don't kiss me," she whispered.

Vulnerability. Where did that come from? Suddenly, she was a raw, exposed nerve.

"Why not?" he asked, keeping hold of her skull, brushing his other index finger down her temple.

"I can't do this again," she murmured in her desperation. "Walking away nearly killed me, Bastian. I know it's wrong. I shouldn't—"

"So don't walk away," he said. "Stay."

"If only it was that easy," she said, touching his dimple before ducking under his arm, liberating herself.

Keep it together. She would get a rein on her horses, she would. This wasn't them. It was external factors, unforeseen things that they would get past. Somehow. They were friends, and that was how it had to stay. She couldn't endure another Bastian drought after such a feast, never again.

FORTY-TWO

Bastian

THE KEYES EVENT had been part of his life since before his memory began. He remembered unloading hampers of food for the kids when he was a kid himself. Charities from all around brought those they cared for, sick kids, those in poverty, survivors of abuse, the list went on. The full breadth of kids in need got pampered and spoiled on this one day of the year.

Yet this time, it was different. Harper was there, with them, with him. She manned the Hunt stall like she'd been one of them forever. Anyone seeing her with his mom or Keely would certainly think she was one of them.

She should be one of them.

After his family's home invasion, the prep and cooking took over and they finished late the previous night. Despite being exhausted when she retired to bed, Harper woke fresh as a daisy. Her enthusiasm for packing up and unloading at their stall encouraged optimism in everyone. How did she do it? Brighten everyone's day like that?

Event over, it was no surprise that after loading up a truck from a local shelter with leftovers, Harper slunk away.

He gave her a few minutes to decompress before going after her. Just around a corner, there she was, sitting on the fountain wall, feet dangling in the water.

Joining her, he sat, facing the other way.

"You okay?" he asked.

She leaned on him, resting her head against his arm. "I'm fine."

"You wandered away."

"Had some thinking to do."

"Thinking about what?"

"My business mostly."

"Business?"

"Yeah," she said. "I mostly do corporate events because that's where the money is. I need to support myself."

"Sure."

"Except there's no heart in it. I don't love it… I've spent so much time fighting for big enough jobs to give me some leeway to volunteer for the charity events… This is what I wanted to do with my life. There's something in all of us that we can share, that we should share."

"Start a nonprofit," he said.

She scoffed. "Yeah, right, where do I get the start-up? I don't have the foundation to—"

"Give me a number and you'll have it in an hour."

She stopped swishing her feet in the water to look at him. "Do you want to have sex with me?"

Just like her to be frank… and smell so amazing. "We're in a public park but the car's just around the corner…"

"Bastian," she said, linking their fingers. "We

can't go into business together. I can't take your money, not with things the way they are."

"What way's that?"

"I won't take advantage of you."

"I'm a big boy."

Her eyes dropped. Oh, fuck, he didn't need any encouragement.

"Things are complicated enough," she said. "We were fake together and broke up to save our families the heartbreak. My family's falling apart. I live in your house. I work from your home. And the cherry? Your family think we're together again… Do you really want to add a business partnership to that? What happens when things get back to normal?"

"Normal?" he asked. "What does that look like? Are you going back to your parents?"

"No," she said. "Another reason I can't take your money. I need mine to get myself somewhere to live."

"I told you to live with me."

She laughed. "Forever?"

If his luck was in. "Yeah," he said. "Why not?"

"This will blow over eventually. Your family will realize we're not together and you can be free of me… again."

"I don't want to be free of you, Harper."

"You're very generous," she said.

She didn't get it. Did he need to PowerPoint it for her? He wanted to open his mouth and lay the truth out bare. But he couldn't. There was too much going on in her life. If she freaked, she'd distance herself. That wasn't happening. Her safety was more important than his urges, his craving to pull her close.

"We're friends," he said. "The offer's always there. No shortage of cash over here, Sweet."

She exhaled. "You're not what I would've thought a billionaire would be."

"You've told me that before."

"It's a compliment," she said. "You're a good man."

"I'd be the same man if I was dirt poor."

Yes, because he was raised right. No matter their financial bracket, Carolyn would've seen to it that he was raised with strong values.

"I suppose I should say you're not what men usually are."

"So long as I'm man enough for you, I'll take it." And her, if she ever offered. "Are you ready to go home?"

She rested against him again, swishing her feet in the water. "Your family were talking about dinner."

"Do you want to join them?"

"Honestly…?" She shook her head. "It's late. I want your big TV and a giant greasy pizza… Not very sophisticated."

"Sophisticated enough for me, Sweet," he said, rising, taking her hands to help her out of the water. "Let's go home."

FORTY-THREE

BIG PIZZA, big TV, big bed… That last part hadn't been part of her thought process. Her conscious thought process anyway.

Somehow, it wasn't weird.

When she'd walked into the darkened room, the lights flickered on, but gave them candlelight rather than the full overhead glow.

That was the moment she paused to wonder if this was a good idea.

Oh, if only she'd listened to herself.

Movies, pizza, being there with him again…

The credits rolled on the TV, that was the end of the second movie, the third? She'd lost track. All she'd been thinking about for more than an hour was how well she fitted against her host. Tucked in at his side, head on his chest, this was home. The strength of his arm across her shoulders felt so good that she didn't want to give it up.

Neither of them moved.

Was Bastian asleep? She could do that. Close her

eyes right there and live in the moment. They'd wake in the harsh light of day, sure, and she'd have to remind herself that Bastian wasn't an option.

He wasn't.

Yet he smelled so good, it was difficult not to turn her face against him and—her fingers opened, splaying against the stomach they'd rarely retreated from all night.

This was why staying with him was a bad idea. More than body heat sizzled between them. Static nipped and sparked in the air when his palm ascended her arm. Was that a conscious choice? If he was sleeping, it meant nothing.

If he wasn't, it meant something, was that what she was saying?

Oh, men. Relationships. Life in general. Why did it all have to be so problematic?

His other hand met her knuckles on his stomach and started upward too. They came together cupping her face, drawing her up, like he just knew to capture her lips with his.

Not asleep. Very awake. And amazing. Completely amazing.

Rising, her leg trailed across his body, locking her pelvis to his as he sat up. His fingers ascended her back, coiling in her hair, pulling it back, exposing her neck to his tongue, his lips, his—

On an intake of breath, she meant to say his name, to say stop, but his hips came up, he grabbed hold of hers and—a long whine left her throat. From way down deep in her center, the whine became a whimper, became a pant and, oh, he felt good. His cock rubbed her just right, right there, that spot, over and over—oh.

She grabbed for his hand still gripping her hip as his other hand did the work of pushing her shorts aside and ah… Pure satisfaction became heat, need raced to be quenched, back and forth, up, he'd slide away and, mmm, ram himself deep.

Warmth, craving, it drove her to move faster until he flipped them over, took his place above her and hammered in fast.

This was them, the home she needed, the grounding point of him on her, controlling the pace, taking a piece of her, claiming it, claiming her.

What was wrong? Nothing. What was right? Him embedded deep inside her, plunging deep, stealing the oxygen that barely had a chance to reach her lungs.

She wanted—she needed—she—oh, she…

"Bastian," she yelped, clawing at his neck, her body braced, frozen then, vigor returned in pure sated lust, a blissful moment where every atom in the universe clicked into its intended place.

All was right with the world.

Her muscles relaxed, her head sank into the bed and there it was, the spark in his eye, the dimple. Reality set in with rigid realization.

With a firm push on his shoulders, she wriggled out from under him. What was she thinking? Where was her sense?

"Babe?"

Showing him a halting palm, she swung herself off the bed. Oh, God. Why was she so weak? That was meant to be a judgment of her character, right up until her legs threatened to go from under her. Dropping, she sat on the edge of the bed.

She needed a minute.

When his fingertips met her waist, she flinched. Not in disgust but in frustrating desire. She wanted his touch, too much. Wanted it on her, everywhere, every minute. She wanted to go back to their Grand suite and lock the door for another four days.

This was dangerous.

Muscles tensed as her gut clenched and—she couldn't trust herself and leaped up from the bed.

"Sweet…" he said, wary and slow. "Don't panic, baby."

Panic? Her? Closing her eyes, she raised an index finger and took a breath. What was she going to do? What would she say if…?

No. That wouldn't go well.

She had to get out of there. Now.

"Harper!"

No. Rushing into her bedroom, she closed the door and flicked the lock. Had that been there the whole time? She paced away, back, away again. What was she going to do?

Fuck. Fuck.

"Sweet," his voice again, right on the other side of the door. "Baby, I'm sorry."

No. Her head shook as she went back to the door and rested her forehead against it.

"You did nothing wrong," she whispered. "*We* did that."

"We wanted it." That he could hear her was some reassurance. Weakness surrendered her weight to the door. "We did nothing wrong. It's not wrong to want this."

"What we want has to be smart."

This was messy. Too messy. They'd been lucky to free themselves the first time. What were they thinking repeating history's mistake?

"Baby, being with you—"

"Don't make it worse," she said, her hand rising to slap down though with barely any force. "Don't use words."

"If you open the door, I wouldn't need words."

Yeah, okay. Did he have to say that? In that tone? With that… Oh, her stomach flipped. The solid door between them made no difference. Hormones communicated without words or actions, pheromones breached the physical to consume her spirit.

Her body still vibrated with the climax he'd driven into her, out of her, in and out and—stop. Stop it. All the thoughts she'd pushed down—deep, deep down—were threatening to spill out. Some sort of peace shook within her, trapped and surrounded by quaking barbs threatening to keep it from freedom.

Keep her from freedom.

"We're supposed to be friends. Friends don't do that." Not the kind of friends they were at any rate. "We can't let this happen again."

Because he had no idea. Talking to Carolyn and Keely, telling them she and Bastian were over, was difficult. Nowhere near as hard as it had been to walk into his office and play it like losing him was no big deal. That couldn't be further from the truth.

"Sweet—"

"We can't," she said. Except how could they stop it? They never planned to have sex, it wasn't like they talked about it. It happened all on its own. "It's lazy. It only happened because we were both there."

In a bed. In the almost dark. A man. A woman. What else did they expect? It was a foregone conclusion, biology, lizard brain and all that… Good try. Chemistry couldn't be faked. Bastian was the only trigger. She'd be able to lie in bed with any other man and avoid getting intimate.

"It meant something to me."

Damn, now she wanted the sexy voice back. The disappointment laced through those words was almost enough to break her heart. She hadn't meant to let him down. It was a kiss. He'd kissed her. Okay, so it was more than a friend kiss, but she'd been the one to mount him. God, he was right to be disappointed.

"Do you want me to move out?"

"I want you to open the door," he said. "Sweet…"

The sexy voice was back. "That's dangerous."

"I'd never hurt you."

Her sharp inhale came before her jaw dropped. On a step back, she grabbed for the door handle. Lock released, it opened and… there he stood, in the dark hall, on the other side of her threshold.

"I didn't mean it like that."

"In any way," he said. With one sure step, he cradled her jaw with both hands. "I'd never hurt you in any way."

"No, you wouldn't," she said, guiding his wrists downward to free her face. He'd held her like that in his bed right before… "We act too much on instinct."

He wouldn't let go of her hand, so linked their fingers instead. "What's wrong with that?"

"It's not that easy," she whispered, emotion suddenly welling on her lower lashes. "We haven't known each other long, I know, but being without you… If you hadn't shown up at my dad's party…"

"Do you know how grateful I was for that invitation? I couldn't function without you by my side. Family, work, it all—"

"If we want to keep each other, we have to stop doing… that."

"You didn't like it? 'Cause I'm damn sure you—"

"I did. I did like it and I did…" Being close to him, just thinking about orgasm threatened to shove aside her resolve. "What happens when we wake up in the morning? When the sun rises? I shouldn't be thinking about how good you feel…"

"Think about that any time," he said with a whisper of swagger as he rested a shoulder on the door frame. "Sweet…"

"We're making a mess of this. A mess of a good friendship with sex."

"Great sex."

"If I've figured out one thing this week, it's that you're my…"

What did Roxie call Zairn? She couldn't—they weren't. That wasn't it.

"Your what?" he asked, boosting himself from the doorframe. "What am I, Sweet?"

What he'd been from the beginning. "My white knight."

His suggestive brow relaxed. "And the white knight would never compromise his princess."

His next step was backward. The wrong way.

No. No. That wasn't what she wanted.

In the times he got closer, her heart raced as her subconscious sped through the tantalizing possibilities of what might come next. Until the moment of his partial retreat, she'd believed distance was good. Experiencing it was something else. And nothing about watching him back off was good.

"I don't want you to go," she admitted.

How bad she wanted him to stay was part of the problem. The biggest.

He raised an arm to offer her a hand. And that was it, the moment she had to choose. Did she take his hand or turn her back? It wasn't even a choice.

"No words. No sex," he said, conveying he'd respect her wishes, not that she'd ever doubt that. "Just let me hold you." She wanted that. "I need you near me. Everything else can wait until the sun rises. And I promise you, Sweet, the sky will not fall, not while you're under it. I give you my promise, I'll always keep you safe."

Tomorrow was coming, no matter what. Would she be ready for whatever happened next? Her arm rose and their fingers touched. While the dark still held them, she couldn't resist the option. As long as his hand was open, she'd fill it with hers.

FORTY-FOUR

"I STAYED IN HIS bed all night," she admitted to her friend on the phone.

"What did he say when you woke up?"

To her shame… "Well, I…"

Roxie exhaled. "You snuck out, didn't you?"

"I didn't sneak," she asserted. "I just left… quietly… while he was sleeping."

"Girl, you have to stop doing that! Did you at least shower and get ready at the house? Give him a chance to wake up and talk to you?"

"I went to the gym."

Her friend was incredulous. "To shower?"

"I worked out." Because she'd been slacking. At least, that was what she told herself. "Then showered."

Unfortunately, Roxie wasn't easily appeased. "You worked out to give yourself an excuse for the shower. Where are you right now?"

She'd hoped to avoid that question, but it had been asked.

Lying was out of the question, though she did

brace herself for a negative reaction. "The library."

"Oh, God, Harper, you're working from the library? I didn't even know there was a library in LA. Is it in a prehistoric tar pit? Geez. Send me the location, that's maybe the one place in LA I won't get arrested. Though I sure wouldn't put money on that. The library! How are you talking to me?"

"I'm in the hallway outside."

"You can't go to your parents, and you're avoiding the solution."

She couldn't think of Bastian that way. "I can rent office space."

"And where do you plan to sleep?"

In her office space? Boy, pathetic, that's what she was. Her bank balance really didn't support LA living.

She growled. "This is exactly why I shouldn't have—we shouldn't have—I was just using him."

"You weren't using him," Roxie said. "Relying on your friends is what you're supposed to do. He wanted to help, I'll bet he still does."

"It screws with everyone's heads. Being with him is easy, it's great, but now his family think we're together again. Adara keeps asking where I am—"

"You haven't told them?"

"I don't trust any of them not to contact him. Adara would say she wouldn't but get Carnell to—it's a mess. A complete mess. His life was nice and easy before I came along. I've wrecked it. I've wrecked his life and my own! Why can't I have an easy life?"

"You can," Roxie said without hesitation. "Pack a bag and go to the airport."

"The airport?"

"I'll send you a phone number, text it when you have what you need. Clothes, work stuff, whatever. A car will come to wherever you are and—"

"Take me where? You said it yourself, I can't go

to my parents, I can't go to Bastian's. I'll go to a hotel tonight. I will get myself together. I will."

"That's what I'm suggesting. Pack a bag, text the number, and you can clear your head here with me."

She didn't even know where Roxie was on the globe. Another example of her being a terrible friend.

"I landed myself on Bastian. I won't land myself on you."

It was so difficult to figure people out. Ordering her thoughts was hard enough without trying to make any kind of plans. Plans? That was a joke. Her life was spiraling; it took everything in her just to dig her nails in and hang on.

"Difference is, we won't have sex…" Roxie said. "Unless you ask really, really nicely. That would be one sex tape to catapult the brand, you'd be doing me a favor. You know what, screw it, let's have sex."

Still pathetic, she could at least muster a smile now. "Thank you. For listening. For calming me down. I don't know why I—it's been more difficult lately to…"

"Function?" Roxie asked. "I have my own theories on that."

"Theories?" She didn't get it. "Everything's happening at once. For so long, my life ticked along…" the best days coincided with Damon being in Australia. Coincidence? Not likely. "Now everything's changing all at once."

"Are you going to a Grand tonight? You said you'd go to a hotel. Will it be a Grand?"

A hotel was the plan to avoid the man who owned those buildings. What sense would that be?

"No." She couldn't afford it, certainly not for more than a night or two, did they do discount coupons? That reason was less important than… "I wouldn't put Bastian in that position."

"I'm sure he'd give you space if you need space.

First time I descended on Z's place without invitation, the staff kept my secret. From everyone. They didn't even tell Zairn I was there. Employees are vetted at the highest levels, they're responsible—"

"You think I should go to a Grand?"

"All I'm saying is, we have an account with the Grand. You can stay in any of them and use our accounts. Check in under a pseudo name if you want. Bastian will never know."

The point wasn't to shut him out, but she also didn't want to go too full on.

"I'm not good at this. At reading people and figuring out when it's too much or not enough."

"And you have no space to breathe right now, I get that. Why do you think I told you to get on a plane? We're all breathing over here. We're hogging the oxygen. Trust me. You can work from anywhere, just like me once upon a time. You can do in-person stuff by video call. We have all the tech you'll need."

"I can't. How can—"

"We have all kinds of people in LA, capable of anything. If there's something that requires a physical presence—"

"I can't afford staff. And that's a bureaucratic nightmare I don't have time for right now."

Her whole body hurt without him. She'd got him back only to wreck it all over again.

"We have staff," Roxie said. "I have staff."

"In LA?"

"Everywhere. Believe me when I say, anything you want accomplished on this earth is entirely plausible. Trust me. You wouldn't believe some of the shit I've seen pulled off. If we can get a plane full of cherry blossom shipped from Japan to the Bahamas in the blink of an eye, anything is possible. Besides, people are on payroll anyway. They might as well earn their keep."

Someone else said that.

The dinner party. Bastian. The night they broke up. The walk away… And the angst that followed. Why was walking away from him akin to trauma? Explained why her insides ached. There was too much. Inside her. Whatever was crammed in there wanted to get out, yet it stayed pent up, pressurized, ready to blow only… nothing came out.

"I don't know…"

"It's that or I get on a plane," Roxie said with such conviction, there was no doubting her. "Is that what you want? I'll get on a plane. Don't believe I won't, Ms. Scott. I'll do it. No problem. No hesitation. I'll bring an entourage like you wouldn't believe. The ground will shake. And you won't be our first stop, honey, no, my first stop will be at your Mr. Hunt's office."

"No—"

"I want to know why he thought it was okay to take advantage of you when you're vulnerable."

"It wasn't like that. It was mutual, I could've said no. We were crazy, it wasn't smart, but… Have you never had a moment like that? When you didn't need words, the moment was just perfect. Everything lined up and it was just… irresistible?"

"I'm married to Zairn Lomond, honey, absolutely every minute I have with him is like that." She sighed. "You can take care of yourself, I get that. But does he? You better figure out what comes next because I guarantee Bastian will track you down. When he does, you have to be ready to stand your ground."

Ground for what? "You just said he'd give me space."

"If that's what you want, tell him. You have to tell him. Demand it. Say the words. Articulate what you want in no uncertain terms. Don't let him drive. Be forceful and sure or he'll walk all over you. Be sure, honey."

She was anything but that. "I'm not ready to talk to him."

"Then get on a plane," Roxie droned. "Just do it. You'll be protected here, you'll get your work done, and no man will seduce you in rapturous silent moments of carnal communication. Although Tripp's always on call if you do need a smidge of that."

"I don't know Tripp."

Which kind of wasn't the point. The words came out before comprehension kicked in.

"Or, hey, go join Zairn," Roxie said. "I don't know exactly where he is or what he's doing, but if you need a hot guy to hold you with no pressure of anything else…"

She laughed. Yeah, it was kind of pathetic, but only Roxie could make something like that possible.

"You're lucky to have a guy you can…"

"Trust that much?" Roxie asked. "No prenup, I get what I want. I'll screw him hard in the divorce if we get one. And not in the way he begs for every night. We're here for whatever you need. My guy'll feel you up if you want that too."

"It wouldn't mean anything to him."

"No, it would be entirely mechanical. But if you close your eyes, he'll give it his best shot."

She would never be that close to Zairn and her friend knew it. It was a tease, a way to cheer her up. The idea was so ludicrous, it worked.

"Because the equipment only functions for you."

"You better believe it. That cock only comes when Lola calls."

Her next laugh was stronger. "And only he can make you call."

"All night long, sister."

This woman deserved complete, submerging

happiness. It was such a wonder how two people could be so perfect for each other while coming from such completely different places.

"Zairn Lomond is one of the most desirable men on the planet."

"Mm hmm."

That must contribute a lot to Roxie's confidence. Not that she got it from Zairn, but being part of a solid partnership. Nothing was shouldered alone. What belonged to Roxie belonged to Zairn too, from their friends, their business, every detail of their lives. Except, somehow, they didn't crowd each other. Nothing felt forced or hostile.

"And you married him."

"Want to know what else?" Roxie's bass dropped just a little. "We started out as friends."

She couldn't let her mind even go there. "He wanted you from the moment he met you. He told me that."

"I didn't say we weren't horny friends. We knew each other six weeks before we had sex. How long had you known Bastian before you two…?"

"Less than that." She quickly followed up. "But not by much."

"Sometimes biology follows instinct. It knows something you don't."

"What?"

Roxie's laugh was short. "Oh, honey, if I tell you that, I'd suck the fun right out of it."

"You're supposed to be my friend," she said on a faux sob for the sake of clarity.

"Get on a plane. Be my friend up close. We'll get through this."

She'd wrecked one friendship, did she want to wreck another? Yet there was something appealing about the idea of running out on her life. It didn't fit and she couldn't figure it out. Something had to change. Roxie was so together, so calm and optimistic, maybe she could absorb some of that by proximity alone.

"I have a client meeting tomorrow morning."

"Take the meeting, then get on a plane."

Maybe it was time to let someone else take the wheel.

"Let me think about it."

"Twenty-four hours," Roxie said. "You better be in the air within twenty-four hours."

She worked well with clear instructions and Roxie delivered. It didn't solve anything but at least gave her something to work toward. Would it be enough to distract her from the mess of her life?

FORTY-FIVE

WHETHER OR NOT she was going to get on a plane, she needed her files. Yes, that's right, from her office at Bastian's.

She'd be the first to admit her headspace was a wreck when fleeing the house. That didn't excuse the insanity of her leaving important things behind.

It didn't matter. She was there now and would do her best to clear out as much as she could. She'd asked the cab to wait by the gate. He would. Wouldn't he? The guy wanted his fare and this would only take a few minutes.

Bastian would be at work.

The house would be empty.

Reminding herself didn't prevent her tippytoeing like a cat burglar in the cartoons. The building didn't exactly echo, but it didn't feel the same without him. Couldn't that be said about any room? Every single breath was razor blades in her throat when her feet weren't taking her to him.

Breathing only got harder as she moved deeper

into the house. She could smell him, almost feel his presence in the air. All she wanted to do was fall into him and it was so selfish. Bastian wasn't a man who needed someone like her in his life.

The trouble was his good heart. Her selfishness may never have had a chance to manifest if he'd been able to walk away from someone in need.

In need? God, it wasn't like she'd been dying.

Ascending the stairs, she rested a palm on the banister then withdrew it. Why? Fool. Bastian wouldn't be dusting for prints, sheesh.

"Robyn, you said this was urgent."

Bastian's voice came from somewhere upstairs, she froze on the spot. He was home?

"And you don't think the rest of our lives is important?" a woman asked, clear as a whistle.

Robyn? He was with Robyn… and quite possibly in his bedroom.

She closed her eyes tight. Please don't say this was post-coital. Oh, she wouldn't be able to handle walking in on that.

"I thought you were in trouble," Bastian said. "You haven't been here for months."

"You said it when we broke up, you said it's time to figure out what's important. I didn't hear you then, I wasn't ready to listen."

"That's fine. You didn't have to call me out of the office in the middle of the afternoon to tell me that."

"People are more important than work," Robyn said. "We had a good thing going, we should never have ended it."

"You were sure you didn't want it."

"What did I know?" Robyn asked on a self-deprecating laugh. "It didn't consume me. Not until I didn't have you anymore. These last few weeks, I can't stop thinking about you."

"I heard you were in Bali."

"I was."

"Finding yourself?"

"You could say that," Robyn said, a smile in the words. "Isn't that what you told me? We have to figure out what's important. What you wanted, all of it, I didn't see it, how important it is to—we have to do this the right way."

"Robyn, we don't—"

"I hurt you. I get that. You were trying to tell me we had a future and I wouldn't listen. It's no excuse, but everyone knows how your mom is…"

"How my mom is?"

That piqued her interest too. Please don't insult Carolyn. If Robyn was trying to win Bastian back, deriding his family wouldn't grease those skids. Walk it back, Robyn. Walk it back.

"She wants you settled down, she wants tradition fulfilled, and an heir and… I wasn't sure I was ready for that. No." Her voice strengthened. "I wasn't ready for that. I wasn't then. To see what I needed, I had to live without you."

"To give yourself time to miss me."

Wasn't that what he'd said to her? Her fingers curled tighter around the metal handrail that was currently holding her up, palmprint be damned.

"Yes," Robyn said. "I did miss you. I missed you so much and… Don't they say if you love something you should set it free? You set me free and this is me, coming back to you. It's all right. This is the time. This is where our life together starts. Right now."

"Robyn, we can't—"

"You have your pride, I understand a man like you doesn't like being spurned. I didn't mean it like that; I didn't mean to refuse or reject you. I just needed some time to get a little perspective." There was that little laugh again. "A lot of perspective."

"Things have changed."

"It'll take you time to trust me again. I'm willing to do whatever you need me—"

"This is not a punishment. You were right in everything you said then."

"No, I'm right now. You were right. When we talked about marriage and a family, I got… I panicked. It's silly, I am sorry."

"The conversation was hypothetical. If we didn't want the same things from the future, there was no point continuing the relationship. We agreed then, our expectations are different."

"Not anymore. It doesn't have to be hypothetical. It's not hypothetical. I'm ready. I'm willing. I want this, Bastian. I want you. And we can have it all. You'll do the proposal. We'll throw a huge engagement party. Everything. I'll involve Carolyn and Keely. We can be a family. All of us."

"It shouldn't be like that, Robyn. You shouldn't have to consciously involve people against your will. Family should be family. You don't have to like everyone a hundred percent of the time, but the love was never there between any of you. I'd have more respect if you'd just say you don't like them—"

"I didn't say that. I never said that! Your mother didn't like me from the word go. Without her approval, it's… I'll do it. I'll find a way. I'll talk to her and apologize for hurting you. I know I'll have to pay my dues. I'll do that. Whatever it takes."

Thing was, if Robyn didn't have Carolyn, then she had no hope of winning her way into Keely's good graces. The women were closer than any mother and daughter she'd ever known. And "family" to the Hunts was on a whole other level.

"I would never let a woman I love be mistreated."

"They didn't mistreat me," Robyn said. "It's a tough circle to crack. They're close, really close and… I could never figure out my way in."

Is that what it was like? A love interest had to wheedle their way in? Was there a dance? A specific combination of moves guaranteed to get through the proverbial door? That hadn't been her experience with the Hunts.

Suppose that was a sign Carolyn and Keely never saw her as a serious contender. She hadn't been shut out or left in the cold. It was hard to imagine those women doing that to anyone. Then again, they loved Bastian so much, it was only right they protect him from people entrusted with his heart.

"We didn't split up because of my family."

"No," Robyn agreed. "Though I was intimidated. You're talking about marriage and kids, and there's your mom glaring at me. How could I be okay with the grandmother of my children disliking me so vehemently?"

Were they talking about the same woman? Carolyn didn't vehemently dislike anyone. Was she capable of being anything but her warm, welcoming self?

"My family weren't the reason we broke up."

"That was part of it, those things add up. But it will be different this time, I promise. I won't be scared of the future Carolyn wants for you. I'm ready to do it all. It's time to figure out what's important. That's what you said. I've figured it out, and you're what's important. I want to be with you, Bastian. Forever with you."

What was she doing? Her files would have to wait, or she'd start new files. She couldn't go up there in case they saw her, and if they reunited there and then— God, she wanted to bleach that mental image from her thoughts.

Backing slowly down the stairs, she hoped more than ever that the cab was still waiting. She needed to get out of there. Fast.

FORTY-SIX

HER NIGHT IN the hotel was fitful. Because it wasn't Bastian's hotel? Maybe. Or it could be that she couldn't stop playing the possible scenarios of his and Robyn's reunion in her head. Did Bastian kiss Robyn first? Touch her? Who made the move? Did they make love in the bed that she and Bastian had—no, damnit, she was doing it again.

After her meeting that morning, she'd come straight to her parents' house. The timing was great actually. Her mom, Adara, and Charissa had a standing weekly appointment at a beauty salon. The guys, her dad and Damon, should be at work.

Still, sneaking in, she didn't dawdle. Through the front door, up the stairs, into her bedroom. A woman on a mission.

Why did she need to hang out with billionaires? God, this was a terrible plan.

Most of her things were at Bastian's. Her daily things. Which was exactly where they'd stay. She wouldn't risk going over there again. Knowing him like she did, there was every chance he and Robyn were still in his room, reuniting over and over and—argh! Enough!

Okay, look forward. The future. What would come at the beginning of her next new chapter. Another chapter or a whole other book?

If she was going to hang with a billionairess, she needed to reach deep into her closet. To retrieve the dresses she feared seeing the light of day. Not because they were shocking, but because their price tags made them museum pieces. That only she got to see. Actually, even she didn't, most were in garment bags.

Should she really go join Roxie? Is that truly what she intended to do?

This could be a bad idea.

She'd lost her mind.

She flicked on the closet light and grabbed a holdall. This would be fast. She flung in some jewelry, cosmetics… What else would she need?

Crazy. Crazy.

The thought went round and round as she filled her bag and zipped it fast. Dresses. Right. Concentrate. She didn't have time to—

"Harper?" Charissa's voice brought her around fast. "What are you doing?"

"Why are you in my room?"

"I heard—I didn't know anyone else was here."

"I'm not here," she said, grabbing three garment bags. "Don't worry about it."

"Are you moving out?" Wouldn't she just love that. "What's happening?"

"Charissa…" she said, fighting to maintain her calm. "Just forget you saw me."

"Adara is worried about you. Why haven't you called?"

"Charissa," she said, draping the garment bags over her arm. "This is none of your business."

"Is it Bastian? Are you moving in with him?" Couldn't this woman get a hint? "Are you staying with him? Or Zairn Lomond? How did you meet those guys?"

"Excuse me."

Charissa didn't move out of her way. "Will you wait and talk to Adara? Please?"

It was nice the woman was worried about Adara, who they both loved. That was maybe the only thing they had in common. They're taste in men couldn't be matched because she'd come to her senses.

Though if she let her cynical side in, she'd admit that telling Adara anything could amount to telling Charissa too. The women were best friends, she didn't know what one confided in the other.

One bonus was with Charissa and Damon on the outs, hopefully he wouldn't hear her secrets as well.

Best plan? Don't talk to Adara. She couldn't guarantee what might come out.

"I'll call her later."

"You haven't called," Charissa persisted. "You said you'd call and haven't. Damon's really worried too. He thinks Bastian and Zairn are a bad influence. You could get in trouble."

"Now he cares about me getting hurt? Too little, too late. And what do you care? I thought you and Damon were done."

"Oh, we…" She shifted, raising a defiant chin. "We're back together."

"Of course you are," she said. "Because where else would he sleep?"

No one bothered to admit their fault or apologize for the mess they'd dragged her into. She didn't care, she just wanted out of there.

"He told me you and him hadn't…"

"No, we hadn't, haven't, never will. Be careful. That doesn't mean he'll never drop you again. Learn from my mistakes, get out before he finds someone shiny new with breasts he hasn't played with yet."

She didn't actually expect the woman to do that, but something had to be said.

"Don't you care about him?" Charissa's innocence was an act, had to be. "He cares about you."

"As his girlfriend, you should be asking why. He didn't care about me when he was cheating on me, but he cares now I have attractive people in my life? My life is none of his business."

"He's a caring person."

Okay, it took all of her energy not to laugh in Charissa's face.

"What is it you want from me, Charissa?" she asked. "My blessing?" She opened her arms as much as her wares would allow. "You have my blessing. Go forth and multiply. I couldn't care less."

"Why are you running away?"

Had Charissa completely forgotten their history. This was hardly the time to start confiding in each other.

"I'm not running away, I'm moving on... for now... for a while."

"How long?"

"I don't know. And, still, none of your business."

"Bastian Hunt is—"

"Someone you don't know in the slightest," she said. "Don't take everything Damon tells you as gospel truth. Think for yourself. I'm not with Damon. I'm not with Bastian. I don't answer to either of them, and I don't answer to you."

"There's no need to get defensive."

"I will stop getting defensive when you get out of my way."

Though she lingered, Charissa did step aside. About damn time. She wanted to be out of there before anyone else came in or the drama cranked up a notch.

Leaving the family home was supposed to save her from conversations like this.

"You can't run out on your family," Charissa said after she passed.

She paused without turning around. "Watch me."

This wasn't a final goodbye, she wasn't cutting herself off from them completely. She just needed some time. How much was anyone's guess.

FORTY-SEVEN

TEXT THE NUMBER.

Easy as that.

She'd done it and as Roxie said, a car came to pick her up without delay. She should've called her friend to check it was still okay to descend on her.

If Roxie knew Bastian was back with his ex… Roxie said she'd never met Robyn, but that wouldn't preclude her from feeling a loyalty to the partner of a man who'd known her partner a long time.

Time to second-guess herself passed in a wink.

Whoever was at the helm of this magically appearing car knew exactly which back gate to go to at the airport. He had the credentials, the know how, and before she could blink, she was ascending stairs onto a private jet.

Shit. This wasn't one of the little shoehorn in planes, no, this thing had length, girth—

"Welcome aboard, Miss Scott. I'm Derek, I'll be your pilot today."

And the pilot knew her name. That was a first.

Standing there, smiling, professional. This was kind of eerie, like an out of body thing.

"Uh, okay, thanks…"

Was she supposed to give an order? Make a request? Tip the guy? Etiquette wasn't clear. This wasn't exactly traveled turf. Nope, believe it or not, she was a private jet virgin. Didn't most people go through their entire life as private jet virgins?

"As requested," the pilot said. "The attendant has been dismissed for the flight."

Just dismissed for the flight. Not their job, right? She hadn't requested anything. Why would Roxie dismiss the attendant? Not that it was a bad thing. Her sitting alone being served by someone just standing there waiting for her instruction? Yeah, that would be weird. She'd hate that.

Roxie proved herself perceptive yet again.

"Please make your way through to the main cabin," the pilot gestured to the door at her side.

Main cabin. Right.

After another smile, she almost ducked her head as she went through the door and—shit.

The door closed behind her, shutting her in with a man she hadn't expected to see.

"Bastian?" What the hell…? "How did you know I…" Was this Roxie's work? No, her friend would never do that to her. "Is this your airline?"

That could be it. One of his people must've told him she was the planned passenger.

"No. Ours are more of the jumbo variety. This is one of Zairn's."

She exhaled a short pant. "I really wanted to avoid this conversation."

"At least you admit you've been avoiding me."

That wasn't a secret. Though she was surprised he'd kept any kind of tabs on her. This would be a respectable gentleman thing again, wouldn't it? The easy, respectable brush-off.

"I know, okay?" she said, hoping to skip to the end.

"Know what?"

"I know about you and Robyn. You're back together and it's okay. My feelings aren't hurt. I understand we can't continue to be friends. You have to prioritize your future with the woman you love."

"Couldn't agree more. This is going a lot better than I hoped. I thought I might have to persuade you." He stood up. "Forget all the bullshit. It's about choice. Zairn says it best. You make a choice. About what's most important and you say to hell with everything else."

Okay, that's good, though had nothing to do with her.

"Why are you telling me?"

As he approached, she recoiled just a little, feet still planted.

"To hell with everything else," he said, stopping just a whisper in front of her. "I'm looking at the most important person in my world. It's you, Harper Scott. You are my to hell with everything else."

Now her recoil was of the physical and mental variety. "Me? What are you—you got back with Robyn."

"I didn't get back with Robyn."

"You did. It's time to figure out what's important."

"It is and I have."

"You picked Robyn."

"No…" His eyes narrowed. "Who told you I picked Robyn?"

"You did." And, oh, oops, she'd just dropped herself right in it. "I might have maybe, heard some of your conversation yesterday."

"You were at the house?"

"You said it's time to figure out what's important and Robyn wants to be with you. Forever with you. Was what she said."

Not that she remembered it word for word or anything. Oh, and look at that, she'd managed to hit awkward all on her own. No attendant or assistance required. She was the star player. Maybe that was Roxie's point.

"You heard that and left?"

"You wanted forever. Marriage and babies. Proposals and big engagement parties. You can have the life you deserve with the woman you love."

"I hope so."

His hand rose, but she bounded backward, spine hitting the door, and, unfortunately, making eye contact in the shock. Damn. Damn. Damn. Double damn. He looked so amazing.

"Bastian," his name left her lips in a quiet exhale.

"If you'd stuck around another five minutes, Sweet, you'd have heard me say I did want all those things, but not from her. I want them from one person. One incredible person. I want them from you and only you."

Thump. Thump. Thump. Her heart battered her ribs. Entranced by his gaze, it was only his dimple that stole their attention.

"I don't understand."

"I know," he said, his smile only growing. "I thought maybe you'd figure it out on your own, but now knowing you better, I've learned it's best to spell things out."

"What are you… spelling?"

"I love you," he said and let that rest for a few seconds. "I've loved you since probably the moment I heard your voice, no, the first time I smelled that lotion." He almost went for a laugh. "I want to be with you,

Harper. No one else."

"But Robyn—"

"Called and said it was important. I met her at the house, she said her piece, but I don't love Robyn. I never loved Robyn."

Clarity. "Your mom knew that."

The explanation just slipped out. That was maybe why Robyn felt the Hunt women didn't fully embrace her.

"Yes, she probably did. She also knew I was in love with you before I did. I want a future with the woman I love, not only as a friend, but as my world. You, Harper."

"I don't understand."

This time he did laugh. "And that's one of the most incredible things about you." His touch trailed down her temple. "Will you trust me? Trust me to know this is the only right thing for me."

"It was fake."

"That was an excuse," he said. "I thought it would be enough to have you, but I'm done with you pulling away and beating yourself up. It's time we sit down and talk about what's important to us."

"For the future? Like you and Robyn?"

"Breaking up with her was a given. We didn't talk about the future in the way you think. I basically said we didn't want marriage and kids with each other, so why were we wasting each other's time? We went our separate ways. It was amicable. I've heard she broke up with someone else in the last couple of weeks."

Hence calling Bastian to the house.

"She wanted to rebound with you, somewhere safe," she said and drew in a long breath. "I can understand that."

"But it's not safe. I'm not safe. I won't be safe for anyone except you."

"I don't want a big engagement party."

Not the point or the time. Stupid brain.

"You can have whatever you want, Sweet. I only ask you to answer one question."

Her shoulders rose. "You're not going to propose, right? Because I'm nowhere near sane enough to—"

"Whether I do or don't depends on another answer."

Was she holding her breath? Her chest hurt.

"What question?"

His fingers laced between hers. "Do you love me?"

Did she…? Thoughts raced, feelings bloomed, and the vault of emotion she'd subconsciously kept locked up tight within her burst. The truth, her heart, all of it sighed in the freedom of liberation.

Instantly, his question alleviated the weight from her chest.

"Of course I love you!" Like duh! Stupid brain! "I've been so goddamn in love with you this whole time and I never…" Until he spelled it out, the pieces hadn't made any sense. "I do love you."

All this time. All the backing away, the fear… it wasn't because of him, it was because she was afraid of losing him. How could anyone love a person so much and imagine ever being without them? She wouldn't let herself think that way, hadn't until… He loved her. God, that changed everything! Suddenly all those things she hadn't let herself feel jarred her whole perspective, flourished with notions of forever.

He scooped a hand around the side of her head. "Good, then expect my proposal to follow."

It didn't matter that she already knew her answer, she appreciated the pause between massive life declarations.

He brought her head up, ducking down and—a chime strengthened her neck.

"Fasten seatbelts," Bastian murmured, explaining the sound.

She gasped. "Oh, God, we're on a plane. We should tell them we're not—I have to call Roxie and—"

His mouth closed on hers, silencing her. They were on a plane and should tell the pilot they weren't going anywhere, but they could enjoy this kiss first. Just a little one. That might get bigger and… Arms around his neck, she held him close, moving in the gentle rhythm of the need she'd missed.

When she lost his kiss, she stayed there, eyes closed, replaying it again in her head. The jolt of movement was what shook her again. She could feel him everywhere, but it still didn't feel real. She had him. They had each other. It wasn't fake anymore.

"We have to tell them to stop."

"We don't," he said. "Why do you think I excused the attendant?"

"That was you? Why?"

Not that it mattered. She wasn't sorry to be alone.

"I'll show you after you answer another question: did you pack any bikinis?"

So they were going, somewhere. Where? Who the hell cared? Kissing her again, he boosted her up, nudging her legs into wrapping around his hips. She hadn't known where she was going when she got on the plane. She still didn't know where the plane was going.

Her future? That path was built on a certainty she'd found in the dark. One she'd never live without.

Read more from the Roxiverse in
Nothing to It…

Thank you for reading this tale!
If you can, please take the time to review.

~

Ask your local library for more Scarlett Finn
novels!

~

For all things Scarlett Finn
check out:

www.scarlettfinn.com